# According to His Deeds

## Annmarie Powers-Vance

Powers-Vance, Annmarie
ISBN: 978-0-7443-1312-3
According to His Deeds – 1$^{st}$ ed.

**SynergEbooks**
11 Spruce Ct.
Davenport, FL  33837
www.synergebooks.com


Capitol Building, Washington DC provided by © Tex Texin,
XenCraft  textexin@xencraft.com
Cover Design by © Michael Ballantoni, MBDesignsinc@aol.com  2008


Printed in the USA

# According to His Deeds

To Chris,
For the courage and faith of your convictions

# PART I

## IMPETUS

*If you remain indifferent in times of adversity, your strength will depart from you. Rescue those who are being dragged to death, and from those tottering to execution withdraw not.*

*If you say, "I know not this man!" does not He who tests hearts perceive it? He who guards your life knows it, and he will repay each one according to his deeds.*

Proverbs 24:10-12

HE WANTED TO know what she smelled like. A scarf of green silk covered the woman's head, yet wisps of dark hair fluttered about her face. He strained to see her mouth as she sipped from a bottle of juice. She tossed bits of what he guessed to be a tuna fish sandwich to a gathering of pigeons.

It was a beautiful October day and City Hall Park bustled with life: business people with brown bag lunches, civilians on break from jury duty, drunks and the homeless with their own bags and bottles. Seagulls perched on the rooftops of Seattle and hovered above the park, their calls merging with the hollow horn blasts of the ferries.

From his bench he saw a chunk of the skybridge linking the King County Courthouse to the County jail. It seemed days ago that he had crossed that skybridge, a jail guard at his side, on his way to the County's work-release facility. In actuality he had only been out for twenty-four hours. He sucked on his cigarette, ignoring the cast-iron monument next to him dedicated to the "Battle of Seattle," a skirmish with the local Indian tribes in the 1850's.

The woman in the green scarf watched as he deliberately flicked his ashes at a pigeon. He watched her watching him and felt the urge. Red and brown and orange leaves twirled from the treetops as he turned up the collar of his threadbare overcoat. Just then, a business man strode past and shot him a look of unmasked contempt; the same look he'd received from the foreman at the crabpot factory that morning. When he left for his lunch break he knew he would not return. Neither would he return to the work-release holding facility. He spent his lunch allowance on cheap wine and cigarettes. He was enjoying living moment by moment. Following his urges. He targeted a pigeon, aimed and threw his burning cigarette. Hit, the bird twittered across a bed of leaves.

Looking up from her lunch, she saw the cigarette hit the bird. He stared at her, challenging, but the look she gave him was not of fear but disdain. It made him angry. He was tired of people looking at him like that. She checked her watch and packed her lunch things into a satchel. As she walked by, he noticed the muscles of her calves work under her nylons. Her wool coat, fashionably large, left the curves of her body to his imagination. He gave the woman a head start then followed her out of the park, keeping several paces behind her until she disappeared through the glass doors of an office building.

The next few hours he spent on a pier smoking cigarettes and drinking strawberry wine from his bottle in a bag. Near the water the wind was quite cold. On Elliot Bay, small whitecaps crested in the wake of the Bainbridge Island ferry boat. He felt its foghorn in his wine-warmed stomach. Above him, the late afternoon sky was blue and streaked with cirrus clouds which seemed to melt into the Olympic Mountains on the horizon.

All of a sudden he decided he wanted the knife stuck in the wood of the pier beside a tackle box several yards away. Two grizzled men leaned on a railing, holding their poles gingerly and watching their lines. At that moment, on Alaskan Way, a trolley car passed, its bell clanging. With feline grace, he padded towards the knife and in one easy motion pulled it out of the pier and into his overcoat pocket. The fishermen watched the trolley as he walked down the pier, crossed Alaskan Way, and settled beneath the freeway viaduct. With his back against a garbage dumpster he listened to cars click across the steel girders of the viaduct.

It was a fillet knife of stainless steel. The blade, measuring ten inches, was similar to a carving knife. Three-quarters of an inch wide at the hilt, the blade narrowed gradually, then curved into a tip. In the shape of a spoon, the handle was used for gutting fish. He wiped phosphorescent fish scales and blood off the blade.

It was getting dark when he sat down at the bus stop at Third and Cherry Streets. He watched the glass doors that the woman had disappeared through hours before. Busses stopped in front of him took on passengers and pulled back into traffic. When the wind came it was in bursts causing pedestrians to look at their feet. Bits of trash bounced amidst the slow-moving vehicles of rush hour traffic. In one coat pocket he felt the near empty wine bottle, in the other the knife. He lit a cigarette while wondering if the Seattle police were actively looking for him. It was then that the woman emerged, securing her scarf in a knot under her chin. He felt a surge of anger as a man came through the doors after her and the woman stopped to talk to him. As he wondered what he would do if the two remained together, they parted, she at a hurried pace down Third Avenue.

He kept pace on the opposite sidewalk, his eyes following her legs in the headlights of idling cars. While most of the people around her hurried into the entrance of the underground bus tunnel, she headed down James Street. He had thought she was going into the bus tunnel. His plan had simply been to snatch her purse, so it was with another surge of adrenaline that he realized there could be other possibilities. He watched as she crossed to Yesler and towards a parking garage that looked like a sinking ship; the stern and upper deck rising several stories whilst the bow disappeared below ground. Parked cars looked as if they might slide sideways the slant was so steep.

He followed her up a flight of stairs to the second floor. Dimly lit, the garage was cold and damp and many stalls were already vacant. As the woman inserted her key into the door of a silver Toyota, the wine bottle struck the crown of her skull, and her body went limp. He caught her from behind and pushed her onto the driver's seat. Snatching the keys out of the door, he opened the passenger door and pulled her over the console onto the passenger seat, laying her on her side as if she were asleep. Then he tossed her bag into the back, next to a child's car seat, and got behind the wheel.

It was at the intersection of Fourth and James that he smelled her. Beneath the noxious dregs of strawberry wine was a faint, clean smell: soap and hairspray. He smiled. Momentarily, he turned on the dome light to glimpse her face. A thin stream of dark ooze trickled down from her hairline, across the bridge of her nose and down her left cheek. He turned off the light and put his fingers to her neck to check her pulse.

Next to the southbound onramp to Interstate-5 sat the King County Jail where he had stagnated the past several months. He laughed as the Toyota gained speed then veered onto the ramp to Interstate-90, heading east.

Forty minutes later, he noticed traces of snow as they climbed the Interstate into the Cascades. There were signs for the towns of Preston and Snoqualmie and the moment he saw the rest stop sign he decided it was time to dump the woman.

The rest stop was vacant, save for a pick-up truck parked next to the bathroom. He parked at the far end of the lot and cut the engine. As the motor became quiet, the woman twitched, then moaned. Quickly, he stepped from the car and surveyed the parking lot and when a man wearing a cowboy hat emerged from the restroom and returned to his truck, he cocked his head like an animal, listening as the truck moved out of the rest area and towards the Interstate. Then there was only wind blowing through the evergreens.

When he opened the passenger door he saw her stockinged legs and his groin stirred. She turned her head and with fluttering eyelids she groaned when he slid one hand under her thighs and the other under her back. He found himself intensely aroused as he picked her up and out of the car. The Moon and the Toyota's dome light illuminated the snowy grass he laid her upon. He observed the curve of the instep on her shoeless foot then he pulled open her coat to appraise her body. As he did so, the wind rippled her dress up her thighs and she moved her hand to her head. She moaned through parted lips and her eyes started to open.

Once he decided to act, it took only seconds to pull off her stockings and undergarments. With the knife's blade between his teeth and his pants around his knees, he mounted her. She screamed suddenly, as she stared up at him in horror. He enjoyed the terror in her eyes as he thrust himself into her. She gasped for air and screamed and tried to push him away. Then she scratched his face with her fingernails so he took the knife and cut her cheek. Finally, with all the strength she could summon, the woman drove her knee up into his testicles. Momentarily stunned, he winced in pain as he stared into her wet eyes. Enraged, he slit her throat and released himself into her.

* * * *

THE COCKER SPANIEL jumped from the van and bounded for the snowy grass at the rest stop off Interstate-90, approximately twelve miles west of Snoqualmie Summit. Ten-year old Paul Laetner watched his dog frolic in the thin blanket of snow amidst the knee-high grass the color of wheat. The dog sniffed the wind as she relieved herself, then scampered towards the edge of the forest.

"Hey! Sunny! Don't run off, you silly mutt!" Paul yelled, hastening after the dog.

Mr. Laetner leaned against the van. "Hurry up or we'll leave without you!" he shouted after his son while watching his wife walk to the public restroom, her breath a trail of exhaust behind her. He surveyed the parking lot as he shivered against the wind and whistled between his teeth. The morning could not have been more beautiful he thought to himself, as the sunlight sparkled on the snow.

Suddenly, the cocker spaniel released a plaintive wail, which Mr. Laetner felt in his bones. He could just make out the crown of his son's head in the distance. "Paul?" he called as he jogged towards his son. "Paul!" The boy did not answer. The frozen grass felt electric as he waded towards the tree line, his shoes and socks wet by the snow.

Increasingly agitated, the dog darted towards him, stopped a few feet away, picked something up in his mouth and sped back to the boy. "Sunny! Here, girl!" he called. When his son turned to face him he saw the terror in his eyes. "Paul?" The dog ran to him and dropped what looked like a cloth at his feet. He bent down and saw it was a mangled pair of women's stockings.

The boy pointed towards the ground at his feet. Everything from that moment on was dreamlike. The dead woman's lips were purplish-black, and long dark hair whipped about her face. Her eyes were open and ice crystals had formed on her lashes. The cocker spaniel sniffed around her head and licked at a gaping wound on her neck. The blood on her face and neck looked black and frozen, and her gray-blue skin sparkled with frost.

Mr. Laetner pulled his son away, "Tell Mom to call the police." The boy did not move. Laetner pushed his son. "Go! Now!"

He took off his jacket and draped it over the woman's naked genitals and legs. When he looked at her face again, a large brown spider crawled out of her ear, moved across her face and vanished into her hair. Her staring eyes never blinked. His stomach heaved and he vomited into the grass. The cocker spaniel ceased sniffing the corpse and investigated his master's regurgitated breakfast.

* * * *

THE CORRUGATED METAL roof covered the grave of his daughter. The day before, at the funeral, rain had come down hard, in sheets, causing mourners to huddle under the portable shelter. They stepped carefully, reverently, around the open hole in the ground.

John Brady was relieved to be alone as he crouched beside the wilting petals of lilies, carnations, mums and roses marking the otherwise anonymous grave. The headstone he had ordered, a large rectangle of gray marble with a cross on top, would not be ready for seven to ten days. With his palm he scooped out a small cup of earth at the head of the grave and placed it in a vase of purple carnations, then patted the dirt about the neck of the vase, making it stand firm. He had asked the florist for anything purple. When thinking of what flowers to bring that morning he had suddenly remembered a passage from a novel by Alice Walker. Something about God; that He had made the color purple so that you could not pass by without noticing it. Brady was determined that Beth's grave would not go unnoticed. He watched the carnations quiver in the breeze and heard the rustling in the tops of the maple, spruce, hemlock and fir trees of the well-tended cemetery.

There were no lights anywhere near the gravesite, and he found himself thinking how scary the wind would sound at night. He remembered the small metal lantern at the base of a headstone nearby. When he had seen it he had not given it much thought. He would find one for Beth, if only for its symbolism. If only for himself.

There was a concrete bench near a hedge of boxwood and rhododendron in close proximity to his daughter's grave. He walked gingerly towards it, through a maze of headstones. He was not used to walking in a cemetery. He did not know how to do it. Was he supposed to walk directly across a grave? Many headstones had Christian crosses, though he also noticed a few Stars of David. Some stones had more than one name. The dates on a simple granite marker caught his eye; birth and death on the same day. A baby girl.

The tears came easily as he reached the bench. Damp and cold, he shivered as he watched the purple carnations. Though his faith told him that his daughter's soul, his Beth, was no longer in her physical body, it was hard to stifle the thought of her fighting for air in the mahogany casket under six feet of dirt.

Later, as he was weaving his way towards the parking lot, he came upon a huge headstone, more like a chunk of rock. Upon it were the words, "William, Chief of the Duwamish Tribe." 1896. For some reason, Brady stood and stared. Somehow the diversity of past lives and religions of the dead under his feet made him feel better. One day maybe it would help him feel that his firstborn was safe and at peace.

\* \* \* \*

THE MORNING DAWNED sodden, a heavy blanket of dew coating grass, shrubs and trees. The mottled gray sky threatened rain. A robin stalked across the lawn in a quirky gait; stopping every few inches, cocking its head back and forth. Up and down. Silent and frozen, its senses alive and sharp. The bird's back was dark gray, its head and tail black. The brick red belly and white throat contrasted starkly with the weather-beaten grass of late autumn. Then, as quick as a shot, the robin stabbed its beak into the ground, but rebounded with nothing.

At the same time, a small house finch balanced on the swaying cedar birdhouse, busily eating a blend of sunflower hearts and cracked kernel corn. Its back, wings and belly were streaked brown, and a touch of red adorned the bird's forehead, breast and rump. Bits of birdseed flew from the feeder as the finch dipped its beak. Seed rained onto the grass near the breakfast searching robin. Again came the sudden stabbing motion, and this time the robin guided a thick, wet worm out of the ground. The house finch flew from the feeder with a spray of seed. The robin stood for an instant, its trophy hanging from its beak. Then it took off over the fence and was gone.

At the kitchen table, Brady sipped his coffee and watched the bird feeder sway. As he watched, it began to rain. He checked his watch. A hard knot of nausea shifted in his stomach. He had never felt real fear before, but he was truly afraid of going to the arraignment that morning. Of seeing in the flesh the person responsible for taking Beth's life. Brady was afraid of his emotions, of what he might do. How seeing this person may make him feel.

The morning Post Intelligencer had a short article on the murder and a brief history of the accused; a twenty-six year old repeat offender named William Jeffries, Jr. Although there were no pictures, the place and time of that day's arraignment was given. The sight of Beth's name in print made him nauseous and light-headed. His limbs felt weak and heavy.

A sudden crackle of static erupted from the baby monitor on the counter, its red sensor lights flickering. There was a sound of rustling sheets then Brady heard his granddaughter sucking her pacifier. There was the turn of the doorknob then muffled footsteps; his wife seemed to keep vigil during the toddler's sleep. He could hear Sarah comforting their only grandchild. Since the murder, two year old Emily and her father had slept in his son Danny's old room. Brady's son-in-law Mark had taken over the top bunk, though at six-foot three his feet stretched out and over the edge. The Winnie the Pooh comforter and some stuffed animals from Emily's room at home now covered the bottom bunk where she'd slept fretfully the past several nights. She knew her mother was not around, though she could not possibly fathom the finality of her absence. Emily was used to Brady's house as Sarah had always been Beth's day care provider during the work week.

Brady folded the paper. Everything seemed surreal to him. In his head he qualified things, events, as coming before or after the murder. He could not step out the front door in the morning without finding cards, flower bouquets, plates of homemade cookies covered in plastic and sometimes even stuffed animals for Emily. The sympathy of others, especially those who were mere acquaintances, somehow humbled him. It made him sad, yet grateful. Ready-to-serve dinners had been dropped by daily.

As he poured more coffee, his wife entered the kitchen. "I thought she was waking up," he said.

"She fell back to sleep," said Sarah.

"The Prosecutor's office just called."

"What for?" she asked as she sat down at the table. She placed a pack of cigarettes and an ash tray in front of her.

"They wanted to know if I'd be at the arraignment. There's going to be a press conference afterwards and they invited me to come."

"What did you tell them?"

"I said I'd wait and see."

Sarah's hand shook as she lit a cigarette. She had started smoking again the day that they found out. Brady had said nothing to her. It seemed a trivial thing and he knew she needed it; something to do with her hands.

When he sat down next to her he noticed that her eyes were dark and sunken. She had been crying again, and as always the sight of his wife's pain caused an ache to form at the back of his throat and behind his eyes. He had to swallow before speaking. "Hey, I've got to go. I'm meeting Mark and Danny in an hour." He looked at Sarah, then out the glass door at the cedar bird feeder. Another finch was feeding. It was strange how the other aspects of life just went on. "You know, I'm glad Emily has you."

Sarah smiled a weak smile then began to cry. "But I should be there with you," she said as she rolled her cigarette along the edge of the ashtray.

He put a hand on her arm. "It's more important that you are here for her."

His wife laughed and then her nose started to run. "I think it's more like she's here for me." She pulled a tissue from her robe pocket and blew her nose. "I just can't believe Beth's really gone," she whispered.

Brady put his arm around her. They were quiet for a few moments then Sarah blew her nose again. "So now, if he gets the death penalty, it's hanging or lethal injection, right?"

"Right," he said softly as he stroked her hair.

"That's good."

Warbled static. "Mama, Mama, Mama," Emily recited matter-of-factly.

* * * *

ON THE STREETS of Seattle people scrambled with umbrellas; holding them horizontally, pushing them in front of their faces against the wind. In the King County Courthouse, the west side of the twelfth floor held the offices of the County Council and their staff, the east housed the Arraignment Court.

John Brady, his son Danny and son-in-law Mark Bennett emptied their pockets before passing through the metal detector manned by an armed County Courts guard. The man nodded his approval as they passed, and then retrieved their belongings.

They entered a room no more than twenty by twenty-five feet, lined with walnut benches which reminded Brady of church pews. Stuffy and warm, the room smelled of wet umbrellas and stale coffee. The three of them took a seat on the only length of bench available, at the very front of the room. The rest of the bench was taken up by camera crews from local television stations. Two cameras were set up inches away from a wall of glass directly in front of them. On the other side of the glass was a wide, yet shallow courtroom. Brady wondered if the glass they were looking through was bullet-proof. On the courtroom's left, in front of an enormous bay window, through which Mt. Rainier was visible on a clear day, was a two-tiered bench, the upper level the desk of the presiding judge, the lower level was shared by two court clerks, busily shuffling through papers and speaking into phones. When using the phones, they covered their mouths as if they were telling secrets.


In front of the clerks, at a long wooden bar like a countertop, stood a deputy prosecutor, a public defender, and the defendant. The length of time in processing an arraignment varied from five to fifteen minutes. Non-violent offenders to be arraigned sat in the same room as Brady. Those accused of violent crimes were led, handcuffed and shackled, by armed guards through a side door within the courtroom, having been transported across the skybridge from the county jail across the street.

Presently, the presiding judge was a gray-haired man with a red face and a black robe. He sat under a large rendering of the Seal of the State of Washington; a likeness of the first President of the United States. His Honor C. Robert Charleston told the defendant before him that he was accused of third-degree robbery and asked what he would plead. The public defender, a woman in her early thirties with close-cropped hair, glasses and a gunny-sack dress leaned towards a microphone and informed the judge that her client wished to plead not-guilty. At another microphone at the bar a young man in a gray suit rifled through a manila folder. In his mid-twenties, the deputy prosecutor accepted the plea and waited for the judge and his clerks to set a court date. Then the defendant nodded his head as he was told his trial date. He thanked the judge then was let through the glass door near Brady into the waiting room. There was movement in the bench behind them as two teenaged boys rose to leave with the defendant.

One of the clerks spoke into a microphone and her voice called out a case number and name over a speaker in the waiting room. From the back of the room a Hispanic man started for the glass door. A toddler cried, "No, Dada! Me go too!" A woman picked up the child and left the room. Once in the courtroom, the man conferred with the same public defender. Brady wondered if most criminals used court-appointed lawyers. The same prosecutor continued to represent the State.

John Brady, Danny and Mark sat through four arraignments which took a little less than an hour. Third and second degree robberies, a forgery and an assault.

"You okay, Dad?" Danny whispered into his ear.

"Fine. Why?"

"You look pale."

"I'm fine." Brady looked past Danny at Mark. "Are you coming to the press conference with me?" he asked.

"You decided to go?" Mark asked.

Brady nodded. "I thought I might." He thought that Mark looked exhausted. Emotionally wrought. As Brady had driven into Seattle he had wondered about the technicalities of legal relations; was Mark still legally his son-in-law? Wouldn't he have to be since he was the father to Brady's granddaughter?

"I'll see what happens here first," said Mark, gesturing towards the courtroom.

"I'm gonna step out a minute," Danny announced rising to leave. Brady patted his son on the back as he passed. More and more Brady noticed how much his son took after him. His mannerisms, his sandy hair and sharp angular features, even the way he walked; father and son had the same gait. How would this chapter in their lives effect his son? Brady would be heartbroken if Danny let the murder hinder his studies at the University of Washington. But how could it not? And Mark, a fourth grade teacher; what would happen to him? Brady tried to shut it out of his mind and as he did so, the television cameras several feet down the row from him clicked on. There was muffled noise from the speaker then, "Case number 4203, State of Washington vs. William Jeffries, Jr."

The door on the side of the courtroom opened and out came an armed guard escorting a handcuffed man in a white jumpsuit and thongs. The shackles on his feet, connected by a length of chain to his cuffed hands, caused him to take tiny steps. The prisoner looked down at his feet as he slowly maneuvered towards the public defender.

Danny returned to his seat. "That's him?" he hissed. "That's the son-of-a-bitch?"

The palms of Brady's hands began to sweat. "Shh," he whispered. He could not take his eyes off the man: approximately six feet, one hundred-eighty pounds. Not a great hulk of a man, but lithe and sinewy. Several strands of thick, greasy hair had come loose from the ponytail at the nape of his neck, falling into his eyes. He continuously twitched his head to get the hair off his face.

As William Jeffries, Jr. stood calmly in front of the judge he turned his head, showing his profile, and Brady noticed two long scratch marks, red-brown and scabbed in the stubble of beard on his cheek. Could his daughter have made them as she fought for her life? Brady felt sick to his stomach. This man had raped Beth. He'd cut her throat and left her nearly naked in the snow. *A goddamned dog had found her.* Brady felt such a strong sense of humiliation and pain for his daughter that he found it hard to swallow, to breathe.

Brady jumped when the door next to him opened and a tall man in dark pin stripes passed into the courtroom walking straight to the prosecutor in the gray suit. Brady could see by the exchange that the new man outranked the other.

"Mr. Dubek, thank you for your promptness."

The tall man leaned into the microphone. "I'm sorry for that, your Honor."

"Ms. Hancock, the defendant, William Jeffries, Jr. is being charged by the State of Washington with committing one count of aggravated murder in the first degree. What is your client's plea?"

The public defender adjusted her glasses. "Your Honor, my client, Mr. Jeffries, pleads guilty." She stepped back from the microphone and whispered something to Jeffries.

"Mr. Jeffries, do you understand that you are pleading guilty to murder?"

"Yes, your Honor," the defendant answered.

The sound of Jeffries' voice made Brady's skin crawl. It was deep and raspy, like that of a smoker.

"Very well," said the Judge. "The plea is accepted. Mr. Dubek, will there be a request for a special sentencing proceeding?"

Brady looked at Danny and Mark. His son chewed intently on his fingernails as Mark clenched and unclenched his jaw muscles.

"Yes, your Honor," Mr. Dubek replied. "The State will be filing written notice of a special sentencing hearing by the end of the week."

"Ms. Hancock?" the judge asked.

"Your Honor, I don't see justification for a death penalty hearing. My client has pled guilty and should receive life in prison without parole. The Prosecutor's office is using this case to grandstand for those TV cameras. We will certainly be filing an objection to a special sentencing hearing."

"Your remarks have been noted. Your client will remain in custody in the County Correctional Facility through the special sentencing hearing."

The slam of a gavel ended the arraignment. The prosecutor and public defender exchanged a few words as William Jeffries, Jr. was led slowly out of the courtroom. Once he was out of sight the TV cameras were turned off. Dubek grabbed his briefcase and headed for the door next to Brady. Once through the door the prosecutor leaned down next to Brady, "Mr. Brady, please come join us in the Prosecutor's office." Then Dubek was gone without waiting for an answer.

Brady did not think to ask how the Prosecutor knew who he was. He remained seated, thinking, "That was it?" The arraignment of his daughter's murderer took only a few minutes? He felt somehow guilty for not knowing how his criminal justice system worked.

The civil and criminal divisions of the King County Prosecutors Offices were on the fifth floor of the Courthouse. Once off the elevator and through the security gate, Brady found his way through the labyrinth of partitioned offices to the door of the Prosecutor's office suite where he was met by a heavyset man.

"Stan Harrel," the big man announced, offering his hand. "I'm Prosecutor McNamara's press secretary."

"John Brady."

"Sorry to meet under these circumstances. I'm glad you came. I thought you had some other family with you," he said.

"My son took my son-in-law home to see his daughter. They couldn't take reporters and cameras right now."

"Understandable." Harrell laid his beefy arm on Brady's shoulder and guided him into the room. "Let me introduce you to my boss."

The room was extremely long and narrow with a giant conference table in the center. Four television cameras from local stations lined the back wall, and reporters from KING, KOMO, KIRO, and KSTW were busy going over the press release and fixing their hair.

At the back of the conference table sat the print reporters representing The Seattle Times, The Seattle Post-Intelligencer, The Tacoma News Tribune, and The South County Journal.

Near the podium sat the radio reporters from KIRO, KOMO and KPLU, which represented National Public

Radio. There was a reporter struggling to affix his microphone to the gaggle of others taped to the front of the podium. A navy blue curtain covered the wall behind the podium, serving as a backdrop for the television cameras.

To the right of the podium, casually surveying the room, stood Prosecutor Stephen McNamarra, his suit coat open and his hands in his pockets. Brady had seen the man on television before, speaking at the same podium. McNamarra was engaged in conversation with Mr. Dubek, the deputy prosecutor from the arraignment court.

"Mr. Brady, I'm glad you came," Dubek said. Then turning to his boss, "Mr. Prosecutor, this is John Brady, father of Elizabeth Bennett. Mr. Brady, Stephen Mc-Namarra."

The Prosecutor's handshake was firm. "Mr. Brady. Please accept my deepest condolences. This is just a tragic, tragic thing."

Brady nodded. "Thank you."

"It's just unacceptable. Something has to be done about these violent repeat offenders. After I give my statement, you may say a few words if you like," said McNamarra.


"Hey, let's go, everyone's here," a woman with short black hair announced. She checked her watch then fiddled with the handkerchief in the Prosecutor's breast pocket.

"Paula, this is John Brady, Elizabeth Bennet's father," said Dubek.

Brady shook her hand.

"Paula Worjowski, Mr. Brady. I'm so sorry for your loss."

"Paula is our Chief of Staff," said Harrel.

"Hey, good work, Stan," Worjowski said.

"Thanks. Finally, a home run."

Brady turned to Dubek, "What does he mean?"

Dubek leaned towards him and said in a low voice, "All it means is that all four TV stations are here. That's a home run. Two is a double. Three is a triple. Getting them here is Stan's job. Pretty shallow." He checked his watch. "Just take a seat right over here," he said leading Brady to a row of seats against the wall. The deputy prosecutor sat down next to Brady and handed him a copy of the press release: MCNAMARRA FILES FOR DEATH PENALTY IN BENNETT CASE. Brady read the words on the page but they had no meaning. He felt like he was dreaming. "How do you think the arraignment went?" Brady forced himself to ask Dubek.

"As well as it could," he answered as he scribbled some notes on a legal pad. "It's hard to get the death penalty in this state, but we'll get our hearing. Especially with all this," he said quickly glancing around the room.

The Chief of Staff whispered something to McNamarra. The Prosecutor buttoned his suit coat. "Well, here goes." He walked briskly to the podium and rested his hands on it. From the back of the room Stan Harrell gave him the thumbs-up sign. "We ready?" McNamarra asked, looking towards the television cameras. "Good morning, everyone. Thank you for coming. A little over an hour ago, we are pleased to announce, William Jeffries, Jr. pleaded guilty to aggravated murder in the first degree. Now seeing that the circumstantial as well as the physical evidence in this case are overwhelming, we believe Mr. Jeffries planned to murder Mrs. Elizabeth Bennett, and this case clearly meets the standards established for the death penalty. Therefore, my Chief Criminal Prosecutor, Mr. Ron Dubek, who will be representing the State, is filing a notice for a special sentencing proceeding. We feel it is our duty within the laws of this state to seek the death penalty. And we will succeed." McNamarra paused then looked towards Brady. "With us today is Mr. John Brady. Elizabeth Bennett, the victim in this case, was Mr. Brady's daughter. We wish to extend to him our deepest condolences and we want him to know we at the Prosecutor's office will do our utmost to see that justice prevails." He motioned to Brady, offering him the podium.

John Brady felt his limbs go numb and heavy as he moved to the microphones. The instant the television lights hit him sweat tickled his brow. He remembered his college speech class, how his hands used to sweat and be cold at the same time. Light bulbs flashed and he saw blue dots in the haze of white light. One of the print reporters took his picture over and over again. Someone coughed. He thought about Beth. He knew this was important.

"I'd like to thank Prosecutor McNamarra and his staff for all their work on this case. And for inviting me here today." He didn't know where the words were coming from. "This is the first time since my daughter was murdered nearly two weeks ago, that I've spoken about it. Um, now Mr. Dubek here," Brady looked at the deputy prosecutor who nodded back, "has told me we'll get OUR hearing. OUR. Well, I'm not sure what I feel about Jeffries getting the death penalty. I know it would mean a sense of closure for my family. But would it solve these problems in our criminal justice system? I mean, the thing that bothers me is why this guy was let out before he had served his sentence. Why? I am told it was because the jail was full and beds were needed."

At this point Brady knew what he wanted to say. Words formed on his tongue effortlessly. "And what, they figured Jeffries was the least dangerous? Let him out on work release even though he had three prior convictions. All violent assaults on women." He felt a stirring in the room: he knew he was on target. "If you ask me, the problem isn't fixed by letting criminals out early. They should do their damned time." Papers shuffled and a buzz went through the room as reporters scribbled.

Suddenly Prosecutor McNamarra was whispering to his Chief of Staff who nodded her head then crossed the room to confer with Press Secretary Harrell. After taking a verbal lashing, Harrell circled the room and stood uneasily several feet away from Brady.

"Our judges carefully meter out these punishments only to have their sentences shortened by parole or work release or this disgusting reason of lack of bed space." It was then he noticed Stan Harrell standing next to him with a worried expression on his face. "I think we should build more jails. Let these guys do their time. Looks like I've said enough. Thank you."

Before John Brady could step back from the microphones reporters shouted questions at him. "Mr. Brady, do you want Jeffries to get the death penalty?" asked the reporter from The Seattle Times.

"What do you do, Mr. Brady?"

"What was your daughter like?"

Prosecutor McNamarra was by his side, sharing the podium.

"If Jeffries is given the death penalty for killing Beth, well, I think that would be fine by me. And my wife." Brady cleared his throat. McNamarra's hand patted his back.

"Ladies and gentlemen," McNamara began.

"Mr. Brady, what do you do?" called out a reporter.

"How is your family coping?"

"I'll just say this, then I'll hand it over to Mr. McNamarra. I'm just a normal guy that has had a horrible thing happen to his child. I'm the Vice President of Human Resources at Northwest Timber. As I've found out today, I know next to nothing about our criminal justice system. But I intend to find out. I intend to find out so that maybe I can change things. What I know is that my daughter did not deserve to die. She has a little girl who right now is at home with my wife. She's only two years old. What does a two-year old know about what really goes on in the world? I also know that her murderer should not have been on the street that day. Something's got to change." Brady stepped away from the podium.

"Mr. Brady—"

"Thank you, Mr. Brady," said McNamarra. "Thank you, everyone—"

"Mr. Prosecutor, is your platform for the Governor's race going to include a tax increase to build more jails?"

McNamarra shook his head. "Hey now, Ted," he addressed the reporter from KIRO radio. "This is not a campaign event. My job is to put criminals away. That's what we're gonna do."

Stan Harrel put his hand on the Prosecutor's shoulder. "That's it, guys." Then he guided his boss out the door of the conference room.

"What the hell was that? I thought he was just going to say thank you!" McNamara whispered to Harrel.

"Sorry, I should have known what the fuck he was going to say. Shit."

"Who do you think will get the air time tonight? A prosecutor running for governor, who everyone will assume is grandstanding on this case, or an honest guy railing against the injustice of his daughter's murder?" asked McNamara sarcastically.

Stan Harrel jotted something in his day planner, then checked his watch. "Let's grab Davis from the Times. He wanted some quotes." As he guided McNamarra back into the conference room, he scoped the crowd. "Hey, Rob!" he shouted. "The Prosecutor's ready for you."

"How's it going, Rob?" McNamarra asked as he offered his hand.

"Mr. Prosecutor," Davis nodded, gripping McNamarra's hand. "What do you think about what Mr. Brady said? Is King County really at the point of releasing inmates to free up bed space? Why was this guy out?"

"Well Rob, I think Mr. Brady was probably right. This man, Jeffries should not have been on the street. And our office intends to make him pay for it. Now you know that it's up to the County Executive and Council to fund jails, but I will certainly look into this. I have always said that public safety is job one. Anyone who has looked at my record…"

Within seconds of turning the key in the ignition, Brady heard his own voice on KIRO radio; "…the problem isn't fixed by letting criminals out early. They should do their damned time." He felt goose bumps cover his arms.

\* \* \* \*

KWR, THE LEADING conservative talk-radio station in the Pacific Northwest, was gaining popularity through Rush Limbaugh's nationally syndicated show and a stable of local conservative hosts, the most popular being Eric Glass. The host of the station's top rated afternoon drive-time show and columnist for several regional newspapers, sat in his eastside condominium scanning the late edition of the Seattle Times. "Hutchinson is a fucking Commie! How the hell can people accept this drivel?" he bellowed, commenting on the liberal views of one of his fellow writers.

"I was waiting for you to read it," snickered Glass' partner as he watched the late news. Ben Olechea, a corporate lawyer, shared Glass' sexual orientation and his conservative politics, having met years before at a Republican fundraiser when Glass was the Washington State Republican Party Chairman.

"He's a Communist," Glass repeated, tossing the paper aside as the story of Jeffries' arraignment came on the screen. "Hey, turn it up."

There was a clip of the defendant in handcuffs and shackles entering the arraignment court, his unremarkable face visible for mere seconds before he turned his back to the camera. The next shot was of John Brady at the Prosecutor's press conference. Beneath his face were the words "murder victim's father."..."What I know is that my daughter did not deserve to die.....the problem isn't fixed by letting criminals out early. They should do their damned time."

Eric Glass sat up and pointed at the screen. "The guy's perfect."

"Perfect for what?" asked Ben.

"My show. The audience will eat him up. People get that weird satisfaction mixed with sympathy. They'll feel sorry for him but glad what happened to him did not happen to them."

"Probably true. But he doesn't sound too profound."

Glass reached for the phone and dialed. "Exactly. He's perfect. Just a second." He held up a finger as he waited for his voice mail at the station so he could leave himself a message. "People find common sense profound. Have Jeff get a hold of John Brady. Dead girl's father. Get him for the show." Glass hung up the phone. "You know what I mean?" he asked. "This guy is saying the same stuff I've said for years. How many shows, how many columns have I done on repeat offenders? On changing our sentencing laws? On all this early and work release bullshit?"

"Don't know," Ben answered.

"A ton. Maybe we can score some points with this guy."

Ben Olechea rubbed his eyes and turned off the television. "I'm going to bed."

Glass plucked the front page of the newspaper off the coffee table. "There must be a story on the arraignment. Where does this Brady guy live? Isn't it the south end? What district? Isn't it Kent? Could we be that goddamned lucky?"

Olechea laughed. He'd seen Glass cook up political schemes before. "Why? What are you thinking? You'd think you're still chairman of the Party."

"Well they keep asking for my help. Remember the Senate Leadership breakfast I went to a few weeks ago? Lobbyists, donors, key people in the Party. Anyway, there are four Senate seats that we have a chance to take. If we can take two of the four we get the majority. Thing is they can't find anyone willing to run in a couple of them."

Olechea laughed. "So what, you think this John Brady will run for office now?"

"Just thinking. I know Kent's part of the 42$^{nd}$ district; that's one of the seats in play. Hazel Newirth is the liberal bitch incumbent. I've always thought we could take her out."

Olechea laughed again and started out of the room. "I'll leave you alone with your politically manipulative thoughts."

"Good night," said Glass. "Hey, as a lawyer, you think this guy Jeffries will get death?"

"Who knows? But they'll have to prove he planned to kill the girl. He'll probably get life with no parole."

"Death is the only punishment good enough for this guy. And most people agree with me." Glass picked up the phone, dialed and waited. "Call Joe Booth, Senate Republican Caucus."

\* \* \* \*

APPROXIMATELY FIFTEEN MILES south, in the city of Kent, John Brady and his wife watched the same local television news. The clip of Jeffries shuffling into the courtroom had been shown several times throughout the day. Brady sipped whiskey as he relived pieces of the press conference; Prosecutor MacNamarra looking stern and professional as he announced his office's request for a death penalty hearing. Then Brady himself. He looked bigger and his voice was deeper than he had imagined. It was as if he were watching someone else. Brady found the sound of his own voice distasteful.

"Do I really sound like that?" he asked.

"Yes," Sarah said. "You did a good job. I'm proud of you."

He finished his drink. "It was so strange, Sarah. I mean, I was there because I had to, you know? This is my life now. Our life. Everybody else was there because they get paid to be there. It's their job."

Sarah pulled an afghan blanket over her legs. "Except Jeffries."

"Yes. It's his sorry life, too."

"Let's hope literally." She wiped her eyes then reached for her glass.

Brady stood. "I need another drink."

Sarah sniffed and pulled a tissue from her robe. "Why not?"

"Why not indeed." He leaned down to pick up her glass then kissed her on top of the head. "But like I was saying, all the people with the Prosecutor's office, the reporters and judges, all of them. It's their work. They see this stuff every day." In the kitchen he poured their drinks. "You and me, our whole family, we're in this new world now. I've totally forgotten about work. Thank God I have the type of job, and Roger, who is letting me take all this time off." Brady handed his wife her drink. "We have to remember that Emily will probably have us up early."

Sarah blew her nose again. "Suppose the Prosecutor is granted this sentencing hearing and we have to testify? I can't even get through a thought without falling apart. I'll be one of those sobbing, bumbling women you see in those courtroom dramas."

"You can't worry about that."

"I keep thanking God that we have Emily. The only reason I get up in the morning is because she is here. Is that awful? We still have Danny. We still have our son. And all I care about is Emily."

Brady studied his wife. "I think it's just that Emily needs us more than Danny does right now."

Sarah took a few swallows of whiskey then laid down on the couch. Brady watched her silently as she dozed off. His sense of powerlessness intensified. Powerless to bring Beth back. To help his wife. To feel like a family again. That afternoon he had noticed that Sarah's hair was turning gray at the roots. He had never noticed gray in her dark brownish auburn hair before and it had made him feel extremely sad.

Suddenly, over the monitor, he heard Emily's blankets rustle. As he listened to see if she would wake up he thought of the scene which had occurred just before dinner. It was dusk and Sarah had gone to answer the front door. She returned to the kitchen in tears.

"What is it? Who was at the door?" he had asked.

"Trick-or-treaters," she said, choking back tears. "Can you believe we forgot about Halloween?" She had crossed the room to where Emily sat quietly watching "The Lion King," and picked her up. She hugged her granddaughter so ferociously that the little girl was scared. Brady went into the front hall and turned off the outside lights.

Sarah slept peacefully now. He reached over and brushed her bangs off her forehead. He turned off the television and closed his eyes. He understood now how grief caused some people to give on life; to believe that God was a falsehood. He would not let himself succumb to it. He thought of Beth's grave on that cold and damp and dark night and he believed with every fiber of his being that her soul was elsewhere. In a bright and beautiful place.

He felt more comfortable believing in a bright and beautiful place with a glass of whiskey in his hand. The ice had melted. He lifted his glass and finished the drink. *How can a person not believe in God? In Heaven? In some kind of afterlife? What would the purpose be to anything?* He thought of Jeffries in shackles. He kept seeing the man on top of his nearly naked daughter in the snowy grass of the rest stop. He saw it over and over and he knew it wasn't only the whiskey making him lightheaded. It was hatred.

With his thumb on his forehead he made the sign of the cross as he had done since a kid in parochial school. *God, please. Give me, give us, the strength to get through this. The son-of-a-bitch raped her and cut her throat. I know that she fought back. I mean, I know if she could , she would. It's probably why he killed her. What I would like to know is what she ever did to deserve this? Such an awful, scary thing. She must have been so scared. I can understand if you felt it was her time, but I don't know, couldn't you have made her sick or something? I could have dealt with cancer. Heart attack. Aneurysm. I could've coped. Why this? How can we get through this? There must be a reason for it. Could you let me know please? I keep thinking of the dog that found her. A dog. I can't get it out of my head. And the scratch marks on Jeffries' face. Oh Jesus, to think what was going through her mind as she realized she was dying. It was the end. Emily. Her little girl would someday know how her mother died. Poor Emily. You'll have her questions to deal with. Please God, just help me know what to do. Amen.*

Brady watched his wife sleep, and as he tucked the afghan gently about her, she opened her eyes.

"You okay?" she whispered.

"No."

"You've been crying." She reached for him as he knelt next to her.

He kissed her and she tasted like whiskey and something he could not name. A memory. She gently pushed him away. He returned to his chair and raked his fingers through his hair.

"I've got to get some sleep," Sarah said as she lifted herself off the couch. She rested her hand on his shoulder just long enough then left the room.

"I'll check Emily when I come up," he called after her. He dragged himself into the kitchen and emptied the last quarter inch of whiskey into his glass. He was searching the pantry for something to eat when a colorful package caught his eye. He knew Sarah must have bought the candy corn weeks ago. As he fought back a wave of nostalgia from Halloween's past, Brady heard a key in the front door. Seconds later Mark entered the kitchen.

"You're still up," he said.

"Mark. You okay?" he asked his son-in-law, though by his haggard, drunken appearance, he knew the answer.

Mark moved to the counter and gently brushed the baby monitor with his fingers. "Sorry I'm so late. Emily okay for you?"

"She's always okay," Brady answered while opening the bag of candy corn. "We forgot about Halloween. Trick-or-treaters came to the door. First time in over twenty years that we didn't give out candy."

Mark sat down at the table and wearily put his head in his hands. "Oh Christ," he sobbed, "And Emily…God dammit." He wiped at his wet cheeks. "I should've taken her out. I should've had a costume."

Brady realized he was swallowing hard so his own tears would not come again, "Mark, hey, she's too young. She never knew the difference. She had no idea."

"Still, I let her down." He pointed to Brady's glass. "Is there any more where that came from?"

Brady shook his head. "Sorry, we finished it. And it looks like you've had plenty anyway."

Mark laughed. "Yeah, and you?"

"Probably."

"You know that concrete bench near Beth's grave?"
Brady nodded.

"That's where I've been. I fell asleep on it. Woke up and it was pitch black. I was terrified." He blew his nose into a napkin. "Wet and frozen. Had to climb over the fence to get out."

"Oh God." Brady could feel Mark's fear. He tried to concentrate on the candy in front of him and when he did he realized he was eating the candy corn the way he had as a child; in three bites. Each color, one bite. Yellow, orange, white.

"I went there to see if the headstone was there yet," Mark said. "It's not."

"Tomorrow," said Brady. "I spoke to the funeral home today."

"And that was a rush order?"

"Seems so. But, I think all their orders are."

Mark rested his head on the table and laughed a deep, wracking laugh that turned into a sob of pain. "Oh God, I miss her so much. I don't know what to do. I can't go back to work. I'm worthless to my daughter."

Tears stung Brady's eyes.

"What am I going to do?" his son-in-law cried.

Brady sat down across from Mark and grabbed his hand and was jolted to find that his own hand was trembling. "It's going to take time, Mark. A long, long time. We have to keep breathing. Keep getting up in the morning and doing the little things. The normal little things. Day to day. We have to learn to live with this. God wants us to. And I think, I hope, the pain will go away in time."

Mark pulled his hand away from Brady and dug inside the bag of candy corn, tossing several pieces into his mouth. "Maybe I should go back to work. Get my mind off this and get back to work. Focus on something else."

Tapping the table with a piece of candy for emphasis, he looked at Mark and said, "You can do that if you want.

That's up to you. But you need time. We all do. The staff at your school is behind you. You can take all the time you need. Your job will be there."

Mark chewed his lip and stared at the table top with glistening eyes. "Thank God for unions."

"Your daughter needs you."

"No shit," he said as he blew his nose again. The silence that followed was broken by the ticking clock on the wall beside them. "What a joke," he continued, "Such the pillar of strength I've turned out to be. Look at me. You can stand there in the glare of TV lights and be strong. You know, saying that stuff that needs to change so this won't happen to anybody else in the future. The Prosecutors office probably loves you."

"Ha! I don't think so," he said, remembering McNamara's face.

"But me. No, I just go and get drunk and forget about everybody and everything and forget all about Halloween for my little girl."

"Mark, she never knew the difference. Sarah and me forgot about it too, remember?" Brady tossed back the remainder of whiskey in his glass and found himself wishing there was more. He knew he had a bottle of rum in the cupboard, but pushed the thought out of his mind. "And if it makes you feel better, I've been ducking press calls all day. Thank God for voice messaging and caller ID. Even some victim's rights groups called. I didn't talk to any of them."

"They're vultures," said Mark, then, "Do me a favor?"

"Anything."

"Let me know if it's too much. Emily and me being here."

"Listen to me," said Brady leaning forward. "Sarah would not get through this if it weren't for your little girl being here. Understand?" Brady closed his eyes. His head felt like it needed a pillow. And as he rubbed his stubbled chin he said, "And I need you guys here, too."

* * * *

HE DREAMED THAT a man was chasing Beth. It was dark and cold outside. Beth was barefoot and wore only a floral nightgown. Their breath white plumes of smoke as she fought to stay mere paces in front of her assailant. They ran down the middle of a street lined with middle-class houses; the windows of which glowed warmly from the inside. It was his own street. He could see his neighbors at their dinner tables, watching television in their dens, making love in their bedrooms; nobody hearing the screams on their street. Beth tripped and fell, screaming onto Brady's front yard. The man, out of breath, doubled-over laughing as he pulled a knife out of his belt. Then he kicked Beth and she rolled across the grass, her nightgown rising above her waist. Stooping, he cut her panties with his knife, pulled them off and tossed them onto Brady's doorstep. Beth screamed hoarsely and the man laughed unzipping his pants. Brady's neighbor across the street, Bruce Aldridge, walked past his living room window without seeing the treachery outside. When the man crawled on top of Beth and began rocking back and forth, she struggled fiercely, driving her knee into his groin. In agony, the man brought his knife to Beth's neck. Suddenly, Brady saw himself, staring horrified at the scene on his front lawn and not doing anything. He couldn't move. He couldn't shout. His daughter screamed hysterically as the world began to shake and vibrate thunderously...

Brady bolted upright in bed as an airplane crossed close overhead, rattling the house's foundation as it descended towards Sea Tac International Airport, ten miles away. His heart banged against his ribs as he saw Sarah's sleeping form beside him. Below, in the valley, a train lumbered, sounding its' whistle at each crossing. On the street outside brakes screeched, tires sounding on wet pavement. He laid his head on the sweat-soaked pillow and watched a beam of light sweep the bedroom ceiling, shorten, stop, turn red then streak down the wall, disappearing as the vehicle passed and braked at the corner. Water trickled down the rain pipe outside their window.

* * * *

MARK HELD HIS daughter's hand as they wound their way around the paved path of the cemetery. Every so often Emily pulled her hand from her father's clutch and ran squealing towards objects of her attention: shriveled-up leaves she needed to present to Mark, large trees she wanted to hide behind, and a mylar balloon floating above a headstone which brought tears when Mark said it was not for her.

The morning had dawned relatively mild and sunny, and the earth, soaked by the night's rain, sparkled. As his family entered the cemetery that morning, Brady had the strongest sensation that it was a Saturday, when in fact it was a Tuesday. He no longer thought of it as being a work week. In fact, as each day passed he wanted more and more to forget about Northwest Timber. All he wanted was to stay at home with his wife and granddaughter. And he was beginning to feel comfortable at the gravesite. Beth's headstone was in place and he felt it was quite beautiful. With the cross affixed on top of the rectangular piece of marble, it stood nearly four feet high. His daughter's grave no longer seemed out of place.

Brady sat next to his son on the cement bench. They watched as Sarah arranged new pots of flowers at the base of the new stone.

"So you think Mark's gonna just stay there indefinitely?" Danny asked.

Brady shrugged his shoulders and tossed a small piece of bark he had been holding in his hand. "I don't know. It's not a problem. I told him he was welcome."

"But what about Mom? You think it's healthy?"

"Absolutely. Emily is her best medicine right now," said Brady.

"Mom's hair is turning gray."

"I don't think she cares. Just don't mention it to her." Brady, however, silently wished she would color it.

Danny shifted his weight on the bench and looked at Mark and Emily making their way towards them.

"Don't mention the cigarettes either," said Brady. "I hope it's just a crutch she'll be able to give up quickly."

"Okay. Do you think I should come home? I will, you know, if you think it would help. I mean, it's not like I can concentrate on school anyways."

"No. Your mother would be even more heartbroken if you were to give up school. And the quarter's almost over. You have to finish, Danny."

"Hey munchkin," Danny called to Emily.

"Me not a munchkin, me Emily!" she yelled and pounded her chest. They all laughed, and their voices carried across the cemetery.

\* \* \* \*

THEY LINGERED ABOUT the kitchen as Sarah made coffee. Mark poured milk into a spill-proof cup. "I'm taking Em up for a nap."

When the phone rang, Danny reached for the receiver. "Hello?" then, "Dad, for you."

"Make it strong," Brady said to Sarah as he took the phone from his son. "Hello?"

"Mr. Brady?" asked a very professional voice.

"This is John Brady."

"Mr. Brady, my name is Jeff Taylor. I produce the Eric Glass show on KWR radio."

"Oh yes," said Brady, "I know the show."

"First I'd like to offer my condolences regarding your tragic loss."

"Thank you. How can I help you?"

"The point of my call, sir, is that Mr. Glass saw you on television last night. At Prosecutor McNamarra's press conference. He thought you made some strong points about the early release of prisoners due to lack of beds, jail space, and so on. Criminal justice issues are his favorite topics. He's involved with the legislature right now trying to make some changes in the system."

"That's good to hear," Brady said uncertainly.

"Mr. Brady, Eric would like you on the show. I know its late notice but he'd love to have you on this afternoon at three o'clock."

Brady paused. "I don't think so. I don't think my family's up to that right now."

"We could call back in a few hours. Mull it over. Talk to your family."

Brady nodded as he accepted a mug of coffee from his son. "I don't think so, and there's no way I could get downtown today anyway."

"No problem. We do interviews over the phone all the time. You don't have to leave your house."

Brady sipped his coffee. He thought about his dream and about watching his daughter get attacked. Even though it had all been in his head, he had not been able to help. And the thing that made him sick was that the real attack was in all probability more vicious. The day before, in front of the press, hadn't he said that he wanted to do something? Something? Could this be it?

"Mr. Brady?" Taylor asked.

"There's one stipulation." Brady said. "I've been asked by the Prosecutor's office not to talk about details of the murder."

"Understood. We'll be calling you at two-fifty-five; Eric will want to speak with you before you go on the air at six after three."

"Fine. Good-bye." He hung up the phone and turned to Danny and Sarah at the kitchen table.

"What?" asked Danny.

"I'm going to be on the radio, live, at three o'clock this afternoon. With Eric Glass."

"Why?" Sarah inquired. She pulled a cigarette from her pack and lit it.

He looked at his wife then down into his coffee cup. "I don't know. I guess I feel like it's something I should do. No, something I'm supposed to do. I don't know. Don't ask me why."

"Oh," his wife said then blew a line of smoke across the table, "Of course not."

"Well, do you mind? Are you going to have a problem with this?" He sat down next to her.

She turned to look at him then turned her focus to the tip of her burning cigarette. "I don't know if I'm going to have a problem with this."

Danny got up from the table and put his coffee cup in the sink. "My opinion?" he asked with his back to his parents.

"Sure," Sarah answered.

"I think it could be a good thing. Let go of some tension. And it's a conservative station. This guy will be one hundred percent for everything you say."

"Probably." Brady nodded. "What time is your class? Don't you be late."

"Twelve-fifteen," Danny said glancing at the clock on the wall.

Just then Mark entered the kitchen, Emily's empty cup in his hand. He rubbed his cheek. "I forgot to shave this morning."

"Eric will ask you questions about your expectations regarding the sentencing, maybe your views on the criminal justice system and how your family's coping. Okay?" Taylor asked later that afternoon.

Brady shifted his weight on the barstool at the kitchen counter. "Okay," he answered into the phone.

"Then he'll take a few calls for you. And I screen the calls, so hopefully there won't be any wackos with off-the-wall questions. Even if there are, Eric will get rid of them."

"Okay," said Brady.

"Any questions? I think that's it then," said Taylor. "I'll put you on hold a second, then Eric will pick up and chat with you for a few seconds before you go on. Thanks Mr. Brady."

"No problem." Papers lay strewn across the counter about him; statistics on the county jail system, quotes from Prosecutor McNamarra and Ron Dubek, a scribbled list of issues he could not touch.

"Bye-bye, Pappa!" Emily shouted. She had her jacket on, the hood fitting snugly around her face.

"Bye, sweetheart, where are you going?"

The hand on his shoulder was Sarah's, "I'll take her outside and push her on the swing so you won't have any interruptions."

"Thanks. I'll come out when I'm done." He watched through the sliding-glass doors as Emily climbed the ladder to the top of the slide then flung herself down the piece of yellow plastic. Then she noticed a soccer ball on the other side of the yard and ran towards it in a short-stepped gait only a two year old has. Suddenly she stopped and squatted, picking at something in the grass. Having been transfixed by his granddaughter, Brady jumped when there was a click at the other end of the phone.

He felt a strange sensation listening to radio advertisements over the phone; Seafirst Bank, a Seahawk season ticket offer, Farmer's Insurance.

The first ten minutes of the show had gone well. Eric Glass gave Brady and his family his condolences, recited numerous statistics on crime and the criminal justice system and he had just begun talking to Brady before it was time for a commercial break. After a vacuum-suction sound they were back on the air.

"Okay, folks, we're back with Mr. John Brady. So, Mr. Brady, what's the deal? Why was this guy Jeffries out?"

"Well Eric, it's my understanding that awhile ago, the ACLU sued the County because the jail was overcrowded. There weren't enough beds. Inmates were sleeping on floors. So to meet the conditions of the court order, the County has been resorting to reduced sentences with home-monitoring and work-release."

"And Jeffries was on work-release, right?" Glass asked.

"Right. He was about to be tried for assault, for the fourth time, and they let him out on work release! I was told he was thought to be less threatening than the other inmates being considered. Less of a risk." Brady sipped water from a cup.

"Unbelievable," said Glass. "Okay John, how would you solve this problem?"

Without hesitation Brady answered, "It sounds simplistic Eric, but we need more jails. We need more jails to put these criminals away. Those convicted of crime need to do their time, and no one should be let out just because jails are overcrowded. Our leaders need to lobby our legislature for more money. We already have tough sentences. We have the three-strikes law. What does any of that matter if we don't have the jail space to carry out these laws?"

"Sounds like you've been doing your homework," Glass boomed.

"No, it's just that when something of this magnitude happens in your life, you tend to, at least I tend to, devote every minute to finding out why this happened. Maybe if we find out why, then we can make some changes. I've been talking to a lot of people in the past several days. People in the Prosecutor's office, lawyers, my County Councilman, Bill Zantz, and Congresswoman Julie Newton's office."

"See ladies and gentlemen," Glass snickered, "Mr. Brady, here, has hit the nail on the head…"

And as Glass rattled off more statistics, Brady watched Emily kick the soccer ball to Sarah. The red, white and blue ball rolled down the slope of the yard, the little girl in quick pursuit. Then instead of making contact, her small foot went over the top of the ball and Emily crashed to the ground. She landed hard on her bottom, and as she did she turned and caught Brady watching out the glass door. Emily's lips puckered and she started to wail as Sarah squatted near her, scooping the child up in her arms.

"…How much longer will people buy this garbage of reform?" Glass said. "Oh, this murderer just needs a little therapy. Well I think Mr. Brady here is correct. And maybe he's the type of guy we need in office."

Brady laughed. "Oh, I don't think so."

"What do you do, John?" asked Glass. "It's Weyerhaueser, isn't it?"

"No. Northwest Timber. I'm Vice President of Human Resources, which is a fancy way of saying I am in charge of all personnel issues, everything from payroll and benefits to hiring and firing."

"Well, I think that you missed your calling," Glass said in a serious tone. "Okay folks, we'll be right back with a few phone calls for Mr. John Brady."

Again, Brady heard a sound of suction then a click.

"John?" Eric Glass asked. "Hey, are you on a cordless phone?"

"No."

"Well, can you speak up a little? Other than that, you're doing fantastic. We have time for about two calls. Then we're done."

"Great," said Brady.

"Hey, and John, I'm serious about you being in office. People like you should."

"You mean, people who've had loved ones murdered?"

"I'm not trying to be rude. I mean it. People who have a passion. A mission, an agenda, whatever you want to call it. Intelligence doesn't hurt either. Be back in a minute."

Then there was a click and Brady heard a commercial for Wal-Mart. With the telephone cradled in the crook of his neck, he moved to the refrigerator. He checked his watch then pulled out a beer.

Sarah opened the door and let Emily into the kitchen. "Sorry," she whispered.

"It's okay," he said. "They're having a commercial break. I'll be done in a few minutes."

"Em wants to try to go potty on the toilet," Sarah said in a confident tone to Emily.

"That's my girl," said Brady. He gave Emily the thumbs up sign.

The first caller was a young man worried about raising taxes. "So, how do you propose we pay for these jails, Mr. Brady? Make honest, working people like me pay for them?"

Brady sipped his beer before answering. "Well, I happen to believe that public safety and law enforcement are the biggest responsibility of our government."

"But where will the money come from?" the man asked.

"Well before taxes are raised, I think the county should be actively lobbying our state legislature for funds. I'm no expert on this by any means, but how often have our legislators spoken of this "rainy day fund? Millions of dollars being set aside and saved. For what? Why can't a small portion of these funds be allocated towards fighting crime?" Brady's mind raced with ideas, but suddenly he remembered the new headstone at Beth's grave and for some reason he felt ashamed. "I think I've said enough."

"And very well, I might add," laughed Glass. "And thanks for the call, David from Mountlake Terrace. Our next caller is Angela in Bellevue. Your question for Mr. Brady, Angela?"

There was a pause. "Hi. Um, I don't really have a question. My name is Angela Lewis, Mr. Brady. My maiden name is Hansen. I was one of Beth's friends in high school. I don't know if you remember me."

He could feel the hair rise on the back of his neck. Suddenly he felt a tug on his trouser leg and Emily was at his side.

"Went pee-pee, Pappa. Me went pee-pee!" Brady looked down at his granddaughter's beaming face and smiled.

"I used to always sleep over at your house," Angela said.

"Yes, Angela, I remember you. It's been a long time," said Brady turning from Emily as his eyes filled with tears. Sarah coaxed Emily back outdoors by showing her a bag of birdseed in her hand.

"We'll feed the birds," she said.

"I just wanted to see how you and your family are coping. How is Mrs. Brady?" Angela asked.

If his memory served him, Angela Hansen was the girl with pale blue eyes and a mop of frizzy hair. Brady fought to remember that the conversation was live on the radio. He lifted his beer can and found it empty. "You're very considerate. Mrs. Brady will appreciate it. She's doing the best she can, as we all are." He looked outside as Emily knelt on the patio, staring wide-eyed as Sarah filled the cedar bird feeder. Then, with an agility adults lack, she waddled about, her stubby hands, pincer-like, plucking up the seed spilling on the ground. "What happened to Beth is not anything you can plan for, you know? You think you know somebody. I mean I've been married to my wife for twenty-nine years. We met in college. And you know, I just thank God for Beth's little girl. She's staying with us. I'm glad we have her. It gives us focus."

"Well, I wish you the best Mr. Brady. Beth was a good friend. I'm really going to miss her."

"Thank you, Angela," was all he could say. The hurt in his throat throbbed.

"And we'll be back after a commercial break," said Eric.

\* \* \* \*

JOE BOOTH, CHIEF of staff of the Senate Republican Caucus, had known Eric Glass since their politically active days at the University of Washington. Both had strident conservative beliefs which led them to careers in Republican politics. Each of them knew a candidate in the making when they saw one.

"He's got this passion building to do something. I just think this rage he has about his daughter's death could turn into a fire in the belly. I think we can get him. You know, hook with what he can do to change the system."

Booth swiveled in his chair and looked out his office window at the capitol dome. Washington State's capitol dome was second only to the U.S. Capitol in terms height and grandeur. He loved his job. "So, did you talk to him about it?" he asked, cradling the receiver on his shoulder so he could take notes.

Glass laughed. "You know me. I dropped about a dozen hints about running. He laughed, but he didn't say no."

"Is he a Republican?"

"I think Brady's the kind of guy who is basically conservative. Works at a timber company, lives in the suburbs. With the murder, he'd be rabid about crime, something Newirth could really be hammered on."

"No shit," said Booth. "How about his wife?"

"Don't know. Haven't met her."

"Okay," Booth said, then nodded his head as an aide entered his office, dropped a folder on his desk and left. He leafed through the folder. "I didn't see the press conference. He's what, 45? 50? Nice looking?"

"He can't be more than 50. Yeah, I'd say he's handsome. Not gorgeous. Clean cut, nice features. Good teeth. Full head of sandy brown hair, little gray at the temples. And he's in decent shape."

Booth laughed at his friend's critique. "Well, if you find him attractive, most people will."

"Fuck you."

"Okay. So he's good in front of the press? Talking one on one?"

"Joe, I'm telling you this guy can be groomed. He's got what it takes."

Booth closed the file and returned his gaze to the capitol dome. The sky was a daunting dark blanket and rain had begun to fall. "Hot damn. I'll get Senator Daniels on this. We'll pull all Newirth's votes on crime and set up a meeting with him and his wife. What's her name?"

"I think it's Sarah," said Glass.

"Your timing, as always, is impeccable. Just this morning we were talking about the 42$^{nd}$. I'd basically given up hope of finding someone. Christ, we've talked to city council members, school board members, and, of course, both those chickenshit House members. This guy sounds too good to be true. I owe you one."

"Wait and see if he even agrees to a meeting."

Booth snickered. "Hey, if there's any interest here, once he sees Newirth's votes he'll want this. I can sell him."

"I know you can."

"Look at it this way. If something like this happened to you or me, what one thing could you do that could really, and I mean really, make a difference so that the awful thing doesn't happen to someone else?"

"Listen to you," said Glass. "Don't sell me—sell him."

"And his wife. We'll get her involved. Let her know she's an important part of this. So, is he back at work?" asked Booth.

"I know the death penalty hearing is soon. I think he's waiting until that's over."

"You think he'll get death?" asked Booth.

"From what Brady said, they have to prove this scumbag intended to kill her, so who knows," said Glass.

"Okay, I'm going to be all over this. Thanks, Eric. I'll be in touch."

"Take care," said Glass.


Booth pushed one of a panel of buttons on the phone. "Genie, Joe Booth here; is the Senator in? Sure." He tapped his fingers on the desk.

"Alex? Joe. I just talked to Eric Glass at KWR and he says he's got our candidate for the 42$^{nd}$. The guy whose daughter was killed by the guy out on work release….Yeah, that's him, John Brady. I'm free for lunch tomorrow if you want to talk about it…. Great, I'll have the staff pull all the votes Newirth has taken the past few sessions. Especially her votes on three-strikes, and hard time for armed crime…. Right, see you tomorrow."

\* \* \* \*

ROGER TATTINGER HAD never been anything but blunt. "When are you coming back to work? What are your plans?"

Brady handed his boss a stiff whiskey. "Are my services sorely missed?"

"You know they are. Conroy isn't as smooth as you. He doesn't exactly rally the troops."

"And I do?"

Brady sat down at the kitchen table with Roger and Sarah. They watched Sarah light a cigarette, and Brady noticed a surprised look on Roger's face.

"We thought he'd go back after the hearing next week," Sarah offered, nodding towards her husband.

"Hey, you misunderstood me. Nobody's rushing you. Actually I guess I wanted to make sure you were coming back." He watched Sarah take a drag on her cigarette.

"Of course I'm coming back. I thought after hearing would be good."

"Yes, I've started smoking again," she said.

"I didn't say anything," said Roger.

"It helps my nerves," she said.

Roger nodded and looked at Brady. "Well that's good; that you're coming back to work." He paused, and then asked, "How's Mark doing? And your granddaughter? Are they still staying here?"

"Yes. He can't stand being in their house. He says he can smell Beth in it." Brady looked into his drink. "He's meeting with a realtor in the next few days to check things out."

"Good." Roger said

Suddenly, in a fluster, Emily stormed into the kitchen. "Pappa? Pappa?"

"And speaking of the little dickens." Brady leaned down to her. "Yes, my sweet?"

She noticed Roger and froze. Brady scooped her into his lap. "It's okay Em, this is my boss, Mr. Tattinger. You met him before. You probably don't remember."

Emily stared at Roger intently, then, digesting the fact of his existence, turned back to Brady. "You help me find

Art?" she asked, referring to her stuffed bear. She wore fuzzy yellow pajamas with feet, the vinyl soles slapping the floor as he put her down. When she pulled his hand, Brady let her believe her strength pulled him to his feet.

"Okay munchkin, lets find Art," said Brady.

"Me not a munchkin! Me Emily!"

Roger laughed as Emily led Brady out of the room. "What a little sweetheart," he said.

Sarah's eyes watered as she sucked on her cigarette, her exhale becoming a sob.

"Hey, hey," whispered Roger as he jumped from his chair and moved around the table to her. He stood behind her, gently placing his hands on her shoulders.

"I'm sorry," Sarah sniffed.

Rubbing between her shoulder blades, his thumbs moved in a circular motion. "No, don't be. I can't begin to imagine what you're going through."

From somewhere upstairs they heard the sound of laughter. Roger leaned down and spoke softly into her ear. "I've been so worried. I wanted to see how you were. I'm here if you need me." As he kneaded the muscles of her shoulders, Sarah leaned her head back into his stomach. He gently kissed the top of her head.

Sarah leaned forward. "Don't," she said.

Roger returned to his seat and sipped his drink. "I just want to help," he whispered. "I care about you."

Sarah went to the sink where she doused her cigarette, then splashed water on her face and patted it dry with a dish towel. "I know." She looked through the window into the darkness of the backyard, but all she saw was her own reflection. She did know how Roger felt. She had known for over ten years, since Brady's transfer to the Human Services division at Northwest Timber. The first time Sarah met Roger was at the company Christmas party after Brady's promotion to vice president. Roger had looked miserable, face gaunt with a five o'clock shadow. He had pretended to be jovial in the midst of a nasty divorce, the details of which he poured out to Sarah over several glasses of potent eggnog. He had broken down and literally cried on her shoulder. That night they had bonded, yet the only time Sarah had ever let herself see him was at office parties or company functions.

The mutual attraction had led to one drunken, yet passionate kiss in the supply room at Northwest Timber. It had been a New Years Eve party and she had pushed him away, swearing to him that she would do nothing to jeopardize her marriage and her family. It had been nearly five years since that kiss, yet she still got goose bumps whenever he was near. She swallowed hard, as if it would make the feeling disappear.

She stood at the sink with her back to Roger and felt ashamed. With the loss of her daughter her life seemed to be falling apart. She thought of Emily and how she repeated the same questions over and over.

"Gamma, where's my Mommy?"

"She's in heaven, sweetie."

"Oh," Emily would say, then move on to another subject. Or she would stun Sarah by stating matter-of-factly, "Mommy's dead."

And with all that was happening she was thinking of the man sitting at the table behind her. How he made her think of things she shouldn't. How she always noticed his hands; long slender fingers meticulously manicured, almost feminine. His hands enthralled her.

As she rinsed her hands and dried them, she heard Brady and Emily descend the stairs. Sarah breathed a sigh of relief and returned to the table.

"Okay Em, go pick one out, okay?" Brady said.

"Kay, pappa!"

Brady entered the kitchen and noticed Sarah's expression. "You okay?" he asked.

"I'm fine," she said. She lit a cigarette and asked, "Could you make me a drink, please?"

"Sure. Roger?"

"I'm fine, thanks. I need to get going."

"Did you find Art?" Sarah asked.

"Yes. He was under the bunk bed. We almost woke Mark."

"He should get up," Sarah said. "Spend some time with his daughter before she goes to bed."

Brady placed a drink in front of Sarah. "He's been sleeping a lot," he said to Roger.

Roger rested his clasped, manicured hands on the table. "You guys, if there is anything I can do..."

"Thanks Roger. That means a lot." Brady sat next to Sarah. "Beth's grave has a headstone now. It's really nice."

Sarah nodded. "Yes it is."

"That's good," said Roger.

Emily ran into the room. "Can I watch, pappa?" she sang as she handed Brady a video. Her arms waved at the air about her excitedly.

"Oh, now we haven't seen Sleeping Beauty for awhile now," Brady said, rolling his eyes.

Sarah laughed and turned to Roger. "She watches the same videos over and over."

Brady grasped Emily's hand and crossed the room to the television.

"She's a lucky little girl to have two such caring grandparents," said Roger.

Sarah watched her husband kneel on the floor in front of the television to insert the video. Emily sat on the floor beside him, fidgeting anxiously. Ice cubes clinked against Sarah's teeth as she sipped her drink. "But it's not like she's an orphan. She does have one parent," she said with a touch of bitterness.

"Sarah, honey," Brady beckoned over his shoulder, "Please?"

"Mark will come around," Roger said to Sarah.

The theme music from the movie wafted loudly across the room. Sarah's hand trembled as she lifted her drink. Roger reached across the table and patted her arm.

"I know you," Emily sang loudly. "...once upon a dream. I know you..."

Tears stung Sarah's eyes. "Oh shit." She wiped her eyes. "This music. This movie. I hate this. It just reminds me of Beth."

Without anybody noticing, Mark had entered the room. "Hey," he said. "Sorry I slept so long."

Hearing her father, Emily leaped from the floor and ran to Mark. "Hey daddy, daddy! Let's dance!"

\* \* \* \*

AS SHE SLID between the sheets, Brady sensed Sarah meant to avoid waking him.

"I'm not asleep," he whispered.

"Oh, I thought you were." She patted the blankets about her and breathed deeply.

He edged across inches of cold sheet and molded his body to hers.

"Mark in bed?" he asked.

"He's still downstairs. Going over mortgage papers."

He buried his face in Sarah's hair. "Em? Did you check Emily?"

"She's fine. Out like a light."

As if his body functioned by its own freewill, he felt his hand moving slowly down his wife's thigh.

"Brady, please. I don't think...it's not a good time," Sarah whispered. "I need to go to sleep." She still felt guilty about Roger. Her face felt flushed even thinking about thinking about him. How would he take care of her in a time of crisis? And his hands. She always thought about his hands. Then she felt her husband's hand, under her nightgown, urgently touching.

"But John," she breathed, "Emily's right down the hall."

"So?"

"And Mark might hear us."

But quietly, gently, he continued feeling, touching; because he knew her and if she did not want him close she would have turned away by now. He knew this. And he was so thankful for it and the minuscule piece of assurance it gave him. A little piece of constancy.

He found himself remembering one Christmas morning when the children were young. Beth had walked into the bedroom when he was on top of Sarah. Only three or four at the time, his daughter had screamed at him for hurting her Mommy. The thought made him smile.

But later, when they were finished, he had a thought that shocked him. It was the revelation that if given the choice of losing Sarah or Beth, he wouldn't change things. It was how he felt and he was angry for even having the thought. Brady loved his daughter more than life but he knew in his heart he would go on. On the other hand, he did not know if he could wake up and breathe in and out every day without his wife to hold onto.

\* \* \* \*

IT TURNED OUT there was a chance that the prosecution would not be granted a death penalty hearing. Assistant Prosecutor Ron Dubek had phoned to brief Brady on two pre-trial motions that the defense filed with the court to prevent a special sentencing hearing from occurring.

The first motion argued that William Jeffries, Jr. had incompetent and inadequate counsel at his arraignment; that he should not have been allowed to plead guilty. The second asked that the request for a special sentencing hearing be denied due to the fact there were no "aggravating" circumstances as defined in the semantics of the State of Washington Criminal Code.

Brady had been studious, almost serene since the call. The house was quiet since Sarah and Emily had left for the park. In the living room he sat in his favorite chair, a rocker his great grandfather had made. It had been refinished and newly upholstered twice since he and Sarah had inherited it. He sat in the chair without moving, momentarily nostalgic about the chair's origin, before his thoughts returned to the present. Staring at a patch of bare wall, he wondered what would become of the person who had ripped a wound into the material of his life. He wondered which sentence would be the harsher; life in prison without parole, or death? Lethal injection? Hanging from a gallows? Life in a cage? In his mind he turned over the scenarios. What was true justice? In all honesty, he did not know. But he knew how Sarah would react. If the hearing was denied she would be outraged. She wanted to live knowing that Jeffries was going to die.

Suddenly, Brady's eyes focused on a movement, a shadow, a spider traveling on the wall. Quarter-sized, more leg than body, it crept with confidence as it sensed no movement within its proximity. Safe.

Brady had always been fascinated at the rapid mobility of spiders. Eight legs working independently, yet in unison. He did not dislike spiders and he marveled at how Sarah's arachnophobia had been inherited by Beth, and through her, to Emily. All three generations of Brady females fearful of the tiny creatures. He startled himself with his own laugh. Sensing sound or movement, the spider froze in its tracks several feet from the protected crevice behind a bookcase.

If only Beth were there to scream for him to help her. He would kill it for her. Protect her from it. He wondered how many times he had been called upon to extinguish spiders for the women in his life. And they always breathed a sigh of relief when the act was accomplished. He would show them the dead spider before flushing it down the toilet. They needed proof of the death.

Rising from the chair, he slowly walked to the wall and in one quick movement, smashed the spider under the sole of his shoe. Then he returned to his chair and watched the late afternoon sun pour through the window, casting shadows upon the inert body, legs and guts smeared across the wall. He felt a minute satisfaction in imposing his own tiny death sentence.

* * * *

WITH THE PUBLICITY his case had generated, William Jeffries, Jr. had landed the pro-bono services of the most famous anti-death penalty lawyer in the northwest. David Allen Green had been counsel to numerous death row inmates. Green had filed the two pre-trial motions which prompted the hearing Brady and his family were present to witness.

Outside the courtroom, the men of John Brady's household instinctively formed a human shield around Sarah, protecting her from reporters thrusting microphones, and television cameras with blazing lights.

"Mr. Brady, do you think Jeffries will get death?"

"What if he gets off?"

"Does Jeffries deserve to die?"

He opted to not answer. "No comment," he barked as he ushered his wife towards the courtroom. As he opened the door he was struck instantly by the weight and quality of its wood; mahogany.

"Mr. Bennett?" a reporter called to Mark, "Should Jeffries die for killing your wife?"

Mark turned and glared at the man, then without a word, passed into the courtroom.

Superior Court Judge Samuel Adams' courtroom resonated with a hushed murmur, like a busy library.

Indeed, from the shelves lining the walls came the smell of old law books; musty knowledge.

As Brady and his family claimed a bench several rows behind the defense table, he recognized David Allen Green from pictures in the newspaper and was struck by how large a man he was; that, and the strangeness of his gray ponytail dangling down the back of his conservative navy blue suit.

"Mr. Brady," a woman said, touching his shoulder. Brady stood and offered his hand.

"Ms. Worjowski."

"You remember."

"Of course," he said, then introduced his family. "What does your boss think will happen here?"

"To be honest, Prosecutor McNamara thought they'd argue pre-meditation at the hearing, not this." She glanced towards Ron Dubek at the prosecution table. "I've got to talk to Ron before the hearing starts. I'll catch you afterwards." Her heels clacked on the black and white tiles as she walked away.

"What did she say?" Sarah asked as he sat down.

"She'll talk to us later."

A door at the front of the room opened and Jeffries entered in manacles. His long hair had been washed, combed and pulled into a tidy ponytail. Above the line of Jeffries' trimmed beard, Brady could no longer detect the scratches he had seen at the arraignment. Jeffries wore civilian clothes; a tweed sport coat one size too small with worn brown elbow patches. His wrists, knobby and naked, hung from the sleeves. The rest of his outfit consisted of a wrinkled white shirt, blue jeans and worn cowboy boots.

As the jail-guard freed the prisoner's wrists, Jeffries turned and nodded to someone behind and to the right of Brady. It was only a nod; no smile, no warmth, and he did not turn again as he took a seat next to David Allen Green.

Brady turned slowly, casually, as if surveying the courtroom, his eyes coming to rest on a woman. She was large, on the verge of obesity, and her hair was like the defendant's, long, brown, and secured in a ponytail. Her wet cheeks shined behind bifocals as she looked from Jeffries to the needlepoint keeping her hands busy. As if through a will of their own, her fingers moved furiously until suddenly they stopped and the woman pulled a tissue from her sleeve to wipe her nose.

It surprised him, the amount of pity he felt for the woman. If Jeffries was her son he was just as dead to her as Beth was to him. He watched her hands work the needlepoint. Perhaps she was making something for Jeffries; a small piece of herself.

Brady knew his assumption was correct when David Allen Green rose from his chair, strode quickly to the woman and whispered in her ear. She nodded, then the lawyer patted her shoulder and returned to the defense table.

"Please rise for the Honorable Samuel Adams," called the bailiff. Everyone stood as the judge; a large, bald African American man entered through a side door, approached the bench and took his seat.

"Good morning ladies and gentlemen," he said

A sense of bewildered shame fell upon John Brady, for since learning the judge's name, he had possessed a picture in his head of the patriot from Massachusetts. A Caucasian.

"Mr. Green," Adams called, "On behalf of the defendant, William Jeffries, Jr., who pled guilty in the murder of Elizabeth Bennett, you have filed two pre-trial motions challenging the state's request for a special sentencing hearing. I have read your motions and the responses from the state. I will now entertain brief oral arguments on these motions. Mr. Green, you may proceed with arguments on behalf of your first motion."

"Thank you, your Honor." Green stood slowly and buttoned his suit coat.

"The first motion filed with the court states simply that Mr. Jeffries had incompetent and inadequate counsel at his arraignment. The public defender in question, Ms. Hancock, should not have allowed Mr. Jeffries to plead guilty because they so clearly had a very good case to make against premeditation, which, as the court knows, is a necessary element of aggravated murder in the first degree. This mistake is so obvious and egregious that unto itself it indicates incompetence. The defense, therefore, asks that the current plea of guilty be set aside, and the case be remanded for trial with a plea of not guilty."

With the air of a courtesan, David Allen Green bowed his head slightly at Judge Adams, unbuttoned his jacket, and sat down.

"Thank you, sir," boomed Adams, "Mr. Dubek?"

Ron Dubek shot from his chair and stood straight as an arrow as he began his response.

"Your Honor, Mr. Jeffries is mentally competent, therefore capable of assisting in his own defense. The public defender, Ms Rachel Hancock, is an experienced criminal lawyer. She and Mr. Jeffries, after carefully reviewing the facts of the case and all their legal options, entered a plea at arraignment that was accepted by Judge C. Robert Charleston. That court certainly saw no 'obvious or egregious' lack of competence in Mr. Jeffries' counsel. Ms. Hancock believed that Mr. Jeffries' best option was to plead guilty to the murder, then oppose the imposition of the death penalty. Mr. Green may disagree with that strategy, but there is no legal basis for the defense to claim inadequate counsel. We request the court deny the motion by the defense."

Dubek sat and whispered into Paula Worjowski's ear.

Brady stared at the posterior of Jeffries' head. His brown hair, pulled taught into a ponytail, had a disturbing quality. The pale skin in the nape of his neck looked delicate and adolescent and feminine. Suddenly, Jeffries coughed and showed his profile, startling Brady.

"She keeps staring at us," Sarah whispered.

"Who?"

"That big woman in back of us. To the side. The one doing needlepoint."

Brady turned and looked at the woman. She looked at Brady over the top of the glasses perched on her nose. Their eyes locked upon one another and Brady did not know what to do. Her hands went slack as she rested the needlepoint in her lap. She mouthed the words, "I'm sorry," then bowed her head, as if in prayer.

Brady took Sarah's hand in his and squeezed it. "It's okay," he whispered. "I think she's Jeffries' mother."

"Anything further, Mr. Green?" Judge Adams asked.

Sarah turned to look at the woman again.

Green remained seated. "No sir."

"Very well. Proceed to your second motion."

Green leaned into Jeffries and whispered in his ear. Their ponytails bounced as they conversed, then David Allen Green stood again, buttoned his coat and addressed the court.

"Your Honor, this motion would obviously only apply if you deny our first motion to set aside the guilty plea entered at arraignment. This motion is also much more complicated than the motion we just discussed. Our motion argues that the state's request for a special sentencing hearing can not be granted because none of the aggravating circumstances as defined in the Revised Code of Washington are present in this case, and thus Mr. Jeffries is not eligible for the death penalty."

Green reached for a large green manual on the defense table, leafed through it, then picked it up.

"RCW 10.95.020," he read, "'Aggravated first degree murder defined. A person is guilty of aggravated first degree murder if he or she commits first degree murder as defined by RCW 9A.32.030, paragraph I, sub A, *and* one or more of the following aggravating circumstances exist.'"

Green looked up at Judge Adams. "Here we call the court's attention to paragraph three of that section. This paragraph enumerates the aggravating circumstance which the state cites as the basis for their request for a death penalty hearing. This is the only aggravating circumstance that they claim exists in this case." He looked back down at the big law book and continued reading.

"'Number three: at the time of the act resulting in death, the person was *in custody in* a county or city-county jail as a consequence of having been accused of or adjudicated guilty of a felony.'"

Green laid the book down on the table by Jeffries. Then, slowly he said, "*In custody in.*" He paused and looked towards the prosecutor, then to the judge.

"What's he doing?" Sarah whispered.

"Shh," Brady patted her knee. "I'm not sure."

Green resumed his argument. His voice was strong and confident. "Now the court knows the facts of this case. Mr. Jeffries killed Ms. Bennett at a rest stop after fleeing from work release, he certainly wasn't in the county jail at the time. And the court knows who writes the laws in this book. Our legislature. The people we elect. Every sentence of every paragraph has been fought over and revised down to every last detail. That would certainly be true in the case of something so important as when to apply the death penalty. *In custody in*, not in the custody *of.* The legislature clearly intended this to cover murder committed in the county jail. They wanted to create a disincentive for someone who has already been convicted of a felony, perhaps already sentenced to life in prison, to kill a guard or a fellow inmate on the assumption that they had nothing to lose. My client was not in jail at the time of the murder, so this circumstance does not apply and there is no basis for a death penalty hearing. We ask, therefore, that the request for a special sentencing hearing be denied, and that the defendant receive a life sentence without parole. Thank you."

As Green resumed his seat, Jeffries slapped him on the shoulder. Green turned to him and gave him what Brady thought was a look of disgust.

Ron Dubek was on his feet even before the judge recognized him. He held a copy of what looked to be the same book Green had read from. "Your Honor, if I may read from the same section Mr. Green cites, RCW 10.95.020, but this time paragraph two. 'At the time of the act resulting in the death, the person was serving a term of imprisonment, had escaped, or was on authorized or unauthorized leave in or from a state facility or program for the incarceration or treatment of persons adjudicated guilty of crimes.'"

Dubek closed the book and held it to his chest. "Your Honor, two points need to be made. First, counties are sub-units of state government. Mr. Green refers to me as a representative of 'the state,' which is true, even though I am a county employee. In matters of criminal justice counties work as part of the state system. Second, when one is in a work release program, one is still considered in custody."

Dubek paused, then resumed with greater passion. "I make these points, your Honor, because although we have cited paragraph three as the basis for our request for a death penalty hearing, you must read paragraphs two and three together in order to understand legislative intent. Perhaps the legislature was sloppy in their drafting of this section, but if you don't read the two paragraphs together you come to the ridiculous result that Mr. Green is advocating. Namely, that if a convicted felon kills someone in a state prison or a county jail, or if they escape from a state prison or a state treatment program and kill someone, then they get the death penalty; but if they walk away from a county work release program and viciously murder a young wife and mother they don't! That is the sort of garbage that undermines public confidence in our legal system! The state implores you to deny the defense's motion and go forward with the special sentencing hearing."

Green lifted the large green manual inches off the table then dropped it with a thud. "Those are the laws of our state, clear and precise. For the prosecutor to even attempt to say the weakness in his argument is the legislature's fault is ludicrous. They were sloppy in drafting? He knows better. These are the laws of our state."

Legal jargon. Technicalities. Brady felt as if he were audience to a theater of the absurd. He folded his arms across his chest in frustration and in doing so felt something in his breast pocket. His fingers extracted a piece of candy corn with lint and shirt thread stuck to it. Brady studied the tri-colored triangle. Three layers. Three stages of life: infant, adolescent, adult. He blinked and looked about the courtroom as David Allen Green's voice filtered back into his ears.

"The language in paragraph two only applies to state facilities. If the legislature had intended it to apply to both state and county facilities they would have employed parallel construction in paragraphs two and three. They did not because it is not what they intended. Yes, counties are sub-units of the state, but in this section of the RCWs, indeed throughout our laws, they are treated as different and distinct entities. Mr. Dubek may not like the result that the law produces in this case, but the law is clear."

John Brady picked the foreign particles off the candy corn and cut the white tip with his teeth. Though stale, the sugary nugget melted on his tongue. It had been the first time in his life that Halloween had just slipped by. Slowly, he chewed the candy and felt a sense of dread at the impending holidays as he watched the circus around him. David Allen Green took a seat next to Jeffries and began to deposit papers into his briefcase.

Judge Adams rubbed his eyes. "Anything else, Mr. Dubek?"

Ron Dubek remained seated. "No sir."

"Very well. We'll recess for lunch. I'll make my ruling at 2:00."

John Brady watched the two courts guards escort the handcuffed defendant from the room. As he looked at the suede brown patches on Jeffries' elbows, all he wanted was to rinse from his mouth the sickly sweet residue of the single piece of candy corn.


"I find no legal basis to grant the defense's first motion," Judge Samuel Adams began, as the hearing resumed that afternoon. "Mr. Jeffries' counsel, Ms. Hancock, is a competent, experienced criminal lawyer. A plea of guilty was made and accepted by Judge Charleston. Mr. Green may not agree with the decisions made at arraignment, but those decisions are not de facto evidence of incompetence. This motion, therefore, is denied."

David Allen Green made notes on a legal pad. Brady tapped his son on the knee to make him stop biting his fingernails; he had noticed that morning that a few of Danny's fingertips were bloody.

"One down, one to go," he whispered out loud.

On the other side of Danny, Mark sat quietly, his jaw muscles working. He leaned forward, as if to enhance his concentration.

"As to defense's second motion," Judge Adams' voice boomed thickly. "Let it be noted that there have only been 15 death penalty hearings in Washington since capital punishment was reinstated, none of them fitting this fact pattern, so there is no precedence to guide me." Adams put on his reading glasses and shuffled papers in front of him. "I agree with defenses' reading of paragraphs two and three of RCW 10.95.020. They are intended to be distinct, separate circumstances – not to be read together. The wording in paragraph three, '*in custody in,*' and the fact that parallel construction between paragraphs two and three regarding authorized leave was not used indicates that the defenses' argument regarding legislative intent is compelling. This court therefore, finds that paragraph three of RCW 10.95.020, cited by the state as the aggravating circumstance in this case and the basis for the request for a special sentencing hearing is not applicable, and the motion to deny the state's request for a special sentencing hearing is granted. Under the law, William Jeffries, Jr. is sentenced to life in prison without possibility of parole, and is hereby remanded to the custody of the Washington State Department of Corrections. This court is adjourned." Adams' gavel slapped his desktop.

Sarah slapped Brady's leg. "What? He gets off? Oh my God!" Several people turned to look. "That's it?!"

"Un-fucking-believable!" Mark said loudly in exasperation, then rested his head in his hands, shielding his eyes. Danny chewed his raw fingertips, his gaze frozen upon Jeffries.

John Brady watched, as for a mere second William Jeffries, Jr. looked up at the ceiling, then turned and looked at his mother. His face was devoid of expression as uniformed guards encircled the defendant's table.

As Brady's family sat absorbing Judge Adams' ruling, the courtroom emptied. Dubek and Green chatted amiably, like two football coaches after a game. Sarah sniffed, "Who are these goddamned laws made for?" Brady put his arm around her as she cried, and he couldn't help but wonder if his daughter's killer had prayed to God in his quick gaze above.

"He's going to live in a cage for the rest of his life," Brady whispered into Sarah's ear. "He'll die there."

She sniffed. "It's not good enough."

As the hot lights of television cameras hit his face, Brady remembered acting in *The Glass Menagerie* in High School. With a protective arm about Sarah's shoulders, they inched towards the elevator.

Each of them were bombarded with questions: Did they agree with the ruling? Was there a sense of closure? Had they wanted the death penalty? Should Jeffries' have died for what he did? Wasn't life in prison punishment enough?

From deep inside, John Brady's emotions, intensified by the heat of the lights, overcame him. Tears stung his eyes. "You know," he said, and when he said it the crowd around him went silent. "You know, I think there is a sense of closure. A little bit. At least for me. In a way, I wanted him to die...and my wife, she wanted the death penalty. I think our whole family is overwhelmed." Brady's throat was dry and he swallowed hard.

"But you know, what the verdict was or could have been doesn't matter. William Jeffries, Jr. doesn't really matter anymore, at least not to me. He'll pay for his crime. He'll spend the rest of his life in prison. I know that God will deal with him. What matters is right now; the present and the future with the kind of justice system that let this happen in the first place. Something must be done."

"Such as?" asked a reporter.

"What would you do, Mr. Brady; or should I ask, what are you going to do?"

Brady was hot and nervous, yet excited, as a bead of perspiration trickled from his hairline down his temple. Sarah tugged at his elbow. Though he knew she wanted to escape the limelight, knew she seethed with anger over the ruling, the press had him hooked. He needed to talk.

"As we speak, the ACLU's case against King County is pending. They're suing because the jail was built for 1,500 and at the current time there are about 2,700 inmates in there. That's the reason prisoners aren't serving their sentences." His heart banged within his ribcage. "More jails need to be built. Convicted criminals must do their time. All of it! And I am determined to pressure the legislature into giving more time and money to this problem."

He turned to ask Sarah a question and realized she had joined Mark and Danny by the elevators. Sarah's expression was incredulous, as if he were a traitor.

"Mr. Brady,"

"That's all I have to say," he said forcefully. As he walked to his family the reporters scattered like gulls when there is no more food to be had.

# PART II

## REACTION

*I refuse to let death hamper life.*
*Death must only enter life to define it.*

Jean Paul Sarte
From *No Exit,* 1947

THE HUM OF the refrigerator. A click of the furnace, followed by warm air pushing through vents. The thump of the Thanksgiving morning newspaper landing on the doorstep, tossed by the old Ukrainian woman who drove her old Buick twenty miles over the speed limit. Stopping to throw a paper. Speeding up. Stopping. Up on a curb. She would nod and smile and show her metal teeth.

As the rest of the household slept, John Brady stood at the kitchen sink in his bathrobe, his arm elbow deep inside the thawed turkey. He could see his reflection in the window against the pre-dawn sky as he pulled the bag of innards out of the bird. His mother used to fry the contents of the icy bag. Necks, gizzards and livers were full of protein she would say, before feeding them to their Labrador retriever.

Brady maneuvered the bulky mass into the largest baking pan he could find, wondering how an object weighing twenty-three pounds could be so cumbersome. As he rubbed vegetable oil on the bluish, goose-bumpy skin, he envisioned his daughter's naked flesh exposed to the frigid mountain air. He shook off the thought and began stuffing the carcass, then breathed a sigh of relief when the turkey was in the oven.

The sun rose, sending shafts of light glistening across the frosty lawn. A brown, non-descript bird landed on the cedar bird feeder, found it empty, and flew away. Brady watched the feeder sway and made a mental note to fill it, wondering what it must be like to search for food. Sipping coffee at the kitchen table, he relished the quiet, knowing there would be movement upstairs soon enough.

He thought of the decision he had made over the last few days, and his plan to tell Sarah and the family at dinner. What would he do if Sarah did not support him? Already, there was a feeling, a presence growing between them. He felt that she was living for Emily. Only Emily. He hoped his plans would draw them together in a common cause.

He had spoken with his boss, Roger, and with Herb Craft, President of Northwest Timber. Each of them felt Brady's idea was a win-win situation. Good for Brady, and the company.

Brady heard a scampering of footsteps. A creak; third stair from the bottom. He smiled. Slowly, the sliding door to the dining room inched open. Running steps, then, "Boo Pappa!" Emily shrieked as she jumped onto her grandfather's lap.

"Good morning!" He squeezed her then looked into her flushed, just-awake face. "Happy Thanksgiving punkin. Wanna see the turkey?"

She nodded, eyes wide, as she followed him across the kitchen.

"Stand back now," he said gently. When he lowered the oven door he said, "Very hot," and they were hit by a burst of turkey aroma.

"Wow," Emily whispered. She grabbed Brady's hand as if the turkey were a thing to fear. "The turkey dead?' she asked.

"Yes, sweetheart," he answered.

Sarah pulled the cork out of the bottle. It slid out easily, flawlessly. No cork crumbs. All morning she had thought about Beth. Whenever she tried to concentrate on the turkey in the oven, the side dishes still to be prepared, or the table settings, Mark or Emily would enter the room and remind her. An emptiness. A void.

Merlot. Sarah swished the wine slowly around her mouth and swallowed. It traveled; warm, down her throat as she watched Brady take the turkey out of the oven. It sizzled in its own juices on the stove top.

"Do you want a glass of wine?" Sarah asked.

Brady looked at the clock as he wiped his hands with a towel. "Why not? It's noon." He wanted Sarah to be happy and he knew she did not like to drink alone. He accepted the glass she handed him and took a sip. "It's good."

"Yes, it is," she agreed.

"I talked to Roger a little while ago. He's going to stop by later. After dinner."

"Oh? How come?" Sarah asked. She felt a hint of the wine in her limbs. "I'll feel rude that we didn't ask him to dinner."

"Oh, no. He had plans to go to his brother's for dinner. He'll just come for a drink. There are a few things I need to talk to you about. And I'd like him here."

"Then it's about work?"

"Partly."

Sarah had felt the blood rush to her cheeks and secretly she was jubilant that she had colored her hair; dark brown with an auburn tint. No more gray. And she had painted her nails. She felt younger and prettier than she had in weeks. She wondered if they had bought enough wine.

Brady sipped his wine, and as if he had read her thoughts, said, "By the way, I haven't told you how beautiful you look. Your hair, it looks lovely."

Sarah blushed again at his compliment and the thought of Roger's presence later. "Thank you," she said. "I was beginning to look like an old woman." She smiled.

"No, you weren't," said Brady. He could not remember the last time he had seen his wife smile.

Just then, wearing Big Bird slippers and a plaid dress, Emily slid into the kitchen. "Me have pumpkin pie?" She traveled the length of counter and being too short to see, felt around with her deft fingers.

Sarah laughed. "Em, sweetie, we'll eat very soon. Let Grampa and me finish with the last few things. Now, go see your Daddy."

"Kay," she said and ran from the room.

Brady poured more wine. "Let's say that for today we forget our troubles and, I know it sounds corny, but let's be thankful for what we have."

"Salute," said Sarah, raising her glass.


Brady liked his son's new girlfriend. Her affection towards Danny seemed genuine and he liked that. There was some measure of satisfaction in seeing his own offspring in a good relationship. He must have done something right.

Emily had pulled Jessie away from the dinner table and led her out of the room. They had taken to each other immediately.

"I really like her," Sarah said when they heard Jessie's laughter from the den. "She seems so down to Earth."

"I like her too," said Danny, his youthful face flushed with wine and emotion as his fingers picked at the label on a wine bottle.

"You're making a mess," Mark said gesturing towards small shards of paper amidst dirty plates with remnants of turkey bones. "Pass me the damn bottle."

"Allow me." Danny reached across the table and filled his glass.

"Your girlfriend seems to get along good with Em. Emily likes her. That's good," Mark nodded.

A silence fell among them. They heard Emily screaming, "Mowgli! Mowgli!"

"Okay, okay!" Jessie laughed. Then from the doorway she asked, "Mark, where are her videos?"

"In the bookshelf in the front hallway, hon," Sarah answered without glancing at Mark.

"I like her," she said to her son. She reached across and laid her hand atop his.

"I know," Danny laughed. "You told me."

Mark shifted in his seat and played with the turkey bones on his plate. "You know, thank God for all of you. I mean, Emily would be stuck with pitiful me if it weren't for you guys." With a leg bone as a rake, he pushed gravy, gristle and green bean casserole into a pile.

Brady leaned forward. "Stop it. You're a good father and she's damn lucky to have you. But she is lucky to have us too. Most kids don't have family like this."

"Things are going to get better. It's just gonna take time," said Danny.

In the quiet that ensued they heard Emily clap her hands as the movie started. "Yay, Jessie!"

Sarah rose from the table. "I need more wine." And like a waitress, she deftly carried several dishes and glasses to the kitchen.


The dishes were done and they had reassembled at the table for pie. Roger Tattinger had arrived, as if on cue.

"Are you hungry? Did you eat?" Sarah asked.

"Oh God, I've eaten enough for an army. At my brother's house."

"Because we have plenty of leftovers." She lit a cigarette.

"Thanks, I'm fine," Roger said. He had taken the seat next to Mark which Emily had vacated. She was sound asleep, curled up on the floor by the television.

"Like I really need to eat pie now," Danny sighed.

"Oh, who cares? It's a holiday," said Jessie.

Brady nodded to Sarah. "This apple pie is excellent sweetheart."

"Thank you," Sarah answered. She did not enjoy zinfandel as much as merlot. When the current bottle was depleted all that was left was a mediocre chardonnay. Sarah found most chardonnays too dry. She did not enjoy a drink that made her thirsty.

"Yes, very good," Roger agreed.

"Okay everybody," Brady proclaimed, "I've got something I'd like to talk to you all about. Actually, it's a plan I've come up with." He drank an inch of wine.

"Should we have a drum roll?" Sarah teased as she offered Jessie more wine. The college senior gladly accepted.

"Ha, ha," Brady mocked. But he felt nervous not knowing how they would react. "Needless to say, we've all been through hell the last few months. Not one of us is the same person we were before Beth died. Now I for one, I simply can't go back to work as if nothing has happened." Though her eyes were locked on his, he couldn't read Sarah's face. He finished his wine and motioned for the bottle.

"Tell me about it. When I go back, all the kids are going to stare and treat me different," said Mark. "Can't wait."

"Tell them about it. Not all the details or anything," said Danny, "But you know kids; they'll probably think it's cool. Scary but cool."

Mark sighed and looked at Brady. "Sorry for interrupting you."

"It's okay," Brady acknowledged, as he took a sip of wine. His mouth felt full of cotton. "Okay. At first I thought it was a crazy idea. But then I thought, why the hell not?"

"Why not what, Dad?" Danny asked.

"Why not do something? Really do something that would matter. For Beth. For all of us. I mean, really make something meaningful come out of all we've gone through." He paused. "I think Beth would like it."

Although her head told her not to, Sarah poured herself a glass of chardonnay. Cold and dry. "So, what are you talking about?" she asked irritably.

Brady fingered a spoon on the table, pressing a fingerprint onto silver. "Some people have been talking to me about running for the State Senate. And I think I'm going to do it."

They could hear bongo drums and shrieking monkeys from the television. Brady watched his wife's face.

"You? A politician?!" she asked incredulously.

"Why not, Mom?" asked Danny, leaning forward, forearms crossed on the table. "I think it would be awesome. So, you guys would have to move to Washington, D.C.?"

John Brady laughed, "No, son, the State Senate. In Olympia. The legislature. No, we would not have to move."

Sarah lit a cigarette, inhaled and blew out smoke. She looked from Brady to Roger to Brady.

Mark's eyes were glazed with wine, yet his interest was piqued. "You're talking about a year from now?"

Feeling his wife's eyes on him, Brady nodded. "Yes, but I would need to start a campaign right now."

"What does that do for Beth?" Mark asked.

"I don't know exactly, but I know there has to be something I can do in the legislature to change the system. It's all I can think of," Brady said.

"Are you a Republican or a Democrat?" asked Jessie.

Sarah's fist hit the table. "Wait a minute! First things first. Why the hell didn't you talk to me about this? You're just going to quit your job? You don't know anything about politics. What if you lose?"

Mark leaned back in his chair and it creaked.

"I approached it this way because it made the most sense. Roger's here to help me explain what Northwest is willing to do to let me run. I just thought that telling the whole family at once the best way."

"Well, you were wrong," said Sarah.

"Sarah, John would not quit his job at Northwest," said Roger. "Doesn't have to. We've met with Herb Craft, and we've checked it out. Businesses do it all the time. Brady can campaign when he needs to and when doesn't, he works at Northwest. If he wins he'll take a leave of absence while the legislature is in session. He'll take a cut in pay equal to a Senator's pay, which, believe me, isn't much. Being a legislator in this state is a part-time job."

The sight of her husband nodding his head in affirmation made Sarah's face hot. Thoughts banged around inside her head. *He had not run his plans by her first... it was Thanksgiving... Roger was here, and Jessie for that matter... how was she supposed to act? He was making big plans without her. Trying to do something good in the wake of Beth's death. And what was she doing? Falling apart. Son of a bitch.*

"You know, I'm sorry, but I'm not up to this," Sarah stated firmly. She picked up her glass and left the room.

Brady stared at his clasped hands for a long moment. "Is this stupid?" He asked no one in particular. "Is this idea stupid?"

Uncomfortably, Roger glanced towards the living room where he could see Sarah fidgeting with the stereo.

"Dad, for what it's worth, I think this could be a really good thing," said Danny. "For the whole family. I think Mom will come around."

Brady nodded, appreciative of his son's positive attitude. "I hope, I mean…maybe I could actually do something to change things. Something to keep these violent assholes behind bars."

"I'll help you," Mark declared. "Whatever I can."

"Me too," said Danny.

"Good. Good," Brady said. He took a sip of wine and looked towards the living room.

Sarah was fully aware that she was drunk as she turned up the volume. She was also aware that everyone else knew it. What she felt was anger. Anger and jealousy. He was moving on, moving forward.

She had played the CD often the last few weeks. The sound of Patsy Cline's voice soothed. Deep, resonant and full of yearning, it somehow gave her emotions an outlet. Her eyes burned as the first notes of *"Crazy,"* plunked from the speakers. As tears welled in her eyes, she laughed and sipped her wine. She knew she was drinking too much.

*"Crazy…I'm crazy for feeling so lonely…I'm crazy…crazy for feeling so blue…"*

Sarah did not care who saw her. She knew that as they sat around the dining table they were trying not to watch her sashay about the living room furniture, hugging her wineglass to her breast.

*"…Crazy for thinking that my love would hold you…"*

She closed her eyes and saw Beth at thirteen or fourteen, here, in this very room, learning to slow dance with Brady. The song ended as she stood at the bay window, looking at the sunset behind the Olympic Mountains, far across the valley and the Puget Sound. It had been a beautiful day for Thanksgiving.

A slow tinkle of piano keys as *"Sweet Dreams"* began. As the slow beat vibrated in her bones, Brady's arms encircled her waist from behind. Burying his face in the nape of her neck, he smelled her hair.

"Are you mad? Do you hate me?"

"Yes and yes. Now go away," she said, pulling away from him. "Don't spill my wine."

Brady stepped aside and put his hands in his pockets.

*"...why can't I forget you and start my life anew...instead of having sweet dreams about you..."*

Sarah thought of Roger watching her from the other room and liked the thought. Then she felt a pang of guilt. "Let's go to her grave tomorrow. We should have gone today," she said.

"We'll go tomorrow," he nodded. "I need to know what you think about my plan."

"Don't," she said. "I'm not going to talk now." She felt dizzy and aroused. "God she had something."

Not knowing if his wife meant Beth or Patsy Cline, Brady said nothing. When *"I Fall to Pieces"* came on, Sarah said, "How appropriate. I'm going outside for a cigarette and fresh air." She laughed. "Isn't that an oxymoron?"

Brady followed her into the dining room. "We'll clean up the rest of this stuff," he said. "Right men?"

"Hey, who said we were done?" Danny asked spooning whipped cream onto a sliver of pumpkin pie.

Sarah set her wine glass on the table and grabbed the chardonnay bottle. "Are we having fun yet?"

"I love this music," noted Jessie.

"Good girl," Sarah nodded and left the room. Once outside she was startled that the sun had nearly set. The air felt cold and good. Leaning on the rail of the deck, she lit a cigarette and blew a plume of smoke into the air, then watched it evaporate. Through the veil of curtain sheers she could see her family at the dining table.

Remembering the wine bottle in her hand she took a swig and felt simultaneously dizzy and nauseous. Then she tipped the bottle over the rail, dousing the dormant roses in the garden.

"Wasting good wine on your garden?"

Sarah jumped then laughed. "Roger. I didn't hear you." She looked at the gnarled, thorny branches of the roses. "I need no more wine."

"Mm," Roger nodded his agreement. "You okay?"

"It's been a long day."

Roger watched the scene Sarah watched through the sheers. Danny, Jessie and Mark laughed as if on cue. Then, worn out, Mark laid his head upon the table.

"I think we've all overdone it today. The wine, I mean." Through the sliding door to the kitchen, she saw her husband pick up their sleeping grandchild. Dead weight. An angel. Even from a distance Emily's rosy cheeks glowed as she nuzzled into Brady's neck. Sarah felt a pang of affection as Brady left the room with the child. Or was it guilt? She wasn't sure. But she did know she should not be alone with the man next to her.

On the television screen a trio of vultures circled about Mowgli the man-cub. Then there was fire and a Bengal tiger. Shere Khan.

Roger leaned on the railing next to her and when his hand touched the nape of her neck, fingers messaging, Sarah jerked away.

She pulled her cigarettes from her pocket. "Don't."

"Don't what?"

"Don't do that. You know what." She lit a cigarette and the smoke was thicker and whiter than their breath.

"It's quite cold out here," said Roger.

"Meaning what?"

"Meaning it's cold out here."

Sarah watched his face as he spoke and wondered what the shadow of stubble would feel like against her skin. His aftershave smelled of leather. What she wanted was to kiss him hard on the mouth. Then erase it. Rewind.

Without realizing it Sarah took a step back from him. She smoked and thought about Brady putting Emily to bed. Tucking her in with Art the Bear. Thoughts of Roger were beneath her. She needed to think of her family. Beth. She was drunk and she was mortified by her own thoughts. "We better go inside."

"Guess so," said Roger.

"By the way," she said grabbing his sleeve, "when did Brady talk to you about this? How long have you known?" She exhaled smoke out over the roses.

"We've talked a few times over the last couple days."

"He should've talked to me first," she said.

Roger nodded then crossed his arms over his chest. "Some Republican staffer in Olympia called him. That's what started this. I think he wanted to see if his job at Northwest was safe if he ran. We met with Herb. Brady wanted to make sure it could be done before he approached you. Your family. I mean, in his defense."

An airplane was passing overhead. "You don't have to defend him," Sarah said loudly over the jet noise. They watched the red lights on the plane blink as it disappeared. "This, his plan, has just thrown me for a loop."

Roger nodded.

"I guess I didn't think he had it in him, you know?" She crushed her cigarette on the railing and dropped it into the empty wine bottle. "I'm just mad at life. Don't mind me."

"I won't," said Roger.

"It's dark out and I'm freezing," Sarah said heading for the door.

Roger opened the door for her. Sarah stepped inside and was enveloped in familiar warmth; smells, noises, voices. Her family. Her duty.

* * * *

BRADY FELT it in his lower back; a soreness that meant he was alive. Sweat tickled his temples as his feet moved on the treadmill beneath him. His plan was to relieve some stress before his meeting with the Senate Republican staff. He had finally talked Sarah into a meeting in their home, hopefully to seal the deal.

Across the bedroom the television was tuned on CSPAN. Politics at every level consumed him now. Brady felt drawn to it for the first time in his life. And it wasn't that he had not cared before. He had just never felt like he needed to pay attention.

According to the digital display panel on the treadmill he had walked two miles. He wondered where two miles would get him if he started walking from that spot in his bedroom, through the wall, into the yard, through the neighborhood.

On CSPAN a gaggle of journalists and cameras were following candidates through school hallways, eaves-dropping while they mingled and ate sloppy sandwiches at a bar and grill. Politics, New Hampshire style. For the first time in his life, John Brady found the run for the Presidency fascinating.

As he watched and walked he also decided he needed a new suit. Navy blue wool. He knew there would be a photo shoot for his brochure and subsequent mailings. Breathing deep he kept walking.

He focused on the crucifix on the wall and he wondered if it was a coincidence that everything was happening at Christmastime. The birth of Jesus. The birth of man. A new life...*Please God, bless my family. And let me be on the right path. For me, my family, Sarah.*

Brady watched his feet as if they had a will of their own. Walk. Walk. Walk away. Sometimes he wished he could.

\* \* \* \*

THE FRIGID MORNING air slapped his sweaty face. Frost covered the neighborhood, the shafts of sunlight poking through heavy clouds made everything jewel-like. Brady hugged his chest with his bare arms as he descended the steps in search of the morning newspaper. Unable to find it in the bushes, he maneuvered carefully on the icy aggregate. It was then he saw the paper, rolled and wrapped in plastic on the sidewalk at the end of the driveway.

Metal dragging on concrete, the sound amplified by the cold, quiet morning. He saw his neighbor a few houses away positioning a ladder against a gutter as he put up Christmas lights.

Reaching for the newspaper, a small, dark object caught his eye. Brady stepped into the street and squatted on the asphalt. Freshly dead, the sparrow had been run over by a car. The tracks of the vehicle were visible on the frosty road. A thumb-sized puddle of scarlet blood on the bird's chest seemed violent. He remembered a time he had been inching in traffic and had seen a dead opossum on the meridian, its' pale, human-like paw, a hand, reaching upward as if for help.

Without thinking, Brady touched the bird with his finger. He thought he could feel warmth.

"Squished flat."

Startled, Brady looked up and greeted his neighbor. "Hi, Jim."

"Sorry, didn't mean to startle you." The man studied the dead bird.

"Saw you putting up your lights."

"Yeah, thought I'd get going on it."

"I should do the same," said Brady. They both nodded in silence.

"I need to get a shovel," Brady said.

\* \* \* \*

HE STARED AT his reflection in mirrors. He studied his profile. Was it a face people could trust? A face they would vote for? Did he have strong features? Did he look honest? He wondered if he was kidding himself with the whole venture.

"Bye, pappa!" exclaimed Emily as she ran into the room, wrapped her arms about his legs and squeezed.

Sarah held the little purple jacket while Emily pushed her arms into the sleeves.

"Be careful walking with grandma. It's very icy and slippery outside."

"Kay!"

"And you have fun playing with Abigail."

"Kay! Bye!"

"Offer them coffee if they get here before I'm back," Sarah instructed.

"Don't worry," said Brady. He stood at the window and watched Sarah and Emily take tiny steps down the slick driveway. He was glad he had disposed of the dead bird. Emily would have been upset to have seen it.

Sarah held her granddaughter's mittened hand. Several of their neighbors with small children had reached out to them, offering to watch Emily. Brady sensed that his wife was becoming more friendly with a few of Emily's friends parents.

Their breath hung in the air for a moment as they disappeared around the corner. His neighbor directly across the street, Ernest, an eighty-four year old ex-Marine stepped onto his porch. Ernest was unfurling an American flag on its pole. Slowly, he wriggled the pole into the holder on the siding of his house. The old Marine pulled the fabric taught, erasing wrinkles, and watched for a few seconds while a breeze rippled the flag. Then he went inside.

Ernest followed the same routine each morning. Presenting the colors. At dusk he took the flag down, wrapping it carefully around the pole with a small bronze eagle on the top. The old man's patriotism made John Brady smile and feel good. It made him think twice about where he lived and what he had.

\* \* \* \*

"HAZEL NEWIRTH IS the last Democrat dinosaur in the forty-second district. Hell, in all of Southeast King County. Besides that, she's old and fat and lazy," Gary Lake, Senate Republican Communications Director, said with a grin. "That helps us immensely."

Joe Booth was a large man with oiled hair and a trimmed mustache. He wore red suspenders. "She won't work hard," said the Senate Chief of Staff. "Hasn't had to campaign in years. Her seat has always been safe. A shoe-in for re-election."

"So, I have a shot because she's old?" Brady asked.

Gary Lake leaned forward. He wore a salt and pepper suit and black shoes with tassels. "That and one other major fact. The district is and has been changing. Used to be solid Democrat. No more. It's swing."

Booth nodded. "Boeing and Microsoft. The success of those two ensure the current trend. Lots of young families moving in who vote Republican."

"How old is Hazel Newirth?" Sarah asked.

Lake looked at Booth. "What? Late sixties? Seventy, even?"

John Brady gulped his coffee, his nerves alive with caffeine. Adrenaline. "Okay. I'm sure you're aware that I know close to nothing about politics. The mechanics. What do I have to do? What about in-depth questions on public policy? Or taxes? Or education? I know nothing."

"Fair question," Lake agreed.

"And who helps him?" asked Sarah fidgeting with the crease in her slacks then crossing her legs. She didn't trust these young staff people.

"Mrs. Brady, we are totally behind John," Lake said. "Our job is to win races and we feel we have a great chance here. It's not in our best interest to have John look like a fool. It's our job to help him. We'll tutor him and give him all sorts of reading material."

Joe Booth motioned to the young woman in the armchair beside him. "Okay, John, Pam, here, has been assigned to your race. She has two others also. Pam, Gary and I will run the campaign. During the legislative session we're all state employees. During campaign season we take leaves and work for the campaign committee."

Pam Naughton smiled as her hand brushed a strand of hair behind her ear. Approximately thirty, she had been Senate staff for five years. "My job is helping you through the day to day grunge work. Doorbelling, yard signs, debates, direct mail, and the big thing: fundraising. I'll help you with all of it."

Booth shook his head. "We will inundate you with statistics and facts. You're quick. We've seen that. You will be as much of an expert as you need to be."

Pen wedged between her lips, Pam Naughton shuffled through her oxblood briefcase. Removing the pen she said, "Here we go." She tossed a paperback booklet into Brady's lap. "Talking points for candidates. Mostly stuff on education and taxes."

"Okay." Brady leafed through the text.

"Oh, and take this. This will be helpful." It was a small hardbound copy of the United States Constitution and the Washington State Constitution.

Pam Naughton wore no makeup and was still attractive. Brady knew his wife would not trust that. He could sense Sarah seizing up the young woman.

"We just need to know you'll work hard. Leave the details to us," said Lake. "Lots of people say they'd like to run for the Legislature. Or Congress. Thing is, they won't work for it."

Brady nodded. He understood. "I think you know I'll give this everything I have. A year ago, in my wildest dreams, I never would have believed I'd run for office. Ever. Any office. School board. PTA. I'm doing this for Beth. And if I win I will do everything in my power to make things better. Especially in the criminal justice system."

Booth banged his knee with a closed fist. "There you go! There's our candidate! And get this- I've had all Newirth's votes on crime pulled. You could practically run on that issue alone. Liberal, liberal, liberal. She is so out of step. On the complete opposite end of the spectrum from you. She's a goner."

There was a high-pitched ring from Gary Lake's coat pocket. He answered his cell phone as he walked into the dining room.

"You have to be willing to call people and ask for money," said Pam.

"Total strangers?" Sarah asked.

"Yes," Pam nodded. "But we'll give him lists. Previous donors to Republican candidates. Small businesses. People with money, and agendas that would benefit from a Republican majority. Don't worry; all they can do is say no."

"More coffee, anyone?" Sarah asked as she excused herself.

She passed through the dining room where Gary Lake stood at the window speaking into his cell phone. "Okay, but there's no way I can cancel. I'm sorry, I was home early yesterday, Cath. What am I supposed to do, not work? I know you're the one stuck bringing him to the doctors. What am I supposed to do?"

Suddenly, Sarah had a different view of this man in the salt and pepper business suit. He looked at her, smiled and gave an embarrassed shrug. Somehow the gesture made Sarah relax; this man understood. He had a family.

\* \* \* \*

WERE LADY BUGS SUPPOSED to be alive when there was snow outside? For several days Brady had pondered the question as he observed the two ladybugs in his bathroom. He had not told anyone because he felt it was special, a sign perhaps; a small miracle in the dead of winter in his bathroom. For some reason it made him recall the dead and bloody bird on the street.

At times the ladybugs were motionless, sitting idly on the edges of the mirror. He noticed them in his peripheral vision. Then they would crawl slowly, opposite their reflections, making four bugs, across the mirror as Brady shaved. Sometimes he heard the faint hum of their tiny wings.

Yet, there was nothing to sustain the insects in the bathroom and Brady observed them for a few more days then he saw them no more.

\* \* \* \*

THE MORNING POST-INTELLIGENCER carried the story that had already traveled through his neighborhood like wildfire. A local high school girl, who lived only a few streets away from Brady, had given birth in a McDonald's restroom. The newborn, a boy, was heard crying in the restaurant's garbage dumpster. In critical condition, the baby was at Mary Bridge Children's Hospital in Tacoma. The girl's parents said they had no idea their daughter had been pregnant.

"Will they prosecute her? With her being a minor?" Sarah asked.

"I don't know."

Brady and Sarah were at the kitchen table having coffee. Across the room Emily held a conversation with her Barbie doll while watching Sesame Street.

Sarah looked up from the paper. "How in God's name could her parents not know? There are too many signs. So many changes. I knew Beth was pregnant before she even told us."

Cradling Barbie swathed in a small crocheted blanket, Emily told them to whisper.

"Shh!" she hissed. "Baby's sleeping."

"Okay," whispered Brady. He kept his voice low as he asked his wife, "Did you see that McNamara announced he's running?"

"I thought everybody knew that already."

"Now it's official."

"Oh."

"Juice?" Emily asked loudly.

Sarah laughed. "Baby awake? Sure you can have juice sweetie. Come in here."

John Brady watched as Emily grasped the spill-proof cup with two hands, sucking on it long and hard. Out of breath, she returned to the television.

"God, I hope that baby lives," remarked Sarah. She folded the newspaper and tossed it across the table. "In some places, I saw a news story, I think it was Germany, but also in this country somewhere, hospitals have a drop-off window. Looks kind of like a drive-thru at a bank. New mothers in trouble can drop off their baby without fear of prosecution. A sensor goes off when a baby is dropped off and a nurse comes to care for it."

"That's a good thing," said Brady.

"So why couldn't it be the norm?"

"I don't know. Maybe it should be."

"If you win you could do something. Pass a law."

"I could try."

Emily burped and laughed.

Brady smiled and nodded his head towards their granddaughter. "You know," he said in a low voice, "It's going to be hard for her to grow up and live with the fact that her mother was murdered senselessly, but can you imagine, I mean, if that baby lives, growing up knowing your mother threw you away?"

* * * *

THE COMPACT RED-LEATHERD manual in his hands looked like a children's book. It felt as if it were made to be held in one hand. Pam Naughton had given him the legislative manual which included the rules of the Washington State Senate, Reeds Rules of Parliamentary Procedure, and the United States and Washington State Constitutions.

Intimidation. The volume had a gold-embossed seal of the state of Washington. It reminded Brady of the book of Cicero he'd had to read for a rhetoric course in college; the only class he had failed. He remembered the book: small, yet daunting.

Once again he felt overwhelmed and bewildered. It was the same feeling he'd had at the arraignment and hearing as he struggled to understand the legal system. Now it was the political system he was trying to learn. As he sat reading the Declaration of Independence and the Bill of Rights, Brady felt meek. He was coming upon fifty years of age and he couldn't remember reading the famous documents; and he was a college graduate. Shouldn't they be required reading in school?

The words he read excited him, increasing his yearning to run for office. He knew it was the right thing. He could make a difference. What a country. An ordinary man like himself could run for office in order to change the system and bring some justice out the murder of his daughter. Then he remembered that this was also a country where an ambitious prosecutor could use his family's tragedy as a stepping stone to run for Governor and his idealism faded a bit.

Brady perused the amendments to the state Constitution and the rules for the legislature. Duties of the individual legislator. Duties of judges. Duties of juries. Rights of citizens. Rights of his daughter and the child she left behind. Rights of the newborn baby boy thrown away in a garbage dumpster with the leftovers from McDonalds.

\* \* \* \*

THE MALL WAS crowded and overheated. The line to have pictures taken with Santa Claus was packed tightly behind theatre ropes. Children and babies dressed in Christmas finery waited in different stages of agitation to sit on the knee of a young, slender, and none too jovial St. Nick.

In a separate line were people who wanted to have their pets photographed with Santa. A big fluff-ball cat attracted the attention of some little girls. There were dogs on leashes, one of which, a pit bull wearing a red sweater growled at anyone venturing near.

John Brady smiled at Emily as she watched the sights from the safety of her father's arms. As Brady tweaked her nose with his he smelled her Barbie toothpaste breath. She wore a new dress of forest-green velvet, black tights, and patent leather shoes.

"John, could you hold these, please? I have one more thing to pick up." Sarah handed him two packages. "How's it going?"

"Slowly."

"They said it would only be a few more minutes," Mark said hopefully.

"Doggie Gramma," Emily said, pointing at the sweater wearing canine.

"Isn't that funny?" Sarah laughed. "Unbelievable. I'm going to Penney's. I'll meet you right here."

When her turn came, Emily was tentative, warily climbing on Santa's knee. All the while she kept her eyes on Mark and Brady. A college co-ed dressed as an elf stood by the camera focusing on Emily.

Watching his granddaughter, Brady was hit by a wave of excruciating emotion. Out of nowhere came the thought of the small poinsettia his family had placed at Beth's headstone. He swallowed hard as he remembered Beth upon Santa's knee when she was Emily's age. She too, didn't know what to make of the strange, bearded man. Then, suddenly, he thought of the newborn in the dumpster. How could somebody throw away even the possibility of a moment like the one he was witnessing?

A light bulb flashed, snapping Brady out of his reverie.

"Almost this many," Emily was in the middle of telling Santa Claus as she held up three fingers.

"So, Emily, what would you like from Santa for being such a good girl?"

"My momma please," Emily said without hesitation.

* * * *

IT'S A JAIL capacity bill. It's perfect. "Beth's Law." That's what it will be called."

Hair prickled on Brady's forearms. "You're kidding."

It was Saturday and Gary Lake wore jeans and a University of Washington sweatshirt. "Nope. Senate Republicans will have a press conference in a few weeks. You'll need to be there. You can announce that you're running. But, we'll deal with that later."

Pam Naughton sneezed.

"Bless you," said Brady.

"Thanks. I wish this cold would go away. Okay, now to the poll." She handed Brady a notebook which was a half an inch thick. "Read this by Monday. It's great news for us. First of all, Newirth has high name ID, close to eighty-five percent. But that's to be expected. It's just that she's been in office so long. When voters were asked their opinion of her, the numbers change. Nobody knows what she's accomplished. And you need to know the stats on crime. It's one of the issues people are most worried about, and it goes without saying, it's the reason for the bill and the press conference."

"Like we just said, your main issue will be jails," Lake said. "Jail capacity. Nearly eighty percent of those polled found it unacceptable for prisoners to be let out early due to lack of space. A majority of the same sample think that a responsible way to build new jails is the answer."

John Brady's head was spinning. He was genuinely excited. "This is the thing I wanted. Something to run on that I believe in, a reason, you know, something to do with Beth. I can run on this."

"We know." Pam smiled. "The Legislature convenes in two weeks. The Senate R's are drafting a bill. And with you taking on Newirth, and her votes on crime, you can't lose." She paused for Brady's reaction. "Before we put Beth's name on the bill, they'd like your okay on it."

The wave of emotion that washed over him was unexpected; the realization that something was happening. Beth's death would literally, officially be of public record. A law in their daughter's name that could actually keep other innocents away from harm. "Of course they have my okay."

"I had a feeling," said Pam Naughton.

Gary Lake opened his briefcase. "Okay, now on to a few mundane items. First, we need to open a campaign bank account. Pam will go with you to Washington Mutual. They're easy to deal with." He paused as he rifled through a stack of papers. "Decide what you'd like for the title of the account. John Brady for Senate. Friends of John Brady. Something for people to write checks to.

"John Brady for Senate would be fine," said Brady. "I don't like the "friend" thing."

"How about the PDC's?" Pam Naughton inquired.

Lake nodded. "That was next on my list. We need to file with the Public Disclosure Commission," he said to Brady. "The mailing to your Christmas card list has brought in around two thousand so far. We need to report it. That's the other reason we need the bank account now. We need to deposit the checks. Now, you mentioned that your son-in-law would like to be your campaign treasurer?"

"Yes. Mark would like to be involved on some level. He teaches math, so he'd be perfect."

"Great. Here are the forms he'll need to fill out. Pretty self-explanatory. Have him call Pam or myself if he has questions." He handed the papers to Brady then checked his watch. "I've got to go. We're having a birthday party for my seven-year-old. I promised I'd be home by two. Okay, last thing; we need to schedule time for the photo shoot. We need to get on that. Doorbelling starts soon. And yard signs. What color do you like? You have a preference?"

John Brady thought for a moment. "Blue. Navy blue. What color does Newirth have?"

"Red," answered Pam Naughton.

"'Cause she's a flaming liberal," laughed Gary Lake.

* * * *

TWINE, GRASS, NEWSPAPER, THREAD and plastic wrap. The pair of finches gathered anything they could carry. Fat and small and black and yellow-orange, the birds labored relentlessly for two days to construct their nest. The dwelling fit snugly into the cornice above the front porch. Swooping in and out, each time returning with a new item for the nest, John Brady watched them create a magnificent, safe haven.

Not long after the nest was built, bits of speckled shell littered the porch steps. Then there were three scrappy heads with bulging eyes, somewhat ugly, chirping wildly each time the mother arrived to make a deposit of food into their open beaks. When the parents left in search of sustenance the infant birds turned silent.

The baby finches grew. Constantly in motion, they nudged each other for more room in the small nest, stretching their fragile wings. Exercising in preparation for flight. Maneuvering their behinds over the edge of the nest, their droppings cascading down the pillar of the porch.

Brady and Emily watched the finch family with binoculars. In no time the babies were small birds with plump orange breasts and black feathers covering their backs and continuing up and over their heads like hoods. At first they flew spastically along the roof of the porch, keeping close by. Each day they ventured farther from the nest. One day they flew away and did not return.

Emily missed the birds. Brady did too. And it was with regret that he pulled the vacant nest from it's' perch and hosed off the bird droppings for the last time.

\* \* \* \*

IT SEEMED TO John Brady that the State Capitol in Olympia was a city in and of itself. A compound where members and staff traversed the manicured lawns and walkways with umbrellas, briefcases and cell phones in hand. Shuttle buses taxied tourists from distant parking lots onto the Capitol grounds. The air seemed physically thick with a feeling of purpose and importance.

Brady stood near an entrance to the Capitol, under cover from the driving spring rain. With him was the Senate Republican Leader, Alex Daniels, the House members from his district, Christine Baird and Randy Taylor, Chairman of the King County Republican Party, Bob Randall, and King County Prosecutor Stephen McNamarra.

Several radio stations and newspapers were covering the press conference along with King 5 television and Northwest Cable News. Both television reporters were women wearing expensive, brightly-colored ski parkas with their channel's logo on the breast pocket.

Brady was amazed at the intensity of the camera lights.

"The Democrats killed the bill in committee. And Senator Hazel Newirth led the charge," Bob Randall said.

"Mr. Brady, now, you plan to take on Senator Newirth this November, is that correct?" asked the Northwest Cable News reporter.

John Brady nodded. "Yes. And I think the timing is perfect to make my candidacy official. The bill which the Senate Republicans introduced was entitled "Beth's Bill," in remembrance of my daughter Elizabeth. It is a good bill. It deals with jail capacity. The Senate Democrats killed the bill in committee yesterday. It didn't even come up for a vote."

The channel 5 reporter interjected, "Why did the Democrats kill the bill?"

"They don't want more jails, or jail space," Representative Taylor answered. "They say they're for rehabilitation, but they're really just opposed to getting tough on criminals."

Brady nodded his agreement. He could feel the cameras on him. "This bill is a very smart solution to jail overcrowding. We need more jail space. This is how it would work." He felt lightheaded and tipsy, as if he had been drinking. "The State of Washington raises roughly seven billion dollars a year from the state sales tax. This is the major funding source for state government. Now, a small portion of this money stays in the county where it is collected. What "Beth's Bill" would do is divert one tenth of one percent of the state sales tax away from the state and funnel it back to counties for jail operations. For King County, this would fund operations for another thousand bed jail. The other thirty-eight counties would each get their share of roughly forty million per year. This could solve our jail overcrowding issue."

"But what about the money the state loses in this?" asked a reporter for KIRO radio. "Something would be affected, wouldn't it? Like education? Welfare?"

Brady cleared his throat. "The state would retain 99.9% of the sales tax it currently takes in. This bill is a good thing. It's doable." He paused, "Several weeks ago we took my granddaughter to see Santa Claus. She asked him to bring her mommy back. This bill would have kept my daughter's killer and people like him off the street."

"And one important point," Prosecutor McNamarra interjected as he moved closer to Brady, "is that most people don't realize that our county jails house prisoners that will eventually end up in state prisons. It makes sense for the state to give county governments a little more help. John Brady is right. This is a good bill. Something needs to be done."

"Prosecutor McNamara, is your campaign for Governor going to focus on this issue of jails also?" shouted a reporter from the back of the pack.

"Of course. It's a huge problem in my current job. Throughout my career as prosecutor, it's only gotten worse. This bill gives each county more ability to fund jails and keep the public safe. Governor Landry has done absolutely nothing to improve our justice system."

Senate Majority Leader Alex Daniels cleared his throat. "With a Republican Senator from the forty-second district and a Republican majority in the Senate, this bill will pass next year."

As if in a dream, John Brady's thoughts were fuzzy and he saw spots when he blinked his eyes. He knew the people, the politicians standing there with him supported him, yet he had the distinct feeling that, in this circumstance, he was being used. Each one of them had their own uses for "Beth's Bill." McNamarra would have a hot issue for his run for Governor. Senator Daniels job was to get on television and trounce any and all Democrats. The same could be said for the county Republican Chairman. And as for the two House members, any day was a good day if they spoke to the press.

As the camera crews packed their equipment and the reporters took more notes, Representative Taylor nudged Brady. "There's Newirth."

In John Brady's head, Senator Hazel Newirth had been a monolithic and formidable foe, someone to be feared. Yet, it was the first time he had seen her in person and the feeling he had was of remorse, not fear. He felt sympathy for her. Maybe he was wrong to challenge her.

Then as if Taylor could sense Brady's thoughts, he said, "Don't let her looks fool you. She's a pitbull. Believe me."

Brady could not take his eyes off her. Nearing seventy years of age, Newirth's physique resembled a pear. Her stubby feet inserted in orthopedic shoes held up thick legs and a large frame draped in a mammoth gray raincoat. The image in Brady's mind was of an aging elephant.

Newirth ambled on a walkway which led to a side door of the Capitol. As she walked, she shifted a stack of papers from one arm to the other, whilst speaking to a younger man at her side.

"She's not what I expected," said Brady.

"Who is?" asked Representative Taylor.

\* \* \* \*

ORDINARILY SHE DID NOT make such purchases on her own. So, it had been with a strange feeling of independence that Sarah bought the small television at

Sears. After Mark installed it under the kitchen cabinet she was able to watch *CNN, Northwest Cable News* and *Oprah.* What a comfort to keep up on issues and other people's problems while making dinner. An escape from Emily's world of inquiry and children's programming.

Her eyes stung as she chopped onions to add to the sautéing mushrooms, peppers and garlic on the stove. Oprah was snapping her fingers as Tina Turner belted out lyrics to a new song. Sarah thought the backup singers looked sixteen and she marveled at Tina Turner's legs. How old was she anyway?

Sarah pulled a bottle of chardonnay from the refrigerator and placed it on the counter. Then she grabbed a glass from the cabinet and set it beside the bottle. A glance at the clock. Almost five. Quiet static from the baby monitor. She rolled her thumb on the volume dial to make sure Emily was breathing. In and out. It was amazing to her how people just kept breathing. When she was young she had worried about never waking after falling asleep.

On the television screen an American Airlines jet broke through the clouds as Oprah's voice stated that her guests flew American. A clip of the five o'clock news to come showed the State Capitol in Olympia and suddenly her husband's face. "When I'm elected, I will help pass this bill," he said. Then came a commercial for Dairy Queen.

Beads of condensation rolled down the wine bottle. Sarah twisted the cork screw in and slowly pulled it out. Pouring an inch into a glass, she took a drink. Emily made a noise and Sarah squeezed her eyes shut against the voice on the monitor as well as the onion on the cutting board. It was not the first time she wondered how a small inanimate vegetable could cause such physical pain.

Watching the monitor, she felt as though she had gone back in time. She was a stay-at-home-mom again. Granted, she had been Emily's day care provider before Beth had died, but this was different. Originally, the plan had been to return to work when Emily started pre-school. That was less than a year away.

It seemed like a lifetime ago that she a job. A career she loved. She was a nurse. For fifteen years she worked at Valley Medical Center only a few miles away. And she was a good nurse; so good that often she felt she was better to strangers than to her own family. She had taken a temporary leave to help out her daughter and spend time with her new granddaughter, now she was her primary care giver. Planning a third birthday party and daydreaming of kissing Roger Tattinger.

She sipped her wine and resented her husband. Not because he was trying to do something noble in the wake of Beth's death, she loved him for that. It was that he did so without hesitation. Without complaint. Without obstacles. She knew her job was to be there for Emily. That was what she had to do for Beth, and she would do it. Yet, she felt jealous of Brady, and sorry for herself.

As she sliced the last wedge of onion, the descending knife blade sliced a finger and scarlet blood stained white onion. Finger in mouth, she tasted her own blood. Rusty metal. She pulled band aides and ointment from a cupboard. It was a small cut and she was a nurse.

"Gramma. Gramma," came Emily's voice over the monitor.

"Goddammit," said Sarah.

* * * *

EMILY'S SKIN GLISTENED, her belly covered with bubbles, her slapping hands splashing water out of the tub. Sponge letters of the alphabet stuck to the tile wall.

"Try to keep the water in the tub, honey," said Sarah.

"Kay," Emily nodded then turned her attention to the small Fisher Price people arranged on the porcelain rim. Sarah noticed the skin of her granddaughter's fingers were shriveled like that of a weathered apple or an old woman's cheek.

Kneeling by the tub, Sarah said, "Head back." Then with a sense of total trust, Emily laid back as Sarah's hand firmly held the back of her delicate neck.

"Keep your eyes closed." She poured water over Emily's head with a big plastic cup from the video store. Next, she lathered her hair with no-tears, cherry-vanilla scented children's shampoo. With the lather, Sarah created a soapy, spikey hairdo then held a mirror in front of the toddler's face. Emily snorted at her reflection.

"I think it looks lovely," Sarah laughed.

For the next several minutes, Sarah watched Emily take lather from her head and pat it about her cheeks, chin and upper lip. Then, with her finger as a razor, she shaved like her father.

When Emily finally stepped from the tub, Sarah held her slippery arm then wrapped her in a thick towel. She shivered and Sarah gave her a bear hug. As she did so, she breathed in the smell of the newly-bathed child and was caught off-guard by the emotional effect. Cleanliness. Innocence. She had visions of Beth at Emily's age and had to bite her lip to hold back the emotion welling in her throat. Pulling Emily close, she hugged her again.

"Granma!" Emily exclaimed as she struggled to be free.

"Oops! Too tight! Sorry my sweet. Okay! Jammie time!"

"Pooh jammies!"

"Of course. Only Pooh will do!"

Emily ran squealing and bare-bottomed from the bathroom. Sarah checked her face in the mirror to make sure her mascara had not run. It did not surprise her to see blood on her lip where she had bit too hard.

The Winnie the Pooh pajama bottoms snapped to the pajama top and the disposable training pants Emily wore to bed made the set a tight fit. Skin could be seen between snaps. Sarah smiled at the large bottom as she followed down the stairs. Suddenly laughter erupted from the kitchen.

"Jessie!" Emily shrieked, concentrating on her vinyl-soled feet on each step. At a sudden burst of sound, ice crunching in the blender, Emily stopped dead in her tracks and turned, reaching for Sarah.

"Its okay, Em, it's just the blender," She picked up Emily and carried her into the kitchen.

"I don't know," said Mark, "I thought it seemed like a nice complex. They have two and three bedroom units. Hey there's my bathing beauty!"

Emily squirmed her way out of Sarah's arms and ran to Jessie. "Jessie!"

The college student was delighted. "Hey, I like those pajamas! I wish my pajamas had feet!" Jessie laughed as she pulled Emily onto the counter beside her.

Danny nudged his mother. "How about a margarita?"

"I would love a margarita. Thanks. Now, what did I walk in on? What were you talking about?"

"Mark's been thinking about moving out," said Brady.

"What?" Sarah was incredulous as she looked at Emily looking at Jessie.

Mark nodded. "I'm wasting money on a house I don't want to live in again." He poured lime-green margarita mix into the blender. "It's money going down the toilet. And we all know what teachers make." He watched as Danny added tequila. "I'm thinking about an apartment, but I'm going to speak to a realtor. Hey, Em, would you like to drop in the ice cubes? And, I also think it might be about time to move on."

Intuitively, Brady put his arm around Sarah's waist. Support. She could feel his concern for her. Yet, hadn't she been thinking of going back to work? Have her career back? Still, all she could think of to say was, "But what about Emily? Would I still have her during the day?" She thought that perhaps she could work nights at the hospital and have Emily all day. At least until she started preschool.

From her seat on the counter, Emily dumped handfuls of ice into the blender.

"I would love for you to keep watching her, no matter what happens," Mark replied. "You're one of the few constants in her life now."

Brady squeezed his wife close as she laughed at Emily cover her ears in anticipation of the blender's wrath.

The lime and buttery taste of the margarita made her breathe easier; loosened the tightness in her chest. "So, what should we do for Emily's third birthday? "she asked. "It'll be here before you know it."

"What do you want for your birthday, Em?" Brady asked.

"A doggie!" exclaimed Emily.

"This needs a little more tequila," Sarah said.

* * * *

"EVER HAD A DOG before?"

"Not since I was about twelve," Brady laughed. "It's for my granddaughter. She'll be three tomorrow."

A small boy, a toddler, wrapped his arms about the man's legs and hid his face from Brady. The man tousled the boy's hair. "As you can see, I've got small children too."

John Brady followed the man and the boy through the sliding-glass door and into the back yard. Several small, golden puppies charged, yapping and jumping. The toddler squatted, giggling, as two of the fuzzy dogs licked his face.

The man, whose name was John White, said, "Golden retrievers are the best dogs for kids. Hands down. They're wonderful."

"That's what I've heard. So, how old are they?"

"Two and a half months. Didn't want to sell them before that. You know, with the nurturing from the mother and all." He pointed. "That, there, is the mother, Dora."

The larger female Golden lay sprawled under a large trampoline. One puppy was nursing.

"Yeah, Dora is a pure bred. Papers and all. Even though she's a little more red than normal. The father is a Golden, but doesn't have papers."

The world of canine breeding was foreign to John Brady. All he knew was that it seemed like more than a coincidence when his neighbor Al Turpin told him of a friend with a litter of retrievers.

"Because of that I'm only charging two hundred per puppy," said White.

"Mmm." Two puppies sniffed at Brady's feet. Then one took a seat on his foot. Gently, he knelt down, scooped it up and looked it in the face. It couldn't have weighed more than five pounds. Puppy-breath. "Oh, how cute!" he cooed, like a woman holding a baby.

"They're irresistible," White agreed. "You looking for a male or female?"

"I don't know. What's this one?" Brady held it up, but could not decipher the young puppy's sex.

"It's a male. It's still kind of hard to tell. That one is pretty spunky. A little more lively than the rest."

"Does he have a name?"

"Nope. Didn't want to get too attached." The toddler hanging on to White's trouser leg began to whine. White patted his son's shoulder. "Hey, now, skat. Go see mommy." The whimpering child ambled to the door. He pulled with all his might to open it, then disappeared inside without closing the door.

That was when Brady first became aware of the ladybugs. By the hundreds, by the thousands, ladybugs covered the siding on approximately half of the back of the house. Some flew in the air, and he thought how strange it seemed to see a ladybug fly. The wings did not seem big enough to hold the bug aloft. "My God," he said in awe. "I've never seen anything like it." He hugged the puppy to himself for reassurance.

John White rubbed his chin as if it were stubbled. "Oh yeah. Damn things. It really beats the hell out of me. Past few years this has happened. It goes on for several days. Something to do with spring."

"Maybe it's an omen, I mean, a sign of good luck," said Brady. "Aren't ladybugs said to be good luck?"

"I don't know. I guess. They're kind of a pain in the ass. I mean, even though they don't harm us or the house, it's kind of gross. My wife's scared of them."

Brady loosened his grip on the puppy and swatted at a ladybug in front of his face. "I've never seen anything like it." The mass of red on the house seemed to move like a wave in the breeze. It reminded him of the cemetery on Valentine's Day, vibrant with red mylar balloons swaying above gravestones. Both circumstances caused him to have goosebumps. "I want this dog," he said.

John White laughed. "Well, good."

The puppy pawed at Brady's chest and tried to chew his collar. "What do I need to know about him?"

"He's had the shots he needs. And, of course, he's not potty-trained yet, so what I'd do, will he be an indoor dog?"

"Um, yes, I guess so." He wondered what Sarah would say to that.

"Just keep your eye on him around your granddaughter for awhile. Until she's used to him. And he's used to her. He may try to nibble her fingers. He'll grow out of it. But get him rawhide bones. You'll find out that puppies chew anything and everything. Look at our deck."

The puppy he held snapped at a ladybug fluttering too close. Brady noticed several of the red insects on his sleeve then a high-pitched vibration, a sensation at his ear. He flinched it away.

"For the training," White continued, "put newspapers down by the backdoor. Let him outside on a regular schedule. Reward him when he does his duty in the right place. Regular Cheerios are good for that. If he goes inside, which he will, rub his nose in it and put him outside. You have to be firm and guide him. Now for food, use puppy chow and go by the guide on the package. Preferably a better brand from a pet store."

All of a sudden, a gust of wind moved through the alders surrounding the yard. The siding on the house undulated like a red flag. On the breeze came the sweet and sour smell of the dogs. The moment seemed familiar to Brady. Lived before. Life.

"Will you take a check?" he asked.

\* \* \* \*

THE WINGS WERE as thin as rice paper. Butter-yellow with traditional black markings resembling Rorschach ink-blot tests. As each car passed, wind lifted the wings, toppling the butterfly, back and forth, on the pavement of the Kent Valley Highway.

John Brady sat in his car waiting to turn into traffic watching the dead Monarch butterfly bounce between opposing lanes of cars like a fly on a fishing line. He felt ethereal watching this dance of death, yet, it was not a new feeling of late. At the edges of the day, there had been flickers. Instantaneous movements or shadows or dabbles of light like the ones sometimes brought on by a migraine. Out there in the peripheral vision. Was he glimpsing ghosts? Spirits? Beth? How many movies had he seen where someone dies and their spirit remains on Earth to fulfill unfinished business?

Then to add to his other-worldly state, he was hit by another sign as he pulled into the cemetery parking lot. The one-way traffic sign was broken. Hanging askew, the black arrow pointed skyward. Heavenward. Brady shook off the eerie feeling with a laugh, yet he noticed his hand tremble as he reached for the bouquet of flowers. Carnations dyed deep lavender. He had mentioned the passage from Alice Walker's book to the local florist. The young woman, a mother of three, told Brady she would have something purple in stock for him, no matter what the season, if he called a day in advance. She agreed that purple was a fine color.

So it was that John Brady placed a bouquet of lavender carnations on Elizabeth's grave to mark the day she had given birth. His granddaughter's birthday. He thought how time could be both wonderful and cruel.

* * * *

HE WAS NAUSEAUS. His palms were wet and cold as if he were to give a speech. His mind raced with answers to an array of questions which might be asked of him. Pulling alongside the curb between two houses, he cut the engine and looked at the neighborhood around him. The Senate staff had explained the "walking lists" to him. From these lists, Brady knew which home owners were perfect voters-those who never missed a voting-or he knew how many times they had voted. One election out of the past four, two of four, three of four and so on. It also listed the number of registered voters in each household.

Brady was to hand out literature and meet voters, one precinct at a time, starting with the most Republican. The Campaign Committee staff had mailed postcards to voters letting them know he would be in their neighborhood on a specific day.

At the first home, a dog barked inside as soon as he rang the doorbell. He looked at the photographs of himself and his family on the brochure. Emily on his knee. In a few hours he'd be home celebrating her third birthday.

The door opened about a foot and a woman with white hair, keeping her body behind the door, looked at Brady inquiringly. "Yes?"

He thrust his brochure at her. "Hi, there. My name is John Brady and I'm running for the State Senate."

"Oh," she said. "Thank you." She grabbed the brochure out of his hand then shut the door.

The next several houses were similar. People said thanks or good luck. A few said they had seen him on television. One said he was sorry that Brady's daughter had died.

The first political question of the day came after a miniature poodle darted from behind a boxwood hedge and yapped and bit at the cuffs of Brady's pants. "Shoo!" Brady hissed.

"Hey! Get over here Louie!" an older male voice yelled from the innards of a garage. The dog ceased its display of ferocity and sat.

"Hello?" Brady felt as if he were trespassing as he neared the garage.

A man of about seventy wiped his hands on a rag as he came into the daylight from what looked to be a very orderly garage. "Sorry," he snickered, "Louie thinks he's a guard dog."

"Well, he's pretty good at it," Brady nodded as he fought the urge to kick the dog. It was at that moment that he decided to keep small stones in his pockets to ward off future animal problems. "Name's John Brady." He handed a brochure to the man. "I'm running for the State Senate."

The man looked from the brochure to Brady then back to the brochure. "Republican or Democrat?"

"Republican."

"You gonna raise my taxes?"

"No sir. I would work hard to lower them."

"Mmm. That's all I need to know." He held out his hand. "Good luck."

After a few hours of ringing doorbells, John Brady grew more comfortable with his new role of political candidate. And though some people seemed grateful, most did not ask questions. They accepted his literature and thanked him. Some said they were Democrats and thanked him anyway. One man slammed the door in his face.

The last house in the precinct had an authentic carousel horse in the living room window. Brady marveled at it as he waited on the doorstep. As he was jotting down a "sorry I missed you" note on the brochure, the deadbolt clicked and the door opened. The woman before him was extremely large. Her hair was thinning and unbrushed. The lime-colored bathrobe she wore hung open to her waist, revealing huge breasts spilling over her tight bra. John Brady could not help staring at all the flesh. The woman smiled and said, "Yes?"

Brady jumped as if bitten then handed her a brochure and darted down the steps. The woman laughed. "Thank you!" she called after him.

He was perspiring as he walked to his car. He wanted to get home and shower before the birthday party. As he walked he thought about the woman in the bathrobe. He was feeling sorry for her when he felt a fuzzy tickle on his hand. A small honeybee was crawling across his knuckles, just below his wedding band. Brady shook his hand to repel the bee, yet it seemed to stick. Looking closer, he noticed minute drops of yellow pollen covering the bee. The bee seemed drunk. Again, Brady shook his hand and the bee stuck. The next instant he felt a sharp pinpoint of pain. He dropped the clipboard and swatted the insect to the sidewalk with his free hand.

As the dying bee crumbled on the pavement, John Brady felt the itchy-pain of the sting and being allergic knew he needed an antihistamine. He picked up his clipboard then stepped on the bee and squashed it.

* * * *

WINNIE THE POOH streamers. Pooh, Piglet and
Eeyore balloons. A giant Tigger birthday cake. The festive
kitchen seemed mysteriously quiet until Brady realized
everyone was in the back yard.

From the kitchen cupboard of medical supplies, he found
a bottle of Benadryl, read the directions and took a dose.
Next he washed the sting and examined it to make sure the
entire stinger was out.

Sarah entered from outside. "You're here," she said.
Seeing the open cupboard and the bottle of Benedryl, she
asked, "What happened?"

"Got stung by a bee." The sting had become a small, red,
itchy knot on his hand. "Dammit, it itches."

Sarah came close and took his hand. She looked pretty
and flushed with the excitement of Emily's birthday. Her
nurse's touch was gentle. "Well, it doesn't look bad. You
got the stinger out. With the antihistamine you'll be fine."

"I know," he said. He could smell cigarettes on her. It
made him remember the previous evening when he had
rolled over in bed to kiss her goodnight. She had tasted like
an ashtray. He had envisioned licking an ashtray.

"Emily and Abigail can't get enough of that puppy. It's
so cute! Danny said it peed all over their place."

"And I'm sure it'll do that here too until he's trained."

"Want a beer?"

"I would absolutely love one."

Sarah popped open a can and handed it to him. "How
was day one of doorbelling?"

He sipped the cold beer. "It's strange. It felt as though I
was trespassing, I mean, even though I was just handing out
brochures. Like I'm invading people's privacy." Brady
watched his wife lift a tray of hot dogs and hamburgers out
of the refrigerator. After only a few gulps of beer, he felt
tingling in his limbs and wondered if he should drink having

taken an antihistamine. Then noticing how fine Sarah's shape was in her blue jeans and striped blouse, he thought of the fat woman he'd seen earlier.

As she cleaned lettuce at the kitchen sink, Sarah looked out the window and laughed. "You know they've named it Toby."

"What?"

"The puppy. They've named it Toby."

"Oh. Why, Toby?"

She shrugged her shoulders. "I don't know."

Brady drank his beer and looked at Sarah from behind. "You should've seen this woman I saw when I was doorbelling. She was huge. Maybe two hundred and twenty-five pounds. Probably fifty years old. Answers the door in this horrendous green robe, hanging open. She's wearing this tattered bra underneath. Just hanging out all over the place."

"That must have been lovely," she remarked laughing.

"Not really, I mean, I didn't know what to do. Where to look." He laughed at how foolish he'd felt. He was feeling affected by one beer. "Should I be drinking if I had Benadryl?"

"Probably not."

"Screw that. This is supposed to be a festive occasion. I don't have to drive."


The body of the puppy was in perpetual motion and like a rolling ball, the two three-year olds tripped over it. The girls laughed as the puppy climbed on them and licked their faces.

Abigail's parents had dropped her off for the afternoon. The beautiful little Vietnamese girl giggled constantly. Watching his daughter and her friend play with the dog, Mark felt grateful. Emily was happy on her birthday. He thought of the Barbie dollhouse she would open later and how much Beth would have loved to play dolls with Emily. But as he watched the activity in the backyard, for the first time he had a strong sensation that he and his daughter would be just fine. They would survive, and he knew it was due to his in-laws.

John Brady was thinking that the smell of meat on a barbecue was one of the best scents in the world. Toby wove about his feet as he monitored the progress of hot dogs and bratwurst. He was pleased that Sarah had bought sauerkraut for the occasion. Suddenly aware of the good smell from the grill, Toby pawed at Brady's pant leg. "Watch out pup," Brady warned as he gently scooted the puppy away with his foot.

"Toby! Toby!" Emily and Abigail squealed as they tempted the dog with fistfuls of potato chips. Toby chased the girls until he became interested in the small sparrows landing on the bird feeder. He barked and the birds flew away.

"How do you like your new friend?" Jessie inquired at Brady's side. Again, he felt thankful that his son had found this particular girlfriend. She just seemed good.

"It's going to take some getting used to."

Jessie sipped from a glass of white wine. "Well he peed on our carpet several times," she said laughing. "Now he's your problem."

Though he really liked Jessie, Brady was still getting used to the fact that Danny had moved in with her. He had to admit that he was pleased that his son had an intimate relationship. He couldn't imagine Danny being old enough to have sex. But didn't it mean that he and Sarah had done something right? They'd raised a good-natured, self-assured, kind young man. Danny had never had a problem with girls. Brady thought that he would like to take the credit for that.

Danny arrived at Jessie's side. "What are you two whispering about? And why is your boss here, Dad?" He lifted a bottle of amber ale to his lips.

"Oh, he said he had a gift for Emily. I told him to stop by," Brady answered. Maneuvering the hot dogs and bratwurst about the grill with the barbecue tongs, he was struck how much the uncooked bratwurst resembled the mottled look of baby skin. "Hot dogs are done; these others need quite a bit more time. Who wants a hot dog?"

"Me," answered Danny.

Jessie nudged him. "We'll get the girls."

Brady carried the plate of hot dogs into the kitchen. Roger Tattinger was standing next to Sarah at the counter. Their backs were to him. Roger's hand was on the nape of his wife's neck as she looked down towards the sink. Brady heard her sniffling.

"Hey, what's up?" Brady asked with a sudden pang of anxiousness in his stomach. Roger took his hand off Sarah with what Brady thought was a self-consciously fast reflex.

"Hey, John. Sarah was just a little overcome when I told her what I got for Emily. She said Beth had the same thing when she was little."

Brady saw that his wife's eyes were glistening. "What is it?" was all that he could think to ask.

Sarah wiped her nose with a tissue. "A Barbie trunk-closet thing. Remember?" she asked, with just a slight tilt of her head. "It has the little clothes hangers for all the outfits? Remember?"

Roger leaned against the counter, hands in his pockets. "I didn't mean to upset you guys. You said anything "Barbie" would do."

It's all completely innocent, Brady thought to himself. "It's just an emotional day," he commented. "You okay?" he asked Sarah. He noticed that her face was flushed.

She nodded. "I think it's time for wine."

Brady felt stupid. As if he was intruding on Sarah and Rogers' privacy. What had he just seen? Suddenly he remembered the tray in his hands. "Hot dogs are done."

Sarah poured chardonnay into three paper Winnie the Pooh cups. "Wine?" she asked Brady.

"Yes." He accepted the paper cup though he would rather have an adult glass. After Sarah sipped her wine he noticed a lipstick tattoo on the rim of her cup. His mind raced. "So did you hear about that teenage girl? You know, the one from our neighborhood who tried to throw away her baby?"

"No," Sarah answered.

"She's not going to be prosecuted. She got probation and she needs to go to counseling. I guess since the baby didn't die that's a good thing. I don't know."

"I don't know either," Sarah said.

"The baby that was thrown in the McDonald's dumpster?" Roger asked. "That girl was from this neighborhood?"

Brady and Sarah nodded.

"I hate wine in paper cups," said Sarah.

"Me too," Brady agreed. "Better check the bratwurst."


A few hours later, John Brady did indeed remember the Barbie trunk Beth had as a child. When Emily opened Roger's gift, memories of birthday parties for Beth came rushing back. He noticed tears in Mark's eyes as his daughter reacted to the Barbie doll house.

Brady thought of his first doorbelling experience earlier that afternoon and looked at his hand. His skin itched under the band-aid. Overcome by a wave of dizziness, he wondered how many times he had filled his Winnie the Pooh cup. He watched the chaos of Toby ripping at discarded wrapping paper. He needed air.

It was quiet on the deck, where he reclined on a lounge chair and closed his eyes. He listened to the festivities inside, but could not keep himself from dozing. His world was spinning. He thought of Sarah tasting of ashes and tried to remember where in the Bible were the words, "*Ashes to ashes, dust to dust…*"

Sarah followed Roger into the foyer to see him out. "Thank you for Emily's gift," she said. She felt dizzy from all the wine and kept her balance by jamming her hands into the pockets of her jeans.

Roger pulled his windbreaker from the closet. "But I'm sorry if it drudged up too many memories."

"Roger, you saw how much she loved it."

"I suppose. Okay, well, goodnight," he said and leaned to kiss her cheek.

At that point, Sarah turned her head just enough and her mouth met his. She kissed him hard and all the while thought how different he felt than Brady and that she should stop before someone came upon them. She pushed him away with her hands just as Abigail burst into the hallway from the kitchen. In hot pursuit, came Toby, his nails clicking on the hard wood floor. Sarah and Roger jumped back and out of the way as if they had been shot. Next came Emily, and the girls and the dog noisily raced up the stairs.

Sarah found it hard to breathe. "Oh my God," she whispered. "I am an idiot."

Roger looked at his feet. "I'm sorry."

Upstairs the little girls squealed and the puppy barked. Suddenly, Mark turned the corner from the living room. "Hey where did those girls go?" he asked. "I've go to drive Abigail home."

Sarah tried to act calm. "Can't you hear them?" she asked with a laugh.

"They'll sleep good tonight. Hey, Roger thanks for thinking of Emily." He offered his hand to Roger. Roger shook it. "It means a lot. Take care," Mark said then headed upstairs.

"Bye," Roger said.

Sarah felt dizzy and hot. "Please leave." Then after she closed the door behind him she whispered, "What the hell am I doing?" to the empty foyer. Upstairs, Mark had the girls laughing hysterically and in the kitchen Danny and Jessie uncorked another bottle of wine

Later, after dishes were cleaned and put away and Emily was tucked in for the night, Sarah poured a glass of chardonnay and escaped to the quiet living room. Brady, Mark and Danny were watching the Mariner game in the den. Jessie slept snuggled up to Danny.

Somehow, just looking at the cozy furnishings in the room made Sarah ashamed. Everything in its place. Framed photographs, favorite novels in the bookcase, current bills on the desk. Each item a part of her. Her family. She felt comfortable and safe here. What had she done? What did she intend to do with Roger? Feeling like a fool, she sipped her wine. Then she got up and turned on Patsy Cline.

Her cheeks burned and her eyes stung as she looked into the foyer where she had stood with Roger earlier. What if someone had seen them?

In the den, the men yelled and clapped their hands. Then from the darkness of the dining room, Toby appeared, sensed her, and sauntered to the couch where he immediately laid down on the floor by her feet. All of his youthful friskiness had been worn out for the day. Within seconds he was asleep, his legs jerking every once in a while. Running with children in dreams.

Sarah closed her eyes and tried to void her mind of thought. She listened to Patsy Cline croon sorrowful lyrics and envisioned the doomed flight the young singer had been on that crashed into the side of a mountain.

She had no idea what time it was when the half whimper, half bark of the sleeping puppy woke her with a start. The living room was dark, save for the front porch light filtering through the oblong frosted glass windows on either side of the front door. Then, raising herself into a sitting position, she noticed the tiny red light on the stereo, an evil eye, seemingly watching her.

Maneuvering slowly in the dark, she turned off the stereo then carried her empty wine glass into the kitchen. The four-watt night light by the sink lit the room as if it were a candle. Standing at the sink, she poured herself a glass of water. She drank it and refilled it again. She needed to brush her teeth. Her reflection in the window, lit by the night light, seemed gaunt. Dark pockets under her cheekbones made her look like an old woman.

John Brady had been dozing when he heard his wife downstairs in the kitchen. He turned to glance at the digital red numbers on the alarm clock on the bedside table. It was nearly four-thirty in the morning. Turning over, he pulled the blankets up to his chin. For the past two hours his mind had been plagued by visions of Sarah and Roger together. What was between them? A queasy, sick feeling churned in his stomach, emanated up through his chest making him think he was having an anxiety attack. Perhaps a heart attack. He began to sweat and threw the blankets down about his feet. The small, hard knot of the bee sting throbbed. He scratched at it.

He was not stupid. He had walked in on something in the kitchen. He'd sensed it immediately. And if he was honest with himself, he had felt it before with the two of them. Yet, if he was wrong, and he accused her, what would happen? Perhaps he should bring it up tactfully in case he was mistaken. Then again, maybe he should accuse her outright and gage her reaction. He heard Sarah come up the stairs. She tip-toed into the room without turning on a light.

"It's four-thirty in the morning," he said.

Sarah jumped. "You're awake," she whispered. "How come nobody woke me?"

"Danny tried before he left."

"Mmm." She ignored the insinuation that she had drunk too much. "Well, it was a nice party, don't you think?" she asked as she flicked on the bathroom light. "Emily had fun." She closed the door and it was dark again. Brady listened to her brush her teeth and rinse with Listerine.

He felt small. A minute particle in the universe with absolutely no control over the direction his life was taking. Why was this happening to him? Then he startled himself by laughing out loud. His hand covered his mouth as if erasing the sound, a muffler to the sleeping souls on the other side of the wall.

The bathroom door opened. "Did you say something?" Sarah asked. She was in the midst of removing her eye makeup and had finished only one eye. It looked small and naked. Someone else's eye. The fact that Sarah spent so much time on her face, on her hair, on her waistline, the fact that she was so high-maintenance, made him feel sorry for her.

"No," he answered. "I just coughed."

She closed the door. Darkness again.

His mind threw out a fact: only a year ago his life, his marriage, his children, his job, everything had been normal. In its place. It scared him.

On his back, staring into the darkness, Brady marveled at his own body. His senses. How his eyes adjusted to the dark, causing dark shapes of furniture to come forth out of the shadows. How he could feel the exact pinprick of the bee sting. How he could tell by the sound of jars touching down on the bathroom counter, what Sarah was applying to her face and her neck.

He thought of her face. Her profile was growing stronger with age, the bone structure more pronounced. Tiny lines of age and stress and worry had begun to creep about the corners of her mouth and at the base of her throat and about her eyes, particularly when she smiled.

There was a thud from downstairs, the sound like a gym bag dropping to the floor, followed by a soft whimper. Toby. Brady had forgotten the newest member of the family. They had used Emily's old baby gate to keep the dog in the kitchen for the night.

The toilet flushed, the light switch clicked then Sarah emerged from the bathroom, slowly making her way like a blind person to her side of the bed. Suddenly the bed shook as she crashed into it. "Shit!" she hissed. "My toe! Can you turn on the light, please?"

Brady did as he was asked.

Sarah sat on the edge of the bed with her back to him and checked her toe. "So, how many times have I done that? It's fine. Just a speck of blood." She turned towards him and her face without makeup looked vulnerable. "Turn out the light."

He switched off the light and both of them settled under the covers. The silence of the next few moments stabbed at him. "So, I have a question," Brady said. Her body tensed on the other side of the bed and he thought carefully about the phrasing of the question. "Is there anything I should know about? I mean, with you and Roger?"

The heavy silence seemed deafening and Brady could feel his heart beating unnaturally in his chest. "Okay, so I guess the answer is yes?"

"It's not what you think," she whispered as if to herself.

Brady sat up. "Please enlighten me."

Sarah turned on the light atop her bedside table. She put a finger to her lips. "Shh. We'll wake Mark and Emily."

"Who the hell cares?" He got up and began to pace at the foot of the bed.

"Okay," she said. Her covered knees were drawn to her chest. "Okay. I kissed him. That's it. That's what I did."

She hid her mouth behind her knees, as if he might punch it. "And that's all I did."

"And that's all you did," he repeated bewildered.

"I swear."

Again, Brady had the disjointed thought regarding her eyes; small and animal-like without makeup. He shook his head. "Oh, well, that's okay then," he stated sarcastically.

Sarah sniffed and pulled a tissue from a box by the bed. Brady laughed. "Oh, great. Fantastic. Let's cry now."

"No, listen, John. Let me explain."

Then she was speaking but Brady was not hearing. A shroud of anger and fear enveloped him as he stood at the foot of his bed in his boxer shorts at five in the morning watching a seemingly foreign woman speak and sob. Then he realized she was looking at him quizzically.

"Are you going to say anything?" She reached for her cigarettes and lit one. "Nothing? You have nothing to say? I know I shouldn't smoke in bed."

"No. You shouldn't smoke at all. I mean, being so obsessed with weight and aging and health and all you'd think you'd be smarter than that."

"What does that have to do with anything right now?"

"Screw you. What the hell do you want me to say? That it's okay? You only kissed him? Only? Do you like him? Do you love him? My fucking boss." Then he laughed. "Or should I say, you're fucking my boss?" Suddenly, Brady thought he might cry so he turned his back to her and feigned interest in the loose change on his dresser. He fingered dimes and nickels and pennies.

Sarah quietly cleared her throat. "John, really, I swear to God, it was only a kiss. And after I did it, even while I did it, I was thinking how stupid I was and of what I could lose. You know, I never thought I could lose more after Beth."

Brady pulled on a T-shirt and sweatpants then grabbing his pillow off the bed he left the room.

* * * *

AS DAWN APPROACHED, Emily sauntered groggily into the den, climbed onto the couch with Brady and snuggled under his blanket. Next, Toby hoisted himself onto the cushion by their feet and Brady did not object. The grateful puppy curled into a ball and fell asleep.

The dependence of these creatures, these living things, made John Brady smile. He loved being a provider. So it was with this feeling, his arm tucked around Emily's sleeping form that he studied her face, mere inches from his own. Her warm, sweet breath, puffs upon his cheek. In the shadowy light he marveled at the length of her eyelashes and at the perfectly angled slope of her nose. With all the muscles of expression slack and relaxed, he knew she felt safe and loved.

A creak in the floor above signaled that Sarah had risen. Moments later, the upstairs toilet flushed and he listened to water navigate through pipes above. Another creak then squeaks from the bed then silence.

As he pictured his wife going back to sleep, Brady thought about the role of protector. He had always felt it was his duty to protect Sarah. His children and grandchildren. His failure to protect Beth from harm had broken his heart. His family's heart. Now something incomprehensible was threatening his family again, just as the healing had seemed to begin. Was it his fault? Should he be angry? Should he forgive?

* * * *

HE HAD LEFT a note on the kitchen counter as Emily lay snug and asleep with Toby under the blanket. As angry as he was, he still felt the need to let Sarah know what he was doing. He scribbled that he was going for a drive and would return by nightfall. As he locked the door behind him he laughed at his sense of responsibility.

It was Sunday morning and there was a line of people at the gas station buying cups of coffee and thick morning newspapers. He paid for his gas and bought a black coffee. The day was beautiful; crisp and sunny, the kind of day one should be happy. As he entered the southbound lanes of Interstate 5 he was surprised at the volume of traffic, most likely weekend travelers returning home.

To the east loomed Mt. Rainier and after about an hour he could see what remained of Mt. St. Helens on the southeast horizon. Brady was glad the day was clear and he smiled as he remembered how Danny and Beth had collected volcanic ash in canning jars. May 1980. So many years ago and he remembered it vividly.

Within another hour he came to the Lewis and Clark Bridge. The mammoth steel structure traversed the Columbia River, connecting Washington and Oregon. It was the type of creation that made Brady marvel at the talent of mankind. Rays of sunlight bounced off wind-whipped waves below the bridge. Above him on a girder a sign read "Welcome to Oregon." On the backside, he turned to see "Welcome to Washington." Two hundred years ago there would have been no lumber mills surrounded by log pyramids. No smokestacks spewing plumes of white pollution. No docks or container ships.

He glanced at the riverbanks in the distance. His cell phone rang making him jump. Caller ID listed his home number. "Yes?"

"Hey," said Sarah. "Where are you? I got your note."

"Mmm. Crossing the Lewis and Clark Bridge at the moment. Entering Oregon."

There was silence. "Where are you going?"

As he came off the bridge he saw a brown National Parks sign for Fort Clatsop. "To Fort Clatsop," he answered.

"Fort Clatsop?"

"You know. The Lewis and Clark Fort? That's where I'm going," he said defiantly.

"Oh. Why? I mean, why there?"

"I don't know, Sarah. Why do we choose anything? It's just that it's here and I've always wanted to go, so I'm going."

There was silence on the other end of the line. He really had always been interested in visiting the Fort. The few times he had passed it before he had been unable to stop. "I just needed to get away for a few hours, is all," he said.

"I know," she said. "It's okay."

His mind said, "*Damn right it's okay you adulterous bitch!*" What Sarah heard was, "All right, I'll be home this evening."

"John?"

"Yes?"

There was silence then a sniff. "I'm sorry."

"I know you're sorry. I'm just not sure what I am," he answered then pressed the end button on the phone before she could continue.

He thought about Lewis and Clark and how truly brave they must have been. Theirs had been a true quest. He felt like he too was on a quest; looking for answers.

The heavy scent of woodsmoke hovered beneath the canopy of fir trees several hundred yards from the parking lot. Brady breathed in deeply. He loved the smell almost as much as meat on a barbecue.

He paid admission at the counter in a small museum and gift shop. One of the Park Rangers gave him a map of the Fort, which he studied then folded and put in his pocket.

The noise his feet made on the gravel walkway seemed obnoxious upon entering the quiet forest. He felt his senses come alive. In day to day life in suburbia, he tended to forget that the smell of nature was out there. Like a memory it all came back. Dank, pungent earth. The world was darker and several degrees cooler. Small sounds echoed; bursts of voices from the Fort up ahead seemed amplified.

A tree, a spruce, caught his attention, pulling him off the gravel path and onto the pine needle-softened forest floor. At least fifteen feet in diameter, the mammoth trunk rose three hundred feet. Grand. Moss, full-grown ferns and small saplings grew on horizontal branches themselves the width of a good-sized tree trunk. Brady guessed the tree was a sapling when the explorers settled the Fort in 1805. His mind formed the words, *My God.* Again, and again. The tree made him feel like a microscopic bug.

John Brady read a plaque attached to a huge log fence encircling the Fort. Each log was at least twenty feet high and each was sharpened to a dangerous point. He thought of Lincoln Logs. Forty men had spent the winter in the original fort and, though the encampment he saw was made to scale, it was hard to imagine so much life crammed into such a small space.

The small, dark rooms were cold and damp and filled with a smoky haze from lit candles and fires. These were the only source of light and heat. There were horizontal spaces between logs in the walls through which daylight and drafts seeped and Brady imagined how cold it must have been.

In the captain's quarters were replicas of parchment maps charting virgin rivers and lakes the Corps surveyed and gave names. There was also a journal describing daily life at the Fort. One room was used as a smokehouse and Brady learned the men lived mainly on elk meat. In the dwelling of Sacajawea, her French husband and baby boy, a papoose of deerskin adorned with beautiful beadwork hung from a peg on the wall.

He came out of the Fort and into a clearing in time to witness a demonstration of an 1803 Harper's Ferry rifle. Tourists with cameras and camcorders lined a split-rail fence giving audience to a middle-aged man in buckskin pants. A volunteer at the Fort, the man was normally a business professor at Indiana University. The man read from the journals of Lewis and Clark. He spoke of how the Corps of Discovery relied on fifteen experimental flintlock rifles Captain Lewis had received from the U.S. Army. Next, the volunteer warned the tourists of the rifle's impending noise, inserted plugs into his ears, then rammed a spit wad into the barrel of the gun. When he shot it into the treetops, the smoky explosion made a small boy with a toy sword cry.

John Brady left the group and wandered down a path to the bank of the Lewis and Clark River. Cattails and tall marsh grass surrounded the clearing where three dugout canoes, replicas of the craft Lewis and Clark had used on the Columbia, rested to the side of a short boardwalk which led to a dock.

He looked about to see if anyone was near then gingerly stepped into a canoe and sat down. The rough-hewn structure was so immense and heavy it seemed implausible that it could float. From a sign beside the boardwalk, Brady learned that the Corps of forty men could make two or three dugout canoes per day using only axes and fire.

He continued sitting in the canoe amidst the weeds. As he sat he thought how incredibly daunting the whole venture must have been. Throughout the duration, only one man of the forty died. It was evident from the journal entries that they all had faith in God. Brady believed God had looked out for the explorers on their quest. He felt it as he sat in the canoe listening and breathing in the nature around him. History had always had a way of putting things in perspective for him.

*They had their mission, I have mine. I don't know what is happening with Sarah, but I can't let it distract me. My job is to win this election and do something for Beth. By God, that's what I'm going to do.*

In the gift shop he bought a parchment map of the Lewis and Clark Trail. On the way to his car he picked a wildflower, yellow, no idea what it was. He put it in his breast pocket to keep it safe. He planned to stop by Beth's grave on the way home and leave the flower as a memento.

Sarah and John Brady hardly spoke that night, or the day after, or the day after that. By unspoken mutual consent, he slept on the couch as a physical silence grew between them.

* * * *

THE METRO BUS Park and Ride was closed to the public, a DO NOT ENTER-CRIME SCENE sign blocking the entry.

His car idling at the street light adjacent the lot, John Brady watched as law enforcement personnel in orange and yellow jumpsuits and rain ponchos swarmed the area. Block-lettered POLICE across their backs, some pulled by leashed German Shepards into the weeds alongside the road.

Dozens of official vehicles cluttered the lot. State Patrol, County Sheriff, Emergency Response units and a Medical Examiners truck. Men and women in an array of uniforms milled about in groups. Under umbrellas, or hats with plastic shower cap covers, they drank coffee from a trailer resembling a fast-food stand. Nearby stood a half dozen portable toilets.

Brady pounded the steering wheel with his fist and cursed the light for taking so long. The scene made him feel sick. He focused on raindrops falling into puddles on the asphalt creating emanating rings of circles. Concentric; like the crime scene commotion, the different agencies involved, all the law enforcement and government officials united for the common purpose.

The light changed and he followed the lineup of cars around a bend like a writhing snake. He now had a view behind the tree line, beyond the crime-scene tape. A bulldozer belched black smoke as its jagged-edged shovel ripped up chunks of earth and debris. More dogs with their handlers. Brady felt nauseas and the only question he let his mind form was whether the food and coffee from the trailer was free. Turning his head away as the line of cars inched past he noticed the license plate holder on the Honda Accord in front of him: COWBOYS HAVE THE BEST BUTTS. He began to sweat. Pushing buttons on the radio, he found the Mariners on-deck show. Lou Piniella was speaking. Sweet Lou was giving pitching statistics. Brady needed statistics. Yet he continued to wonder whether cops had to pay for doughnuts and coffee.

John Brady absorbed the gruesome articles in the newspaper over the next several days. A recreational fisherman, wading the swollen stream a few dozen yards from the busy road, had found the remains of a human foot. The investigation that ensued was huge. More remains were found and identified as those of a young woman reported missing for several years. Brady was fascinated by DNA matching. How could a person be identified from a bone chip?

He was genuinely thankful, that unlike the current case, everything with Beth had happened quickly. He and Sarah had not been tortured for years wondering what happened to their daughter.

Dwelling on all of the evil in the world, Brady continued to think that some kind of goodness had to come from it. One might strive harder to find something good. To achieve something good, or at least to give thanks for the ordinary good in everyday life. He was re-minded of his old neighbor putting up his flag every morning and taking it down every evening. A small and good thing. That belief kept him going through long days of doorbelling and fundraising calls.

Over the ensuing weeks and months, after all signs of law enforcement had gone, one sign remained: a short length of yellow crime scene tape. It clung to a tree branch mere feet from the road. Brady found himself traveling the road more than usual. He went out of his way to take it. The tape was a gruesome reminder that his family's situation could have been worse. He was scared that some day he would drive down the road and the tape would be gone.

\* \* \* \*

SARAH HAD ALWAYS been somewhat of a hypochondriac, and her worries had intensified since Beth's murder. Every small ailment seemed cause to fret. It did not help that she and Brady would turn fifty in a matter of months. She thought of her life in the time frame of half a century. She thought about death. The subject seemed to permeate every part of her life. She was beginning to find comfort in routine trips to the cemetery.

Like her husband, all of the media regarding the girl's body found only miles away consumed her. She traveled the road in question nearly every day. She dwelled on the vicious murder, yet she could not stop questioning. Was her death the same as Beth's? She was ashamed to have the thoughts in her head. Deep down, she just felt the facts were different. Had this girl deserved what had happened to her? At least more than Beth? The girl had been a prostitute. Beth, a working mother.

Sarah worried about making such judgments. She worried about worrying; worrying was stressful and stress could lead to many a health problem.

Then there were the signs and symptoms of menopause which sent her to the computer to peruse medical websites. Hot flashes overcame her several times a week, and many nights she woke dripping wet as if she had been in a sauna.

She felt out of control of herself, her physical body. Her periods were slight and sporadic.

Twice she had panic attacks while shopping at Wal-Mart. Each time she had left a shopping cart full of unpurchased goods and rushed out of the store. It was an uncontrollable panic. Panic that she could not pinpoint the reason for, yet which made it hard to breathe. She felt anxious when she thought of all that had come to pass over the past months. She was a different person from the woman she'd been.

In her husband, she saw a distinguished man whose grief had brought out a sincere effort to do good. That's what the new obsession with politics was all about.

And her? More and more she found it hard to care about anything. Her husband ignored her. Why bother trying when God would just up and ruin things anyway? The idea of having an affair with Roger seemed more reasonable every day.

But then there was Emily. Emily seemed to be the only thing that gave her life dimension. She felt physically ill when she thought about Mark buying a new home. Yes, God had taken Beth, but maybe she could find the way through Emily. The little preschooler taught her new things everyday.

Sarah decided that what she needed to focus on was Emily.

\* \* \* \*

THEY DECIDED THAT EMILY was old enough to color Easter eggs. Sarah had made the hard-boiled eggs the previous evening so that they felt cold and fragile as he placed them on the newspapered kitchen table in front of Emily.

"Kay, Em, we have six colors here, see? You can make these eggs whatever color you want." Brady watched her eyes widen at the expanse of possibilities before her.

He felt like a hypocrite. Though thankful that the modern coloring kits made egg decorating simple, he did not understand the reason for coloring them and what, if anything, it had to do with Easter. What did a rabbit and jelly beans have to do with the Death and Resurrection of Christ? Yes, eggs could be the beginning of life, or a sign of Spring. He supposed that was the link.

All he could think about as he watched his granddaughter dip an egg into a cup of purple dye whilst humming along to her Peter Cottontail video was the campaign. He felt guilty, like he was wasting his time. He should be doorbelling or working on his speech for the upcoming kick-off breakfast.

"John, show her how to use those wax crayon things before dunking the eggs in the dye," Sarah suggested as she washed a pan in soapy water in the sink. "Write her name or something."

"Okay," he replied.

"Hey, I bought Emily a frilly little yellow Easter dress today. Isn't it beautiful, Em?" Sarah asked.

"It's like a princess!" Emily shouted then chewed on her lower lip as she concentrated on her egg.

Sarah smiled at Brady.

He returned the smile but it felt fake. They had still not spoken of Roger and their situation. They skirted the subject, making it a tangible void between them. A void filled with endless, superfluous comments and conversations. Sarah extolling a myriad of Easter traditions from her childhood. Easter hats adorned with ribbons and plastic flowers. White gloves and patent-leather shoes, stiff and uncomfortable for Sunday Mass. Blisters.

"Isn't it funny how people wear jeans to Easter service these days?" She laughed to herself as she wiped off the counter and folded a dishtowel. Brady watched his wife pour a glass of cabernet. "I'll be back. I'm putting my sweats on before I start the casserole for tomorrow."

She walked out of the room, sandals hooked over the fingers of one hand, wine glass in the other. Brady noticed how good his wife's figure still looked in jeans, then feelings of anger, embarrassment, agony and lust churned inside him when he remembered he was still sleeping on the couch.

Later that night, with Emily safely asleep, Brady and Mark sat on the floor of the den filling pastel plastic eggs with goodies. Since Mark knew three-year olds could handle only so much chocolate, the innards of the eggs consisted of tiny graham cracker bears, cheddar fish crackers and jelly beans. Brady loved the small fish crackers shaped like the kind of fish he drew as a kid. He had a habit of cracking the seam of each orange fish with his teeth, creating two halves. A little challenge in each cracker.

The salty snack made him crave a beer and pulling one from the refrigerator he spied the Easter ham. "That ham's big enough for an army," he remarked.

Sarah looked up from the diced cubes of bread on the cutting board. "Well, we want leftovers for sandwiches, don't we?"

"Of course we do," answered Mark.

"I suppose so," Brady agreed. "I've never understood why we always have ham on Easter."

"Tradition," Sarah answered.

"Mmm. Like our tradition of attending church on Easter. Over the past few years it's been Easter and Christmas. At least for me," Brady added as he took a swig of beer. A few seconds passed and he was surprised his remark failed to get a rise out of Sarah.

Mark tossed a plastic egg onto the growing pile. "I think we have enough eggs. Remember, this is all for one kid."

John Brady caught himself before he blurted "lucky kid."

He momentarily pondered the meaning of Easter, before the campaign again crowded out all other thoughts. He thought about the week ahead and what would be the official start of his campaign. He had spoken to Gary Lake earlier that afternoon. He figured they had roughly two hundred affirmative responses thus far. The price was twenty dollars for admission to his kick-off breakfast at Emerald Downs, the local thoroughbred track that had the best banquet facilities and parking in the area.

"I can't wait until this week is over," Brady said. "At least the speech part."

"Give the speech to us," said Mark.

Brady sipped his beer. "I'm still trying to put it together in my head. But maybe tomorrow. After ham. Gary says to keep it to ten minutes. I don't want to put anyone to sleep. I guess they just need to know that I can speak coherently. String reasonable thoughts together." He grabbed a handful of eggs. "Come on," he said to Mark. "Let's hide these before Em wakes up and sees that there's really no Easter Bunny. And remember to make it really easy for her."

Toby followed Brady and Mark, jumping and sniffing at eggs placed just out of his reach. Brady laughed as the puppy grabbed the egg he had hid behind a plant and ran into the kitchen. "Okay, this is going to be harder than I thought," he said.

"Toby! No!" Mark scolded as he pursued the dog. With the egg still in his mouth, Toby laid his head on his paws.

At the kitchen sink where she stood peeling carrots, Sarah said to herself more than anyone in particular, "Who'd have thought we'd ever have a dog?"

* * * *

IT WAS SIX-THIRTY in the morning. John Brady was glad he had a few minutes to go over his speech. He picked a vacant dining table next to the wall of glass. His coffee and his speech in front of him, he turned to stare out at the desolate track.

The track had a strange feel. The grandstand was empty, the betting windows were closed. A light rain was falling upon the muddy track. With the whir of activity in the restaurant, it felt more like a place of business and less a place of recreation and entertainment.

Brady took too large a sip from his cup of coffee and burned his tongue. He swore under his breath with the knowledge it would be sensitive the rest of the day. He studied the words on the paper in front of him, smoothing it with his hands. The sentences seemed foreign even though he had recited them numerous times in front of his bathroom mirror. He had also given the speech to Danny and Mark. Sarah had put him off every time he tried to run it by her.

If he stared at a word long enough, it no longer seemed like a real word. At the moment the word that did not seem like a word was "ordinary." It did not seem ordinary.

People getting off the elevator milled about tables manned by Republican staffers. After signing in, each guest was given a name tag to stick on their chest.

Though John Brady had always hated name tags, he looked down at the plastic pin with white embossed letters: JOHN BRADY- CANDIDATE. Gary Lake had presented him with the pin upon arriving at the track. The words on the pin made him even more nervous.

He folded his speech and returned it to his coat pocket. Across the room he saw Sarah, Danny, Mark and Emily standing in a cluster near the head table. Emily was in the process of taking glasses of ice water from the empty places and lining them up at the end of the table.

Event staff in white coats had finished setting up the buffet breakfast which spread over four eight foot tables. Brady crossed the room and perused deep metal trays of wet and slightly bluish scrambled eggs, platters of bacon and sausage links, mixed fruit and a large assortment of muffins and doughnuts.

People were lined-up and moving down the length of the tables, filling plates. It amazed Brady how poorly some people ate. Mostly the overweight, unhealthy-looking people. Middle-aged men with massive stomachs and women with rotund backsides making choices of fried meat and doughnuts. Extra creams for coffee; Half-n-Half. He felt ashamed making crass judgment of his supporters.

As he scooped a small pile of eggs onto a plate, someone nudged him. "You're going to eat more than that, aren't you?" asked a woman with a heaping plate. Brady glanced at her name tag hoping to spark a memory, yet he came up blank.

"Stomach's kind of nervous this morning," he answered.

"Oh, understandable," she nodded. "You'll do fine. And it looks like a great turnout."

Brady smiled and nodded as he surveyed the room. There had to be two hundred and fifty people in attendance, of which he recognized many friends and acquaintances. Neighbors from both his current and past neighborhoods. Coworkers from Northwest Timber. Lobbyists from his company and all the other timber companies in the northwest. House member Randy Taylor from his district. Prosecutor Stephen McNamara. Sprinklings of legislators from around Puget Sound. Brady knew these people worked the room with their own agendas.

With the plate of eggs in one hand, he moved about the room greeting people, shaking hands firmly and answering questions. Adrenaline high, he was not sure if the answers coming out of his mouth made sense. With his tongue still raw from the hot coffee, he thought he might be lisping.

There were pats on the back and hugs. Eyes were on him. He wiped his brow with one hand and spied a table to deposit the uneaten eggs.

He discarded the plate and looked up to see Sarah staring at him. She was across the room with Emily in her arms, and she was scowling. She clearly wasn't enjoying being the candidate's wife and all that it entailed. Brady knew he had neglected her lately, but the campaign was all consuming. He started to make his way to her when Gary Lake grabbed his arm.

"Hey, Representative Baird won't be here. She has the flu. So Randy will MC and McNamarra's here, "Lake said. "He'd like to do the pitch for money. It would be a good thing, though he just wants some limelight." Lake wore the salt and pepper suit he had admired at one of their first meetings.

"It's okay by me," said Brady.

"Good." Lake looked about the room. "Look at this room. This is great. Pam's done a great job, don't you think?"

Pam Naughton was responsible for Brady's yard signs, brochures and anything with his name printed on it. JOHN BRADY navy blue and white yard signs lined the walls for people to take after the breakfast. Tables covered in white linen and heavy silverware were packed with people eating and drinking coffee and talking. JOHN BRADY brochures and business reply mailing envelopes enhanced each place setting.

Just then House member Randy Taylor stepped up to the podium on the stage. He gently tapped the microphone, buttoned his coat and cleared his throat.

"Good morning," he said.

People ceased mingling and returned to their seats with plates.

"What a great turnout this morning," Taylor said. "If you would kindly return to your tables we will begin. We will start with the Flag Salute and to lead us this morning is a man very comfortable with this role. This is because he is a public school teacher. He is also the candidate's son-in-law and part-time treasurer for the campaign. Mark Bennett."

Mark made his way to the podium through applause and yells of "Yay, daddy!" from Emily.

On the stage he adjusted his tie, and said, "Good morning, please stand and join me in the Flag Salute." Then with his voice strong and firm and with his hand over his heart, he recited the words which were part of the curriculum, his daily routine for years. Yet, he knew this was different and he had to fight back a wave of emotion threatening to overcome him.

When he was finished he stepped aside for Father Jeffrey O'Brien, the priest from Brady and Sarah's church who had married Mark and Beth. He wore a black suit and shirt with the white Roman collar, and he touched Mark's shoulder as he stepped towards the microphone.

After asking the crowd to bow their heads, he asked God to bless each person in the room and in particular John Brady and his family. "God has given this man, this family, the strength to overcome a horrific personal crisis," he said with a hint of Irish brogue. "Now John is moving on to do something important. One must have a calling to enter public life and John has had that. God bless him on his journey, we who know him know he will be successful."

Representative Taylor returned to the microphone and Father O'Brien and Mark made their way back to their tables.

"Thank you, Father," Taylor said. "Now as you eat your breakfast, and please help yourselves, there's plenty left, I would like to acknowledge several state and local dignitaries present here this morning." He went on to point out a few members of the city council, the State House and Senate and the county prosecutor.

John Brady drank coffee and watched people reading his brochures. He felt jittery and he had a headache. Suddenly, people were on their feet, clapping and looking at him.

"John, come on up and give us a few words," Taylor said.

Sarah nudged him, waking him from a daze.

On the stage, he was momentarily blinded as a camera flashed. He took a drink of water from a glass in front of him and felt the burn on his tongue.

"Good morning and thank you for being here. I'm John Brady. I'm running for the State Senate." He cleared his throat. "I'm an ordinary man. But I do not believe that I'm an ordinary candidate. I think most people run for office to BE something. A U.S. Congressman. A member of the legislature or city council. I would like to be in office to DO something. That may sound presumptuous, but I have the passion, or should I say a cause behind my reasoning."

"I will do everything in my power to improve our transportation system. And our schools. There are many things I would like to help make better. For my family and yours. But my main focus will be crime and its prevention.

"As most of you here today know, an important bill died in the Senate this year. That bill was entitled "Beth's Bill," after my daughter Elizabeth who was murdered several months ago. "Beth's Bill" is a good bill. The idea behind this bill is to divert $1/10^{th}$ of 1% of the state sales tax back to the counties. This small percentage, for example, would give King County about 40 million dollars more per year to fund jail operations. The other 38 counties in Washington State would each get a share of roughly 60 million dollars annually. This is just one idea. There are many other options. But the one option we don't have is to do nothing.

"My opponent, Hazel Newirth, helped kill this bill. She does not believe more money should be spent on jails. She believes in rehabilitation of violent criminals. I just don't happen to believe that criminals and violent offenders deserve a second, third, fourth and fifth try."

The room erupted in applause. Someone yelled, "It's about time!" More applause and scattered whistles.

As the speech went on, the fact that people were applauding and whistling for him seemed humorous. He nearly laughed. Nearing the end and fighting for something to do with his hands, he jammed them in his pockets and his fingers touched a foreign, rubbery object. His natural instinct was to extract it; subsequently he pulled free a 2 ½ inch green Gumby figurine. Brady laughed out loud. The chunky, pointy-headed doll wore a frozen yellow smile.

He felt the anticipation of the crowd waiting for his next words. Across the room he spied the culprit, Emily. Sitting between Mark and Sarah, she was stirring ice cubes in her water glass with a spoon.

"Remember Gumby?" He asked with a laugh. He held it up for viewing. "And wasn't the horse, Pokey? Now, this is not mine, though I do like Gumby."

There was laughter.

"My granddaughter, Emily, must have slipped it into my pocket. Can Gumby be considered a good-luck charm? Thanks, Em."

Realizing Brady was addressing her, Emily put down the spoon and waved to him. "Hey, Gumby!" she exclaimed.

Sarah laughed and said, "Shhh!" with a finger to her lips.

Brady cleared his throat. "Seriously folks, I guess this little green guy could be a symbol for my race for the State Senate. My granddaughter. My late daughter. I can't change the past. If I could turn back time, I would. But I can't. What I can do is go forward and try to make things better for my family. And yours. Thank you."

That's all they wanted. He felt it. They wanted someone in office that would work hard for what he believed in. For him it came down to the family he had watching him, applauding for him. It came down to the little girl content to play with ice cubes in a glass of water who had put Gumby in his pocket.

He would change the justice system for her. He would work to make schools better for her. He would be an environmental advocate for her. This is what he could do.

This is what he would do. More than ever he felt like a man with a mission.

Several moments later, after the applause ceased and Brady was back in his seat next to Sarah, Prosecutor Stephen McNamarra stepped up to the microphone, buttoned the jacket of his navy blue suit and placed his hands on the podium.

"Just a few words and we'll release you to your busy lives. I am King County Prosecutor Stephen McNamarra and I'm honored to be here today. It is an exciting day. It's not often that a candidate with real potential comes along. What I know of John Brady after going through the day to day hell of his daughter's murder, is that he is a man of character. A strong family man. A natural leader."

Now, my job this morning is to make a pitch for money. Granted, you've paid to be here this morning, but what we're asking for is above and beyond. Having a function like this, having brochures and yard signs printed, any kind of direct mail, it is all incredibly expensive. If John Brady is going to win this fall, if he is to unseat Hazel Newirth, he needs money for his campaign to get off the ground. Please write a check this morning or bring one of the envelopes in front of you home and mail it on payday."

"The thing is, and here is a little pitch for myself, is that I want John Brady in the Senate, in hopefully what will be a Republican majority, when I become Governor!"

There was applause and whistles throughout the room.

"Thank you; now please get out your wallets and checkbooks."

\* \* \* \*

THE TRUNK OF HIS CAR smelled of the clean-cut 2x2's. John Brady loved the smell of new lumber. After doorbelling, he now liked to spend an hour or two putting up and repairing campaign signs. He pulled out two yard-signs, a small sledgehammer and a tire iron. He felt less self-conscious putting signs into the ground on roadsides since the breakfast had raised nearly fifteen thousand dollars. They supported him out there. Not just the Republican staff, but real people. Voters in his district. Voters in his neighborhood. Voters with families.

He found a good, visible spot in the knee-high grass and dropped the signs. Then taking the tire iron he staked the spot and pounded the piece of metal into the earth with the sledgehammer, driving it down approximately half a foot. After removing the iron he pushed the pointed end of the yard sign stake into the hole then hammered on the top of the 2x2. He liked it when a sign stood nice and firm and in a good place.

As he was walking down the shoulder of the road with the last sign, a car passed and Brady saw a woman looking at him with an uncomprehending look on her face. He smiled to himself. Then, while driving the tire iron into ground which consisted of much more rock than the terrain mere yards away, he thought how he used to view politics, particularly local politics. He had never really paid attention. Yard signs had always been somewhat invisible to him.

Also, he had never realized how much litter was strewn in the weeds on the side of the road. Beer cans and candy wrappers and what looked to be a used condom, which startled him so thoroughly he brought the sledge hammer down directly on his thumb. The pain was instant and excruciating. Brady was simultaneously embarrassed and mortified; first that he might have been seen hitting himself, second that he may have broken his finger.

As he drove home, the sun had begun its descent and he had the vague feeling he was returning home, wounded, from battle. The thought made him laugh, as his only injury was a split fingernail and the beginning of a blood blister.

At the traffic light he studied his bruised finger. Intuitively, he stuck his thumb in his mouth and sucked it, feeling at once infantile and repulsed by the bitter metallic taste of blood. Across the intersection and through the evening traffic Brady stared at a yard sign he'd put up a few hours earlier. Turning with the traffic, the sign remained visible in his rear-view mirror. Rays of light from the setting sun hit the area around the sign like a spotlight. His name, in large white letters on the blue background, seemed to glow.

* * * *

THERE WERE MANY EXCUSES, and to Sarah, they were clear and sound. She needed to talk. She craved the attention. The physical contact. Brady had become so absorbed in the campaign that she felt irrelevant. Her marriage felt irrelevant.

Standing before the bathroom mirror in her bra and panties she spat mouthwash into the sink and listened as it trickled down the drain. It seemed to sizzle, which made her wonder what it would do to her insides if she swallowed it.

She stared at herself for what seemed a long time, her face inches from the mirror. New wrinkles appeared daily. Unexpectedly she asked her reflection, "What are you doing?" She was shocked she had vocalized her thought.

Her mind swarmed with thoughts. Reflections. Facts. She was almost fifty. She was menopausal. The muscles in her body, her skin was turning soft and slack. And no matter how strictly she watched what she ate, her waistline was getting a little thick. She thought of Brady doorbelling and putting up yard signs after work. Then she thought of Emily, who at that moment was at Abigail's house probably playing with dolls. Or blocks. Or dress-up clothes. She started to cry so she fanned her eyes with her fingers and blinked the blurred vision away. She had to fish her makeup out of her purse to touch-up her eyes, then brushed her hair and put on lipstick. Slowly, she got dressed.

She wondered if she was entirely evil. One day Beth was alive and the next day she was gone. What if she, Sarah, died tomorrow? What if what she was doing was meant to be? Again she felt the weight of tears and vowing she would not cry, busied herself picking tiny chunks of eyeliner off her puffy lids.

Suddenly she was dizzy and she sat down on the edge of the bathtub. She laughed. She was a middle-aged woman with a family to look after. A granddaughter. A husband and a marriage. She felt pathetic. The thought struck her that she was turning as ugly inside as she was becoming to herself on the outside.

She wanted a glass of wine. Or a shot of bourbon. Next came the urge to pray. Sarah closed her eyes and the words flowed in her head. Heartfelt and sincere, she asked for help. Then the guilt of not having prayed since Beth was killed washed over her. Why pray to the Entity she held responsible? She concentrated on her breathing and tried to relax, then she asked for forgiveness for what she had done, and for what she had not done. And for blaming God and everyone other than herself for anything and everything.

Warbled voices from the television seeped through the wall. Distorted. Sarah took a deep breath and felt her heart slap against her breastbone. Checking her watch she knew she must get up. She stood and opened the bathroom door.

"Okay, I've got to go or I'll be late picking up Emily," she announced.

"You were in there a long time. Everything okay?" Roger asked. Turning off the television with the remote, he then reached for his robe and got out of bed.

"Sure."

He followed her down the stairs of his condominium, shooing the Siamese cat out of the way on the landing. "You hungry, Stuart?" he asked the cat.

The moment felt unreal to Sarah. It was so quiet in the condo that she heard her own footsteps on the carpet. She retrieved her jean jacket from a barstool at the kitchen counter, then unable to look Roger in the face she pretended to search for something in her purse. She chewed her lip then accidentally bit down and tasted blood. "Dammit," she whispered, fingering her mouth and tasting blood.

From the opposite side of the counter Roger studied her. "Are you okay?"

"Hmm?" Sarah touched the cut with her tongue and at the same instant noticed that the refrigerator's hum was too loud.

"I'm asking you what's wrong. Are you okay?"

"Well no, I can't really say that I'm okay." She slipped an arm into her jacket. Then she struggled to get her other arm into the jacket for the sleeve was inside-out. She fought with it until all of a sudden she burst into tears. "No. No. I'm not okay. What we did is not okay. I can't do this. Can't you see? This is not going to happen."

Deflated, Roger came around the counter and sat down on a stool. She saw the look on his face and knew she had hurt him. She felt worthless and pathetic.

"I'm sorry," she said gently. "And it's not that I'm not attracted to you. Or that I don't care about you." She sniffed. "Do you have any tissues?"

Roger went into the kitchen and grabbed a box of tissues off the top of the refrigerator. He placed them on the counter then busied himself making coffee. "I'm the one who's sorry." He dumped scoops of coffee into the filter. "I know you're in a bad place. I know you're vulnerable. But I'm not sad it happened." He tossed the scoop into the coffee can. "I care about you."

Sarah blew her nose. It felt wrong that she should pity him, yet she did. She watched him pour water into the coffee maker and wipe the counter.

"I'm sorry," she said. "I just can't. I can't. I couldn't live with myself. God, I need to grow up."

\* \* \* \*

THE SEVENTY-FIVE POUND leather bag dangled from a thick chain bolted to a rafter in the rear of John Brady's garage. He'd had a punching bag as a teenager, and when he told his son he might like one again, Danny helped him insert the heavy-duty bolt and manipulate the chain until the bag hung correctly.

His hands, taped and sweating inside fat boxing gloves, felt foreign as they struck the bag. Hitting the dead weight, hollow thud after hollow thud, helped eliminate the tension. Helped ease the tightness in his shoulders and his neck and his mind. The release, then, gave way to a feeling of momentum, one jab leading naturally to another. One gloved fist protecting his face while the other found the target. Shifting about the bag, Brady moved by instinct, though he knew only the bare bones of boxing.

He let his mind wander. It didn't bother him that he was feet and inches away from trash and recycling cans, shelves of paint thinner and automotive oil, bags of donations for Good Will. He became mesmerized by the red leather bag with white letters: EVERLAST. Pummeling the letters, they became faces. He envisioned Roger's face. And he thought of Sarah, yet he couldn't get himself to picture her face on the bag.

Moving about the bag, he jabbed. Recently, Sarah's demeanor led him to believe something had happened. She was more attentive and open to talking. And they both agreed that maybe they should seek out counseling. The change felt ominous.

He jabbed, and his thoughts shifted to Hazel Newirth, his aging and extremely large opponent. Their first debate was only a few days away. He needed to study. He needed to fill out the candidate surveys sitting on the kitchen counter. And he needed to do the minimal amount of work at Northwest Timber. Again, Roger came to mind. Roger his friend. Roger his boss. Roger who had urged him to run for the Senate and had persuaded the company to support him. Now this thing with Sarah. It seemed that Roger had too much control over his life. As if Brady's life was a game of chess.

He did not know how long he had been pounding on the bag but suddenly he was out of breath and felt sweat trickling down the small of his back. He took off the gloves, threw them across the garage and went inside, the bag still swaying on its chain.

* * * *

NATIONAL FEDERATION OF Independent Businesses. Washington Taxpayers Association. National Abortion and Reproductive Rights Action League. Affordable Housing Council. Washington Council of Police and Sheriffs. Washington State Council of Firefighters. Log Cabin Republicans.

John Brady had been sitting at the kitchen table filling out candidate questionnaires. Mundane answers to every imaginable policy question. Does life begin at the moment of conception? Are you against raising taxes under any circumstance? Do you believe gay/lesbian couples have the right to legally wed and benefit from the same tax breaks as other legal unions? Do you support a light rail system? Would you support a tax to fund said system?

Though he answered each question honestly and to the best of his ability, he did not comprehend how his naive answers could earn him the endorsements of such organizations. Political Action Committees. He had never realized how important PACs were to a campaign. Endorsements, he'd been told, could make or break a candidate.

"I'm taking Emily to lunch. McDonald's. Would you like to join us?" Mark inquired upon entering the kitchen.

Brady stretched and clasped his hands in back of his head and glanced at the clock on the wall. "Give me one minute and I'll be done with this survey." He patted a stack of papers on the table in front of him. "I want to mail these tomorrow."

"How's it going?"

"Okay, I guess. I just can't fathom how some of these questions, let alone my answers, are relevant. You can't tell me candidates wouldn't make up answers to get the endorsements they need. For example, obviously I'm not homosexual, but who's to say they shouldn't get tax breaks if they are a longstanding couple? Now, should they legally be able to marry? I don't really know. But to be honest, I don't see why not. Who the hell am I to judge?"

Mark laughed as he grabbed his keys and wallet off the counter. "I think you should run as a liberal Democrat."

"Great. That's really great. Helpful."

On the way to McDonald's they counted yard signs. Brady vs. Newirth. They counted signs wherever they went.

"We're winning the sign wars," Mark announced. "Say "yay" Em!"

Buckled into her car seat, Emily looked out one side of the car then the other. "Yay!" she yelled clapping her hands with enthusiasm.

"Yep, two more there!" Brady said pointing out two blue signs in an abandoned lot. Then pulling into the parking lot, he said, "John Brady seven, red-flaming liberal Newirth three."

Mark put two trays down and doled out the wrapped and boxed food. Their table was in the glassed-in Playland. Childless adults and packs of teenagers looked at them from the other side of the glass as if they were zoo animals.

"Em, c'mon!" Mark called to his daughter. She climbed out of the ball pit and ran to the table.

"Where's the toy? Where's the toy?" she asked fidgeting in her chair. She watched her father pull a plastic-covered creature from the latest Disney movie out of the Happy Meal box.

"That's the one I wanted!" she exclaimed.

Mark tore off the wrapping and handed it to her, whereupon she seized it and started back for Playland.

"Hey! Get back here and eat!" Mark yelled.

Emily returned to the table and Brady arranged her food. He made her a small mound of ketchup after emptying many miniature packets.

"Thank you, Grandpa."

"You're quite welcome. You talk more like a big girl every day."

Mark took a large bite from his Quarter-pounder with cheese. "I finished updating the website," he said, with food in one cheek.

Brady thought that Mark was looking better lately. He looked healthier. "Thanks. How does it look?"

"I think it's good."

"I'll take a look at it later."

J.BRADYFORSENATE.COM. He found it hard to believe that he had a website. He found it harder to believe that anyone would use it. But people did use it. They sent him email all the time. There really were people, constituents, who wanted to be involved. Wanted to be informed.

Emily gobbled fries, took a monster bite of her cheeseburger then, with her mouth stuffed, sucked chocolate milk from a straw. "Now can I go?" she asked chewing.

"How about a deal," Mark suggested. "You go play for a few minutes, then come back and eat some more."

"Kay." She ran across the floor in sock-feet and dove into the pit of balls as if it were the surf. The balls about her undulated, causing a little boy resting on the surface to bolt upright and flounder about; trying to keep afloat in the sea of many colors. Emily spoke animatedly to the boy and they both giggled. She grabbed his hand as they trudged towards the slide.

It never ceased to amaze Brady how easily Emily approached children strangers and became instant buddies. "It's incredible how trusting kids are," he said.

"It's scary."

"Can you imagine adults acting that way? Holding hands and hugging within minutes of meeting?"

Mark dipped French fries into ketchup. "I wasn't like that when I was a kid."

"I wasn't either."

Mark had a faraway look in his eyes. "I was shy. Or scared. Probably both."

Brady nodded. "You know, not to change the subject, but doesn't this stuff taste damn good once in awhile?" He felt the guilty pleasure of fatty chicken McNuggets smothered in honey dissolving in his mouth. He momentarily did not care that what he consumed had zero nutritional value. Processed foods. He thought of the packaged cheese Sarah bought for Emily's lunches. PROCESSED CHEESE FOOD. There was an uncomfortable knot forming in the pit of his stomach.

Mark motioned to Emily as she waved from a space-bubble window in the tube extravaganza. He mouthed the words, "Come eat your lunch," and pointed to her uneaten food. "Are the talking points Gary sent helpful?" he asked turning to Brady.

Brady gulped Diet Coke. "Yes and no. I've got to get the stats on taxes down."

"You'll do fine."

"The debate is in three days.

Emily erupted out of a tunnel-slide and ran to the table. Without a word she grabbed her cheeseburger with two hands and took a bite. Surveying the food before her, she chewed in earnest. Mark reached over and brushed a lock of hair out of her eyes.

"Having fun?" he asked.

She nodded in the affirmative and swallowed. "Where'd my toy go?" she asked looking under wrappers and behind her carton of chocolate milk.

"It's under your napkin," said Brady.

Tossing the napkin aside, she giggled and then was off to Playland. Brady watched her in what seemed like slow-motion. A film, grainy with age. But he wasn't seeing Emily. He was envisioning Beth, young, probably first or second grade with her hair pulled back into a ponytail. They had frequented the same McDonald's, yet at the time it was new.

He was remembering one day in particular. It had been just he and Beth, Dad and daughter time. Brady had noticed nothing out of the ordinary that day, certainly no danger, so it was shocking when suddenly the parking lot was full of police cars. He remembered that the officer who had come into the play area asking for everybody's cooperation had seemed exceedingly young. Everyone was to stay in the play area until the police had asked some questions.

The children, in the presence of so many law enforcement officers were pop-eyed and quiet as mice. It had seemed surreal: quiet, attentive children at a fast-food Playland. Some children started to cry. Not Beth, she stood in the play kitchen, her arm protectively draped over the shoulders of her friend.

When it was Brady's turn to be questioned, he stated he had not noticed anything unusual. The young officer had said in low tones that a man had tried, unsuccessfully, to abduct a small child, a girl, in the restaurant. The man had approached the child in the girl's bathroom. Brady wondered if the term "sexual predator" was used at that time.

Presently, sitting with his son-in-law watching his granddaughter, Brady could still feel the fear. He had only felt it four times in his life. That day at McDonalds. Then there was the time there had been a call from the police and from St. Francis Hospitals Emergency Room. Sara had been in a car accident. Though she only suffered a laceration on her forehead, she had required sixteen stitches and Brady had been scared to death arriving at the hospital with Beth and Danny in tow. And as a teenager, Danny had totaled his car, yet miraculously emerged unharmed. The last, and hopefully final, time he'd felt real fear was the ordeal with the murder.

"Hey, where are you?" Mark's voice broke through his clouded thoughts.

Brady blinked. "Oh, sorry."

"Have a cookie." Mark tossed a few McDonald Land chocolate chip cookies onto the table in front of him.

When Brady bit down on one of the cookies, a shooting pain made his tongue seek out a back molar. "Dammit. I think I'm getting a cavity. Aren't I too old for cavities?"

"No. Go to the dentist."

"Cavities. Tooth decay. Physical decay. God, I'm getting old."

\* \* \* \*

AS THE TINY DRILL invaded his mouth, hot and metallic tasting, as he swore to God that any second it would hit a raw nerve, John Brady wondered if there was such a word as "toothdust" or "toothsmoke." If there wasn't he thought that there should be. There should be a word to describe the foul smell of decaying or dead tooth tissue.

Dr. Evan Wozniak shifted on his stool, giving him a new angle into Brady's mouth.

"So, how was your mother with all the hoopla?" Grace the dental hygienist asked the doctor.

"She was okay," he answered slowly and without diverting attention from Brady's teeth. "She's just getting so old. You know? She sat in the same overstuffed chair all night. Observing. I think she was more amused than anything. But most of the time I wonder if she's even all there."

"Mmm," Grace acknowledged in a knowing tone as she adjusted the yellowish goggles perched on the bridge of Brady's nose.

Brady watched tiny pieces of decayed tooth fly out of his mouth. Tooth flesh wafting about his head like dust motes. He hated the dentist and hygienist for having a conversation as if he were not there. The dead tooth matter settling about him, the smell of hot metal and antiseptic and the ghoulish face of Dr. Wozniak , masked and upside-down, made Brady want to escape. Flee. He remembered the lecture on "fight or flight" in college. He strained his eyes to see out the window just beyond his right foot.

The office was on the tenth floor of a medical building in downtown Seattle. Brady could see a corner of a brick building. The top of another. A seagull. But mostly he saw brilliant blue sky, the hue of which was made possible only by sunshine.

Suddenly there appeared, (or was he just thinking it?) a bubble, translucent yet sparkling, mere yards from the window pane, float up then out of view. Then another. And another. It was wonderful and he would have smiled if he could. So he just felt the smile. He pictured someone on the sidewalk ten stories below, a child or perhaps the child's mother dipping the small plastic wand into a pastel bottle of soapy solution. They would take turns blowing their breath into the shimmering circle of soap giving birth to a stream of bubbles. The bubbles would spin haphazardly, most bursting before they got far. Some triumphed, spiraling up and up. Up past tenth floor windows.

Dr. Wozniak turned off the drill and Grace suctioned foreign particles and saliva out of Brady's mouth. The doctor then maneuvered a small mirror about his teeth, surveying his handiwork. Then he began tapping and smoothing. Picking. Tapping again.

"Bite down," he said.

Brady obeyed, though one side of his mouth and nasal cavity remained numb.

"Are you ready for Mrs. Delaney's crown?" Dr. Wozniak asked Grace. "This is just about done."

"Everything's set," Grace answered.

Brady felt the primal urge to spit. He wanted to spit and then he wanted some water to drink. He wondered about the particles that had flown out of his mouth during the cavity demolition. The matter not sucked up by the white suction hose. Where did it go? Had it settled, like volcanic ash, in a fine dust about the office? Or was it airborne being breathed into other peoples' lungs? If there were no roof above, would the particles rise like the bubbles outside? Up and up until there was no more atmosphere? To Heaven? To Beth? He knew he was meant to see those bubbles.

Dr. Wozniak pulled down his mask. "Okay John. I think that'll do it. Looks good." He lifted the yellow goggles off Brady's face and pushed a lever. Brady rose to a sitting position.

"The Novocain should wear off within the next few hours. Just be careful what you eat, you could bite your lip." He turned off the monster-head lamp above the chair. "So, what's it like to run for office?"

As Brady rubbed his numb chin in an effort to stimulate feeling, he saw more bubbles float up and out of view. For some unexplainable reason he felt at peace. And he smiled.

\* \* \* \*

COLONEL MUSTARD WITH THE WRENCH IN THE LIBRARY... John Brady laughed as he entered the library, remembering the board game CLUE he'd played with his children. It was past dinnertime and the building hummed with the hushed tones libraries naturally have. With modern access to computers and the Internet, it surprised him how many people still used the public library.

An elderly gentleman, alone at a table, slowly turned the pages of The New York Times. Several yards from the front desk where Brady stood, two teenage girls hunched together in front of a computer. One of the girls giggled forcing the other to elbow her friend in the ribs while hissing, "Shh!"

There was a small room behind the counter. Brady saw a small sink and a microwave. A middle-aged man with a ponytail was stirring something in a large mug. He looked up and noticed Brady and smiled. "Oh, hi, sorry." Carefully, he carried the steaming mug to the counter and set it down.

Brady could smell chicken noodle soup. "Dinner?" he asked.

The librarian chuckled showing big white teeth. "Exciting, huh? What can I do for you?"

Brady hated that expression. "I'm one of the candidates in the debate tonight. Can you tell me which conference room?"

"Oh right!" Conference Room B." He pointed towards the back of the library as he spoke. "To the right of the men's bathroom. Some people arrived awhile ago to set up."

"Good. Good."

The librarian was about to speak when he paused and turned his head and sneezed.

"Bless you."

Pulling a tissue from his jeans pocket, the man blew his nose. "So, you're the guy running for the Senate."

"Yes. That would be me."

"I've seen you on TV. I hope you win. Even though I'm a teacher in real-life and I usually vote Democrat, I think we need some new blood."

"Well then, wish me good luck."

"Good luck."

A small group of people were busy setting up the conference room. Gary Lake, wearing his salt and pepper suit, was straightening a row of metal chairs. The words COUNTY LIBRARY were stamped across the backrest of each chair.

"Nice tie," Gary commented.

"Thanks," said Brady as he pinned his candidate nametag above his suit coat breast pocket. "Sarah thought it was too conservative."

"Is she coming?"

"She was waiting for Danny to get there to watch Emily. Mark had something going on."

"You nervous?"

"Yes."

"Get some coffee," Gary suggested. He pulled his cell phone from a clip on his belt, pushed some buttons and left the room.

Brady crossed to a table with a large aluminum percolator and plates of cookies. As he poured coffee, his back to the door, he was certain Hazel Newirth had entered the room. A loud, heavy presence. Then his feeling was confirmed.

"Rory!" she bellowed to her aide busy at work attaching microphones upon two small podiums. "I need you."

The aide left the room and Brady could see Newirth speaking in hushed tones to him and a man holding a Starbucks coffee cup.

Gary Lake was back with a stack of Brady's brochures. "Hey," he whispered, "I've got a few people to ask the right questions."

"Who?"

"You don't need to know."

"What questions?"

"Why she killed Beth's Bill. Her record on taxes. You're ready."

"Feels like cheating. This is the standard, huh?"

Gary Lake laughed. "It is SO the standard, John. Don't worry. I know this is your first debate. But it's not Kennedy-Nixon. All we need is a quote or two for the Valley News and you've done your job." Lake began placing brochures on chairs.

Brady checked his watch. The debate was due to begin in twenty minutes and only a half dozen people loitered about the room. He poured coffee into a Styrofoam cup and with the first sip, again, burned his tongue. An omen. "Dammit," he hissed.

A tap on his shoulder made him turn. Elmer, his elderly neighbor stood grinning at him.

"Hi, Elmer! How are you, sir?"

"Good evening, John," he said offering his hand and giving Brady a strong and cold and skeletal handshake. "I'm good, John, real good." Elmer chewed his lower lip as he surveyed the room through bifocals. An American flag pin on his windbreaker reminded Brady of the flag on Elmer's house.

"I couldn't miss a debate. Nobody takes the time to debate anymore. It's a lost art," said Elmer.

"Well, this is my first."

Elmer nodded and gazed at Brady as if he had not heard him. "You're a bright young man. Just state the truth."

Brady found Elmer's description of him as a young man humorous. Elmer jangled change in his pocket. Brady noticed a flesh-colored hearing aide behind his neighbor's left ear.

"Well, if it isn't the candidate's wife," Elmer announced as Sarah entered the room. Brady thought she looked like a college co-ed in a black sweater and jeans.

"Why, hello, Elmer, so good of you to come." Sarah offered her hand to Elmer.

He held her hand. "Oh, my dear, I was just telling your husband that I love debates. Wouldn't miss it for the world." Elmer released her hand and resumed fingering coins in his pockets.

"So Danny got to the house on time?" Brady asked.

"Yes."

"Jessie with him?"

"No."

"Mmm." He checked his watch and counted heads in the room; twenty-three. He carefully sipped his coffee.

"Coffee any good?" she asked.

"No. And I burned my tongue. There are tea bags over there."

Sarah turned to Elmer. "Would you like to come get some coffee?"

"Yes, I would, thank you." He shuffled along with Sarah to the refreshment table.

Brady left the room to use the bathroom. The hallway smelled of chicken noodle soup. He paused between the women and men's restrooms to glance at a bulletin board covered with notices and announcements. Beneath it ran a counter littered with pamphlets and brochures, including his. The photograph of his somber self, mere inches from a pamphlet of a support group for single parents. Thinking of Mark, he tucked one into his pocket.

Pamphlets for battered women, drug addiction, alcohol addiction, big brothers and sisters. He wondered if people with any of these problems would actually pick up his brochure. He thought not.

Just then a young sweat-suited woman erupted from the women's room with two small boys and a baby balanced on her hip.

"Hungry Momma," one of the boys whined as he pulled on the woman's pant leg.

The woman maneuvered the baby in her arms and said, "Shh," rather loudly. "Okey dokey, artichokey, but first we need to check out books. So let's be good kids and we'll be quick."

Hazel Newirth sat in a metal folding chair two feet away from him. John Brady crossed his legs and gazed at the tassels on his shoe. Subsequently, he found himself staring at his opponents thick ankles. Encased in thick translucent nylons several shades too pale, they resembled bratwurst he cooked on the grill.

Repulsed by the thought that Hazel Newirth's leg reminded him of food, Brady quickly turned his attention to the man raising his hand in the second row. The man repeated, "Mr. Thatcher, Mr. Thatcher!"

Bill Thatcher, editorial page editor for the County Valley News gestured and said, "Yes, sir. The man in the second row. Who is your question for, sir?"

"Mr. Brady."

"Go ahead."

"Mr. Brady," the man began as he stood and put his hands in his pockets, "you've said you are running for office to do something about crime, the criminal justice system and so forth. But isn't it true that you're employed by one of the biggest industries in this state? Doesn't the timber industry have a vested interest in the state legislature? Logging rights and restrictions, the spotted owl, etc. So, to get to my question, couldn't you end up being a tool for big timber to get exactly what they want?" The man sat down.

Save for someone slurping coffee, the room was quiet. Next to him, Newirth fidgeted in her chair. Brady stood and clasped his hands calmly in front of him. He remembered what Gary Lake had said about the sole purpose of the debate was to get a story in the paper. A good quote or two. He was not there to sway anyone in the room. Everyone there was a partisan of one side or the other. His face was hot and he felt defensive.

"First of all, sir, I've worked for Northwest Timber for nearly two decades. I work in management. Personnel. I have nothing to do with legal, technical, political or harvesting aspects of the company. And I don't want to. Yes my company has lobbyists and some of them are acquaintances, but mind you, if I win this race, the only relationship I will have with them will be on a purely professional and legal basis. The same would go for any other lobbyist no matter what the interest.

I'm here, I'm running for this office because it's time for a change. I want to help make changes in the criminal justice system. I want to help cut the bureaucracy in our schools so we can reduce class size and put more money in the classroom—"

"Mr. Brady," Thatcher interrupted, "time."

Brady sat down.

"Your rebuttal, Senator Newirth."

Brady looked at Sarah who nodded her approval.

Though it took visible effort for her to stand, Brady had to admit that Newirth had presence. She stood like a large bear, legs two feet apart, stretching her gray skirt taught. The stance gave her hefty frame balance as well as the appearance of a man.

"Mr. Brady, here," she began in a crotchety voice, "has lost his daughter to a senseless crime. I feel bad for him. He says he is running for this office to do something about it. I respect that." She turned her head on her neck like a wise owl and gave him a penetrating look. "But Mr. Brady is a novice. And not being politically savvy, he may think that working for one of the biggest industries in the state won't be a problem, but inevitably it will be."

"Time," Thatcher announced.

As her weight hit the chair, Brady heard Newirth exhale as if deflating. She caught his glance and smiled. He smiled back as if they were friends. He'd decided that politics really was acting. At least partly. Charades.

Elmer, holding his hand purposefully in the air, was called upon next. He slowly rose and cleared his throat. "Good evening. I would like to address Senator Newirth. Ma'am, I have always prided myself in being keenly aware of local and national politics. I have followed your service in office and I know you have voted for every single tax increase that has crossed your desk. Now, I am an eighty-five year old man with a wife and a fixed income. I have grown children and grandchildren. If my property taxes keep going up, I won't be able to stay in my house. Thank you." He sat down without asking a direct question.

Bill Thatcher nodded politely at Elmer. "Thank you, sir. Senator Newirth, would you like to address this gentleman's comments?"

Newirth inflated into a standing position. "I'm very honored that you have followed my political career so closely. It's nice to know..."

Brady tried to concentrate on her answer. He needed to pay attention, yet all he could do was scrape his coffee-burned tongue with his teeth and stare at Sarah. At that moment he adored her and her attentiveness to Elmer. It was endearing. Sarah always tried to be kind. She meant well.

"...and how does Mr. Brady expect these jails he wants to be built without raising taxes?"

"Mr. Brady?"

"There is a plan that lets counties receive more funding for jails without raising taxes. That is what the bill that Senator Newirth was key in defeating this legislative session was all about. It is entitled "Beth's Bill" after my daughter Elizabeth. If this bill ever becomes law, $1/10^{th}$ of 1% of the state sales tax would go back to each county for jail operations. Now when-"

"Time."


He had been daydreaming. Newirth was in the midst of answering a question on education. Public schools. Charter schools. He was warm and his shirt was damp under his suit coat. Reaching into his pocket for a handkerchief he felt the small rubber Gumby doll. He carried it with him all the time now. It made him smile. And it reminded him of the reason why he was sitting in the warm, unventilated library, smelling of chicken soup and stale coffee, talking about issues on which he was no expert.

"More money needs to be put towards teacher salaries. How are we to get good people interested in teaching when salaries are so low? And class size. We need to reduce—"

"Sorry, Senator, time," said Thatcher.

Brady was momentarily distracted when he looked up and found Sarah staring at him. The surprise must have shown on his face because she smiled. Then his face grew hot as he felt the audience's cumulative eye as they waited for his rebuttal.

"I admit I am not an expert on education," Brady began as he rose from his chair. "But it seems to me that all Hazel Newirth has ever said about education is that we "need more money." To her and to her fellow Democrats in Olympia that translates into more bureaucracy in the system. More government involvement in our schools. I disagree with this thinking. What do we need? More school counselors and psychiatrists or up-to-date, quality textbooks and supplies for our children to learn what they need to know?"

An abrupt, "You're right!" from Ernest elicited laughter in the room. Sarah laughed too as she nudged an embarrassed Ernest on the knee. Brady had the urge to hug his wife. He experienced an instantaneous memory-scent of her shampoo.

Afterwards, a handful of people mingled as they nibbled on shortbread cookies. Crumbs covered the carpet. The librarian approached Brady. He sneezed then wiped his hand on his sweater then offered the same hand to Brady. "I thought you did really well for not being a politician."

Brady shook the hand he envisioned covered with germs. "Thanks." He put his hands in his pockets to wipe off invisible viruses and felt Gumby.

Suddenly, with a sense of urgency, a young man approached. "Mr. Brady, sorry to interrupt, but I'm on deadline." The man wore a jean shirt and a bad tie. "I'm Alex Azeltine from the Valley News. It sounded like you knew what you were talking about. And you say you're not an expert?"

"I just call it as I see it," answered Brady fingering the Gumby doll in his pocket. "Senator Newirth is a tax-raising, old-time, liberal Democrat with no innovative ideas…"

Afterwards as Sarah got into her car she motioned to Brady as he got into his. "Follow me."

Ten minutes later he found himself sitting across from her in the bar of Las Mexicali family restaurant. Though the dining room they had passed through was quite empty, the cantina was lively.

Brady watched the Mariner game on the wide-screen TV. Seventh-inning. Second baseman Brett Boone swings at a pitch from Mike Mussina as though his life depended on it. Strike. Damn Yankees, Brady thought to himself.

Rena, their politically correct Spanish waitress appeared with their drinks and a basket of tortilla chips and a bowl of salsa. Brady liked Rena's white peasant blouse and thought that Sarah needed one.

Sarah licked salt off the rim of her margarita glass then took a sip. "I'm glad we're here," she said.

"Me too." Jack Daniels on the rocks soothed his coffee-burned tongue and warmed going down.

"So," said Sarah.

"So."

They both watched the big screen.

"What did you think about the debate?" he asked.

Sarah dipped a chip into her margarita and stirred. "I think Hazel Newirth is one scary woman."

"I agree."

"And she's too old. And fat. She could barely get up from her chair." Sarah rummaged through her purse and extracted a pack of cigarettes and a lighter. She tapped one out, lit it and inhaled deeply. Then she exhaled and for a few ongoing seconds trails of smoke seeped from her nostrils.

"It's going to be hard for you to give it up again," he said.

"Please don't start."

"I wish you wouldn't."

She took another drag. "I know you wish I wouldn't. I'll stop soon."

"They're cancer sticks."

"Okay, John, please? Enough," she said with finality.

"All right then, what should we talk about?" he asked. "There are a few topics I can think of."

They drank their drinks in silence. Brady eavesdropped on the conversation at the table behind him.

"No, it was Olerud. Yeah, he had a tumor or something."

"That's right. I remember."

"They put a metal plate in his head. That's why he wears a batting helmet all the time."

"Wow, that's amazing," said a female voice.

"I think he almost died."

Brady realized that Sarah was staring at him. "What?"

"I wanted to come here so that I could apologize. I'm sorry. I've wanted to apologize for a long time."

"Okay."

"For what I've done. To you. To us."

Brady downed the remainder of diluted whiskey. He felt its heat in his chest.

"I know, Sarah."

Magically, Rena the Spanish girl appeared at the table. "Another round?" she asked.

"Please," answered Brady as he watched Sarah take a puff off her cigarette, squinting so that smoke would not get in her eyes. He debated where to go with the conversation.

"How long have I been sleeping on the couch?"

Sarah stared into her empty glass. "I don't know. Seems like a long time."

"Okay. I need to ask this. How many times? You know, did you sleep with him?"

"John, don't—"

They sat in silence until the waitress invaded their space a few minutes later, depositing fresh drinks on the table. Brady picked at a fingernail until she was gone.

"John, don't," repeated Sarah. "Don't do this."

"Don't I have the right to know?"

She met his glare and her eyes welled with tears. "It was only one goddamned time. Okay? Isn't that sick? Isn't that absolutely sad?" She used a cocktail napkin to dab under her eyes. Tiny black mascara marks stained the napkin.

Laughter from the table behind him. He wished he could watch baseball and swill beer without a care in the world. "How the hell could you? Even once. With everything we've gone through. With the campaign."

Sarah looked at him and gulped her margarita. "Fuck your campaign."

"Thank you very much. What the hell does that mean?"

"It means fuck your goddamned campaign. How do you think it makes me feel? It's all you care about. You're gone all the time doing this great, noble thing for your dead daughter. My dead daughter. When you and me, we don't talk anymore. It's not my campaign. It's like we have nothing in common anymore. Except for Emily. Emily is our only topic of conversation. Emily is all I have." She tapped another cigarette from the box and lit it.

"Why did you have to turn to Roger? We could have changed things."

"He was there. That's it. He was attentive, you know?"

He wanted to scream at her. Scream at her and shake her. But then she may clam up and there would be no talk. No negotiations. No truce. He wanted to tell her of the other-worldly thoughts he'd had of late. Thoughts usually alien to his way of thinking. Visions of oneness, of being alone in the world. Individuals and their actions and their connections with him could not deter him from his own quest. His destiny. Ultimately, in the end, he believed he would be judged on his own merit. His own life and how he lived it....HE WILL REPAY EACH ONE ACCORDING TO HIS DEEDS. Brady found a cool serenity in the words from Proverbs. He made a mental note to pick up his Bible more often.

He thought maybe he was going crazy. Maybe he needed to eat. The bourbon was strong and his stomach was empty. He weighted a chip with salsa and picked up an appetizer menu.

"What are you thinking?" asked Sarah. "Please say something."

Brady shrugged as he chewed a chip. "I don't know what to say. What do you want me to say? That it's okay? That everything's okay?"

"Maybe."

"Well, it does say on this menu that it's happy hour." Brady sipped his drink and ice clinked against his teeth.

"That's stupid. Please don't do that."

"Do what?"

"Be sarcastic."

"I like being sarcastic. Good defense mechanism."

"You need a defense mechanism because you can't say that you forgive me." Again, she stirred her drink with a chip. "That's okay, because you know what? It's my own fault. I think I'm evil. I swear. Look how many people I've hurt."

A pain evolved in the corner of his eyes and his throat grew tight. He would not cry. He stifled the emotion by downing his drink and signaling for another round. *Let me be the bigger person. Turn the other cheek and all that. Don't let me push her away. Help me.*

"So what am I supposed to do whenever I see Roger, which, by the way, is quite often, since he is my boss? I can't exactly beat the shit out of him, can I? What kind of pathetic loser does that make me?"

Sarah lit a cigarette as Rena placed new drinks on the table.

"I don't know. I've ruined everything. I've sinned. And for what? Because I'm a weak, pathetic person. I'm not strong, like you. What does that feel like? Always being good."

"Sarah, stop it. I'll be right back. I'm going to the men's room. Could you order some food? We need to eat something. Quesadillas or something."

Sarah watched him maneuver around tables and chairs and disappear down a darkened hallway.

She wanted to cry; get drunk and cry. But she had to drive. She could just have him drive home and get her car tomorrow. Guilt. She felt so guilty. At times of the day, when she thought the guilt was behind her, that she could cope with it, a new wave of shame and self-condemnation washed over her. It had to be something about being raised Catholic. Always the guilt. About anything. About everything. *Thou shalt not commit adultery.* She had broken a commandment. She had broken her commitment.

Brady moved his fork through mounds of sour cream, salsa and guacamole, making his plate like a palette of oil paints. Whorls of color.

"Eat something," he said to Sarah.

"I'm not hungry."

His plate looked like a mosaic and he wondered if anyone had painted with food before. "So. Do you still love me?"

"Yes."

For several minutes they picked at their food in silence.

"You're not evil. Don't even think that. We were both wrong," said Brady. "I've been using the campaign to deal with the pain. I never asked you or included you. I'm sorry."

"Okay. So, I guess we have work to do."

"I guess we do."

Sarah stood and came around the table and when she leaned down her hair brushed his face. She kissed him softly. He kissed her back.

"Okay?" she asked.

He looked at her face. "Okay."

She sat down.

"Why don't you work on the campaign with me," Brady suggested. "We can share this. We'll just tote Emily along."

Sarah tucked her hair behind her ear. "It might be a good thing."

"It might be a very good thing."

\* \* \* \*

IT WAS A Saturday in mid-summer, but it felt like October. The lean-to shed attached to the side of Claude Elliot's garage provided rustic shelter from the unseasonal wind and rain. Brady, Mark, Danny, Jessie and some of their college friends were at Claude's to build another batch of campaign yard signs.

Claude Elliot was an old man with old-school conservative views. Immersed in local politics, Claude donated his sign-building shed with naked light bulbs suspended by wires, and electric staple guns to any Republican he liked and had the guts to ask him for the favor.

A crabby and ill-mannered man set in his hard-right views, Claude did not trust anyone who disagreed with him. Inevitably, this meant all forms of media. The media was evil, save for FOX news and Rush Limbaugh. He was an extreme patriot with an enormous portrait of Ronald Reagan above his mantle.

John Brady did not understand Claude Elliot's type of patriotism. It seemed more like a hatred. Yet, Brady had to admire the ferocity of his dedication to the political system. He was a critical cog in the wheel of most local republican grass-roots campaigns for the legislature in Western Washington. He knew everybody; who to call to get things done and connections with businesses willing to donate materials. Two of his friends owned printing shops and were willing to offer incredibly low prices for signs, brochures and mail pieces to candidates Claude endorsed.

Though a crucial player, Claude was not an appealing person. Brady was baffled by the man's demeanor, since it seemed, from an outsider's viewpoint, that he had a good life. Retired from a successful career, politics was his hobby. Food for thought.

His home was beautiful. It sat on an acre and a half of land, part of which was fenced pasture roamed by two horses. Claude and his wife Louise had four grown children and ten grandchildren.

Physically, the man was a specimen of vitality. People were flabbergasted upon learning he was seventy-nine years old. Fit, trim and sinewy, he had a vice-like hand shake and a mind like a steel trap.

He had devised a very particular and neurotic system for sign building. The effort consisted of two stations, each station comprised of specific jobs. At the first station were two electric staple guns plugged into outlets in the rafters by long orange extensions. Persons at this station took sign faces and stapled them to pieces of wooden lathe. With the lathe secured to the top and bottom of the sign, it was ready to be drilled onto a 2x2 stake with heavy-duty screws. The drills and staple guns became so hot that gloves were needed.

Claude walked about the lean-to, hands clasped behind his back; a yard sign commandant. While passing Jessie at station one, he witnessed her apply a sloppy staple. Brusquely, he took the staple gun from her hands and said, "Here, the way you're doing it, the sign will come off in the slightest wind." Then he proceeded to show her the proper way. His way.

Jessie and Danny exchanged glances as Claude leaned over the sign to examine his handiwork. Jessie bit her lip to stifle a laugh.

"There. Understand?" Claude handed the staple gun to Jessie.

"Yes sir, " Danny answered militarily.

"Yes sir," Jessie answered.

Then to Brady's surprise, Claude giggled. "There is a method to my madness."

Brady delighted at the fact that he was building his own signs and subsequently, his campaign, his future. It was an adrenaline rush watching the college students work in silent dedication. Talk would erupt in spurts. Wooden stakes plunked down on the assembly line. Staples shot like gunfire. Within a few hours there was a respectable mountain of finished signs on the driveway.

"We've done a ton," Brady said.

"Oh, this is probably about two hundred, on top of the hundred and fifty we built a few weeks ago to get you going," Claude estimated as he rubbed his chin. "You need more. Being the challenger and all. You need at least five hundred pre-primary. Then roughly three hundred and fifty more after. Now, McNamarra needs thousands, being a statewide race."

"You're doing his signs too?" asked Brady. He held a group of ten finished signs together as Claude tied them tight with twine.

"I'm just helping with the signs for King County. There are several people helping. Joe Tinkerton is covering the eastern part of the state. He lives in Moses Lake."

"You think McNamarra has a chance?"

"Sure I do. And I think you're going to help him win it. With your daughter's case and your campaign."

There were no age spots on Claude's hands. His hands were not youthful, just well-worn like good leather. Strong hands; capable.

Brady looked at his own hands holding the signs. The joints in two of his fingers had bothered him lately. His father had been riddled with arthritis in his hands, feet and back. Brady would not complain about the mild swelling and pain. He did worry, though, that his hands might become disfigured and grotesque. He prayed that they would not.

Claude adeptly pulled a knife from his back pocket, snapped it open and cut a length of twine. The man seeped physical vitality. It was as if the strength of the old man's convictions, his political beliefs and sheer will to eliminate candidates and initiatives he believed evil, not just wrong, kept him vibrant. Body and soul.

After tossing another bundle of signs on the growing pile, Brady said, "Claude, thank you for everything."

"Hell, I've built signs for many new candidates. Can't begin to remember them all. Now go put one of your signs on the wall in the garage," he instructed, pointing.

The wall was adorned with dozens of sign faces. Candidates for state legislature, city council, county council, fire and water districts, school levies, statewide initiatives, governors. Republican presidential candidates all the way back to Goldwater.

"There's a small staple gun on the workbench," said Claude. Then he turned just in time to witness Danny's friend Brian bend over to pick up more stakes. The young man's jeans were oversized, hanging limply from his hips and exposing striped boxer shorts.

"Young man, your pants are falling down," Claude snapped.

Brian laughed. "I like them like this, sir."

Claude shook his head and looked at Brady. "It's just plain wrong," he scolded. "Go, go put up your sign."

It was hard for Brady to feel his age around Claude Elliot. He felt more like a fifteen year old constantly scrutinized by an adult. Carrying a sign, he entered the oily-smelling garage and began searching for a staple gun among the rusty tools. Suddenly, Jessie came up behind him. She was giggling.

"What?" Brady asked smiling at his boy's girlfriend. "What's so funny?" He was thrilled Danny was attracted to a happy and positive person. So many young people of Danny's generation seemed morose and unfocused. His son's high school class had been a mixed lot and quite a number of them had not gone to college. Several of his son's crowd worked retail jobs at the mall.

"He's got a pink toilet seat!" Jessie laughed and had to stop to catch her breath. "You know, the inflatable, squishy kind?"

"Who, Claude?"

"Yes! You know, he seems so mean? So know-it-all?"
She looked about to make sure she was not overheard. Then
her tone decimated to a whisper. "I asked to use his
bathroom. Well, the man has a pink toilet seat! And I think
it's their main bathroom!"

Brady laughed at the vision in his head. It was
incongruous to everything about Claude's character.
"Under it all, he's probably just a kitten. Now get back to
work. We're almost done," he jokingly ordered.

Claude entered the garage, passing Jessie on her way out.
She erupted in laughter again.

"Can children these days ever be serious?" he asked.

"Oh, sometimes they can," Brady answered. He pictured
a serious Claude Elliot sitting on a pink toilet seat. It was
amazing to him how you never really knew a person.

"Lots of signs. Lots of campaigns, heh?" Claude crossed
his arms and looked upon his wall of signs with affection.
"I think you've got enough going for you that you can take
her out."

"Newirth?"

"She absolutely must be the most liberal of liberals in
Olympia. She's an old, worn-out hag," he said, though
Newirth was at least ten years his junior. "You'll have
timber and business behind you. Obviously. That's huge.
Have to be careful, though, it could look like you're a
bought man."

"Of course," Brady agreed. "I could never be influenced
like that. It's corrupt."

Claude laughed. "Happens all the time. Can't trust
anyone. Remember that."

"Okay." Brady thought how sad it would be not to trust
anyone.

"All right, time to get back to business." Claude
examined his watch. "I've got McNamarra's people coming
at two o'clock." He exited the garage with an air of
importance.

Brady found a stepping stool and maneuvered it so he could place his sign within the political mosaic.

Outside he heard tires crunching the gravel driveway. The sound ceased and car doors opened and shut. Then there was conversation and it was indecipherable, yet he knew the voice. The tone. Nuances. Then another voice. High-pitched; a child. It was an instinctive, feeling. The sensation reverberated in his head, his chest.

"Hi, there," Sarah greeted as he began stapling his sign next to one for the local water commissioner.

"Hey. Where's Em?"

"With Jessie. Naturally."

"Naturally."

A gray spider balanced in its web obstructed the placement of where he had yet to staple. Brady could have stapled right over it, trapping the spider in its lair. He could have squashed it. Instead, he shooed it away with the stapler and it crawled quickly up the wall and into the rafters of the garage where it would start constructing a new web.

* * * *

BRADY SAT IN a chair on the patio mesmerized by the fire, its flames haphazardly licking the iron grate of the portable fireplace.

Sporadic pops and bangs sounded about the neighborhood, and on the air was a modest twinge of sulfur; anxious revelers unable to wait the remaining few hours until the Fourth of July. Toby, uneasy with the sounds and smells of fireworks, whimpered as he skittered about the yard and returned to lay by Brady's feet.

"One more marshlego?" Emily asked, white pasty goo ringing her small mouth.

"No, no more marshmallows. You've had enough," said Brady. "You'll have a sick tummy for the parade tomorrow. We don't want that."

"Can Toby come tomorrow?"

"No, Toby can't come."

Fourth of July as a first-time legislative candidate; hot dogs and speeches and sweaty handshakes and dunk tanks. Decorated bicycles and pop corn and yard signs and balloons. He had his speech memorized yet he had jotted a few key phrases on note cards.

Suddenly there was an explosion. A strand of Black Cat firecrackers. TNT sounding like rounds of machine gun fire. Toby whined and disappeared under a fir tree by a flower bed.

"Here Toby!" Emily called. "Here boy!"

"Toby doesn't like the fireworks, Honey."

Emily clapped her hands. "Toby! Come!"

As she continued to clap above the din of firecrackers, there came a commotion under the fir tree. There was growling and gnashing of teeth and Brady feared for Toby. He whistled and rose from his chair. "Toby!"

Though the yard was dark, Brady could just make out something white, a creature, roll from under the tree and lay still in the grass. Emily screamed.

The screen door opened. "What's going on out here?" Sarah asked.

"Turn on the outside light. Toby come!" Brady called.

A floodlight lit the back yard. Tail between his legs, Toby ran for the back door and Sarah stepped to the side to let him in. Emily, crying frantically, reached for Brady. He picked her up and could feel her small body shaking .

"It's okay, Em. Toby's fine. He's fine."

"What is it?" Sarah asked as she came outside with a flashlight. She focused the beam of light on the still form in the grass.

"A rabbit. Or a possum. A possum playing possum. You two stay here," he said putting Emily down. She ran to Sarah and grabbed her hand and held it.

Flashlight in hand, Brady walked across the lawn towards the still and quiet form. Toby barked and whined inside the house.

Expecting to see a wounded and bleeding animal, Brady was surprised to see a very peaceful opossum. It appeared to be dead, but it was not. Brady saw that it was breathing. MARSUPIALS HAVE POUCHES TO CARRY THEIR YOUNG. The only fact he knew about the animal kept repeating in his mind.

"Grandpa!"

"It's okay, honey. It's an opossum. It's just pretending to be dead. It's acting." He walked several yards from the nocturnal creature, keeping the beam of the flashlight upon it. Quietly, they all watched the animal as Toby barked and barked behind the sliding-glass door, his breath, hot and wet, fogged the glass.

Suddenly, after a few long minutes and more exploding Black Cat firecrackers, the play-acting animal slowly, eerily raised its head and looked about. Paws, like human hands with slender fingers, stretched towards the night sky then turned giving it momentum to roll and stand upright. It gazed unafraid, relaxed, into the beam of light, with pink eyes. A peaceful vampire.

Emily squirmed and whined. "Go away!"

"It won't hurt us, honey," said Sarah.

Toby pawed at the glass door, barking frantically.

Then in an almost casual manner, the opossum turned and waddled under the trees and disappeared into the darkness. Under the fence and into another world.

"Well, that was amazing," said Sarah. She set Emily down. "Let Toby out, sweetheart."

"I've never actually seen a possum play possum," said Brady. *If only Beth could have done that. Would he have slit her throat?*

Emily pulled open the sliding door and Toby burst into the yard like a bull from a corral. He ran about the yard crazily, on the scent of a rarely glimpsed ghost.

\* \* \* \*

APPROXIMATELY NINETY-SIX hours until the polls opened for the September Primary Election. Brady ticked-off minutes in his head as he stood on the busy corner of Pacific Highway and 272nd, two of the busiest arterials in his district . He had a yard sign in one hand, a cup of coffee in the other. He found it incredible that some citizens had already cast their ballots via absentee. How many people had filled in the little circle by his name with black ink while sitting in their kitchens?

It was 6:00 am. The headlights of commuters inching their way to the freeway onramp blinded him. In the early light of dawn, people in vehicles looked like shadows, shades. He could not make out their features. Someone would honk and he would wave to a faceless soul. Morning was better than late afternoon rush hour. Faces were visible then. Smiles. Grimaces. People honked horns and waved. People honked horns and gave him the finger. Democracy.

Gary Lake had told him that waving signs was the best use of time at this point. His last mailing would hit that afternoon. The campaign had ended up with enough money for five mass mailings. The first went to senior citizens. The remaining pieces went to all two-of-four voters; registered voters that had cast ballots in two of the last four elections. Of these, one was an introduction piece, a short biography of Brady. Posed family pictures. Two other mailings were comparison/contrast pieces differentiating himself and Newirth on the issues of taxes, education and especially crime. The last piece, which would hit that day was a get-out-the-vote postcard to Republicans from the State Party.

Brady did not mind standing and waving his sign. It was actually relaxing and gave him some thinking time. He daydreamed about the General Election and how it would feel to win. When he reflected on the past year and why he was where he was, a definite awareness, a sensation came over him that he was not alone. As if there was a figure, a shadow in his peripheral vision. He would turn instinctively and there would be nothing. The feelings did not scare him, in fact he was comforted by them. It was just a presence. Safe.

The waitress at Denny's was named Norma. A sturdily-built older woman with fair skin and visible facial veins, she looked as if she'd smoked her whole life. She looked Swedish.

"You're the one, aren't you? On the corner with the sign?" she asked with an accent from somewhere on the east coast.

"Yes, ma'am."

The fact seemed to impress her. "That's you? The name on the sign?"

"Yes. My name is John Brady. I'm the candidate."

Norma poured him a cup of coffee, placed the pot on the table and pulled a small pad of paper from her apron pocket. "What are you running for?"

"The State Senate."

"I've always loved the Kennedy's."

"Mmm."

"Every single person in my family is a Democrat. What are you?"

"I'm a Republican." He lifted his coffee cup to his lips and was careful not to burn his tongue.

"Well, not that it really matters. One way or another, you know? I mean, basically, we all want pretty much the same things."

"That's the truth," he agreed. He liked Norma. She reminded him of his grandmother. He believed the world would be a better place if more people thought like Norma.

"I think so. Anyways, enough about that. You ready to order?"

"Yes, ma'am. I'd like two poached eggs on wheat toast."

"I can do that." She scribbled on her note pad then picked up the coffee pot.

"Thanks."

"What's your name again? I'll tell my friends to vote for you."

Brady felt himself blush. "My name's John Brady."

"Okay then." She winked and nodded and retreated to a table on the far side of the restaurant.

He sipped his coffee and watched traffic in the soft morning sunshine. He saw his reflection in the window take a sip of coffee.

The campaign, the months of doorbelling, had made it clear to Brady that the majority of the general public had no idea how their political system, the government worked. He was not judging his fellow Americans because he too was ignorant, although he liked to believe he had become a little less so in the past few months.

Stirring drops of cream into his coffee, he watched it turn a lighter shade of tan. Witnessing Norma and her fellow waiters interact with their clientele made Brady appreciative. Just sitting at Denny's made him thankful. Thankful to live in a free country. The freedom to be informed, or ignorant. The freedom to be involved, or apathetic.

He felt corny, almost juvenile, having such thoughts, but as he got older they came more often. He compared America to places like Bosnia or Liberia or Iran. How was it that he was lucky enough to be born on the Pacific Coast of North America? Most people he knew were comfortable. Or at least they had the capability of being comfortable. His family had often donated food to shelters and food banks, yet he personally knew no one that used them. He wasn't naive, of course there were innumerable people around him that needed help. He was fortunate enough to have money. Health insurance.

Acquaintances of his complained about taxes and city government and bad roads. Some of these people were proud to say they did not vote. Well, they had that choice but more and more Brady found them obtuse. Complacency. When people have it good they can afford to be lazy. Most average citizens had no reason to get excited about politics.

Gary Lake estimated 40% of registered voters in Brady's district would vote in the primary. That number might double for the general. Complacency. Brady was tired of being complacent.

He had just finished his coffee as Norma appeared with his food. "Here you go," she said. "Two poached eggs and wheat toast."

"Thank you."

"So when's the election?" she inquired as she filled his coffee.

"Well, Tuesday's the primary."

"Holy Mary. I really do need to keep up on things."

Brady laughed.

"Like I don't have enough to do," she said with a wink.

\* \* \* \*

IT WAS GOD'S ironic humor that the first week of school brought with it the hottest, most beautiful weather of the summer. Kids came to Mark's classroom in the latest

Fall fashions only to peel them off in layers. Balled-up items of clothing bulged from back packs by days end.

Though he had taken Emily school shopping for a few new outfits, he knew enough to dress her in summer clothes on her first day of preschool.

He had chosen a Montessori preschool, the structure of which focused on students learning as individuals as opposed to one of a group.

"Okay, munchkin," said Mark pulling into the preschool parking lot.

"Daddy!" Emily yelled, exasperated. She was strapped in a booster seat holding Art the Bear and a new Winnie the Pooh back pack.

"Sorry," Mark apologized, "you're a big girl now. I shouldn't call you that." He turned to look at her, "You know that Mommy would be very proud of you today."

"I know," she remarked in a sure-footed way that made Mark want to cry. He would not have been upset if she had cried at the thought of her mother.

"Daddy! Daddy! There's Miss Janice!" Emily screamed as she tugged at the seat belt holding her back. "Miss Janice!"

The woman Mark and Emily had met at open house, who had wanted to be known as Miss Janice, was standing by a chain-link fence surrounding the red school house. It looked like a school out of Little House on the Prairie. The schools atmosphere seemed to ooze goodness. It, and Miss Janice looked wholesome.

"Daddy! Help!"

Mark stepped from the car and opened the rear door. "Okay, now remember," he said unbuckling her, "Grandma will be here to pick you up in a few hours."

Emily kissed Art the Bear on the nose and set him on the back seat.

Mark held her small hand as they crossed the parking lot. Emily was unfazed when they passed a boy clinging to his mother's skirt.

"I don't want to! I don't want to!" the boy screamed hysterically as he rubbed his snotty and tear-stained face in the floral fabric. The woman's tense face looked skyward, searching. For mercy? Patience? She met Mark's gaze, shrugged her shoulders and smiled. He smiled back.

Miss Janice wore a denim jumper with large pockets and a wooden beaded necklace. On each bead was a letter of the alphabet. With one arm she opened the metal gate, with the other she waved them inside. "Good morning Emily!" she welcomed cheerfully.

"That boy is sad," answered Emily as she pointed to the boy in the parking lot.

Miss Janice knelt down to a three-year-old size. "That boy's name is Jonathan. He's just a little nervous because it is our first day. But we're going to have such a great time that he will forget all about being nervous. Okay?"

"Kay!" Emily squealed.

"She's pretty excited," said Mark.

"And she should be!" laughed Miss Janice, the epitome of nice.

Emily pulled on his hand in an effort to forge ahead.

"I won't stay long. She wants to show me the classroom again," Mark explained.

"No problem, Mr. Bennett. She can put her back pack on her own hanger. And if you brought her extra change of clothes, she can show you her cubby."

"Great."

The classroom reminded him of the dwarf's lodgings in Snow White. Everything geared towards little people. Little hands. Coat hooks and toilets and chairs; miniature. Toy-like. Pictures and charts and mirrors, hung at Mark's waist.

Emily let go of his hand. "Don't help me Daddy."

"Okay, munchkin, oops! I'm sorry." He backed-off reluctantly and watched her eyes scroll down the drawer-like "cubbies" on the wall by the bathroom. When she came to her name in large block letters, she gasped. On each child's cubby was a photograph of that child. Emily's photograph was from her first birthday party. She was in her high chair wearing nothing but a black cowboy hat and chocolate cake with white frosting. To the side of the high chair was Beth, in profile, hands together in mid-clap. She was smiling and proud.

"Oh Mommy," Emily whispered.

The emotion in her young voice took Mark's breath away.

"What's your name?" asked a little girl who had appeared at Emily's side. She had large and dark and beautiful eyes.

"Emily," she answered pointing at her name on the cubby.

"My name is Jasmine. Wanna see Peter Rabbit?"

Emily's face brightened. "Okay!" Then she looked at Mark.

"Go ahead, sweetheart. I need to get to school. Remember, Grandma will be here to pick you up."

"Kay, Daddy." She hugged him tightly then accepted Jasmine's hand. Her new friend pulled her across the room to a large cage which held a big white rabbit, albino-like, with red eyes and a pink nose.

Mark watched his daughter interact with the other children. Emily and Jasmine laughed as they poked a leaf through the wire of Peter Rabbit's cage. The large-eared mammal greedily sucked it from their fingers.

"Are you a daddy?"

A little boy in a red striped shirt was looking up at him.

"Me?" Mark asked. "Yes I am."

The boy pulled a plastic bag out of his Mickey Mouse backpack. "Whose daddy are you?"

Mark pointed to Emily at the rabbit cage. "Her name is Emily."

The boy nodded then stuffed his plastic bag into his cubby. "I'm Brendan." He pointed at his name and photograph. "I don't have a daddy. I have a mommy."

Mark shook his head. "That's good. That's good."

* * * *

SPARROWS OR SWALLOWS, he was not sure. He really didn't know the difference. Brady heard the birds chirping as he shopped for wine and other items on Sarah's list, the Sunday before the Primary. Anything to get his mind off the election. He'd seen birds in the rafters of grocery stores before but they just seemed so out of place. Like in a dream. Later, in the car on the way home he wondered if maybe it was a game to the birds. Waiting for the automatic doors to slide open then swooshing in. Maybe signaling to each other in bird-talk, amazed at the human race below.

In a Volvo in front of him, a woman lit a cigarette and a plume of smoke wafted from her window. At a stop light it looked to Brady as if she peered at him in her mirror. Red light turned green then yellow then red, allowing only the smoking woman in the Volvo to pass through the intersection.

As Brady gripped the steering wheel and waited, a mosquito landed on his hand. Just behind his knuckle. Instead of flicking it off or slapping it dead, he sat mesmerized as the insect poked its stinger through his skin and commenced sucking his blood. A living syringe. The sensation was one of stinging heat. How fascinating, Brady reflected, that God would create a living thing that fed on the life-blood of other living things. Predators. Then he thought that perhaps he was losing his mind to be so enthralled by a bug.

Suddenly the driver behind him honked his horn and Brady looked up at a green light.  As his foot hit the accelerator, he smashed the mosquito dead.  The flattened body stuck to his knuckles in a small red smear of blood.

* * * *

ANXIETY OR HEARTBURN, he wasn't sure which caused his present state, but the Alka Seltzer had no effect. Thus it was that Brady opened the bottle of Jack Daniels and, uncharacteristically, downed a shot.  Then he made a drink.

"Hey, easy does it," Sarah remarked as she prepared a tray of appetizers.  Something with shrimp.

"I hate the waiting.  I feel like I'm going to jump out of my skin."

The small primary night gathering had congregated in the dining room, sampling the spread of food.

Danny, deep in conversation with Gary Lake, was grazing from a meat and cheese tray.  He washed down mouthfuls with Budweiser.  "So, I still don't get why tonight's so important when Dad has no Republican opponent.  Isn't that what a primary's supposed to be for?"

In shirtsleeves and loosened tie and hands in pockets, Gary Lake appeared relaxed.  "Most people don't get it. Washington is the only state with a blanket primary and no voter registration.  Anyone can vote for anyone.  Don't ask me why.  But it's totally unique because it's an exact preview of the general.  Your Dad has to get about 45% of the vote to show this race is close and remain a top target. If he doesn't, he's toast.  The money will go to someone who'll win."  He picked up a glass of diluted ice and took a sip.  The ice clinked on his teeth.

Brady entered the room.  "Another drink?"

"No, thanks, I need to stay on my toes.  I'll wait until the first returns," Lake answered checking his watch.

Danny observed his father. "Nervous?"

"Nauseous."

Emily pulled Jessie into the room by the hand. "Let's get cheese!" she exclaimed. Toby fidgeted by the child's side, tail wagging, waiting for dropped edible scraps.

Brady saw the look of adoration on Danny's face as he watched Jessie with his niece. He sipped his whiskey and took a deep breath.

Jessie filled a plate with cheese and crackers and sliced turkey and roast beef. Emily munched a cracker. "Sit Toby!" she ordered.

Toby sat.

"Here boy!" Emily exclaimed as she threw a piece of cracker across the dining room.

Brady laughed. Suddenly, as he perused the table, he realized he was hungry. He peeled a slice of roast beef off the plate and rolled it and salted it. His system needed something. Whiskey and beef and salt would fix the deprivation. Toby sat at his feet, staring at the meat in his master's fingers.

"Scavenger," said Brady.

"My wife does not like to go out at night. Even if it's only next door." Elmer stood at the kitchen counter holding a glass of red wine. "Here's to your husband, my dear. No matter what happens tonight, he's a very brave man."

Sarah tapped his glass with her own then finished her wine and poured more. When she lit a cigarette she felt like a child in front of her parents.

"You must be proud," Elmer said.

She thought about his words as she exhaled smoke. "Yes, I am proud." She felt herself blush, thinking of her betrayal.

At eight-fifteen they assembled in the upstairs office. Mark sat at the computer scanning the King County Elections web site. Gary Lake moved a chair next to the desk and took a seat. Numbers and percentages scrolled down the screen.

"Okay. There. Stop," said Lake. He scribbled on a piece of paper.

"Oh shit," Mark whispered.

"What? What do we have?" Sarah asked. She felt queasy. People had voted yes or no on her husband.

"We're at 43.5"

Brady felt a crushing weight in his chest. "Dammit!" he hissed, then, not realizing he'd been chewing his lip, tasted blood; dirty metal.

"Hey," Lake said, "remember, the first report is only absentees. And they tend to run Democrat. These are the ballots mailed in weeks ago. Second report is at nine. Our numbers WILL go up."

At nine-twenty,, the second set of numbers had yet to be seen. Mark watched the monitor and sipped beer. Trays of food from the dining room table had been brought upstairs and placed around the room.

"Anyone need a refill?" Danny asked holding up a bottle of wine.

"Please." Pam Naughton held out her glass.

"Looks like we're in for a bumpy ride," said Danny.

"It's going to get better," Pam said matter-of-factly.

"Me too, hon," Sarah held her glass out to her son. She looked at Pam Naughton and again thought about how much time she, Sarah, spent in front of the mirror. Applying creams, gels and makeup in the eternal quest for beauty and youth. The hide and seek of wrinkles and sagging skin. Why even bother, really? She took her wine to the window, opened it a few inches and lit a cigarette. She blew smoke through the screen, ghostlike, into the darkness.

Having scrolled through the same numbers for what seemed an eternity, Mark jumped back in his seat when the change came. "Here we go!" he exclaimed.

A tight circle formed around the desk only to find that John Brady's percentage had risen to 44.1%.

"Oh my God," Brady whispered, realizing that he had, in fact, been praying. But was it appropriate to ask God to let him win? For his numbers to go up and Newirth's go down? With 44% was it possible Heaven did not support his endeavor?

Pam Naughton's cell phone rang. A piece of Beethoven. She answered the call stepping into the upstairs hallway.

*I'm not going to make it*, Brady thought to himself.

Jessie popped her head in the door. "Um, excuse me, but your neighbor, the elderly gentleman? He said he needed to get home. He said to tell you 'good luck.'"

"Okay, thanks," Brady said.

"He didn't want to bother you guys." Jessie added.

"I should have gone down to say goodbye," said Sarah.

"I'm not going to make it. I'm not going to make 45%."

Gary Lake used his pen as a pointer, tapping on the monitor screen and looking at Brady. "John, listen. I'm not worried at all. Look at this. Believe me, this is typical. King County Elections is stupendously slow. They've only counted, what, 3,000-3,200 votes in our district? That's why we've barely budged. You're going to go up." With that, Mark stood and made way for Lake to take over the helm of the computer.

On his way out the door, Mark said, "I need to get Emily ready for bed. I keep forgetting she has school now."

"Good luck getting her to bed with Jessie here," Sarah said.

"She'll be part of my strategy," he called back from the hallway.

Danny laughed. "Let her help. She loves Em."

Lake swiveled in his chair. "Next report should, and I say 'should' be at ten o'clock. I'm going to check on a few other races. Everyone go relax. I'll yell when new numbers come up."

Pam Naughton returned. "What are the numbers from the 27$^{th}$? And how is Moen doing?"

"Let's see," said Lake.

Brady grabbed the cold-cut tray and left the room, leaving the political pundits to calculate data. Create war plan strategies. Descending the stairs felt like going down in defeat. A leader, a commander come to address his troops.

To his apolitical mind, the numbers seemed disastrous. How in the world would he get backing for the general election? Who would take him seriously?

Out of nowhere, Toby appeared, tail wagging, as he sniffed at the tray Brady carried.

"You're getting fat," said Brady. "Go away. I have nothing to give you."

At ten o'clock everything changed. As suddenly as the gloom had descended on the house with the first numbers, it lifted when Gary Lake yelled, "Yes! Yes! Yes!" Simultaneously, Brady's home phone and cell phones about the house started ringing.

"Hot damn! We're at 48%," Lake exclaimed from the top of the stairs.

"Dad! Phone!" Danny called from the kitchen. "It's a reporter!"

By eleven o'clock, Brady was at 49.1%, with 90% of the vote counted. He had given telephone interviews to four local reporters. One television crew taped an interview on his front porch. And he had agreed to do the Eric Glass radio show the next day.

Mark, having downed many beers, tapped a spoon against his empty bottle. "Excuse me folks. But I think a toast is in order."

"Hey, I haven't won yet, guys," Brady laughed. He was relieved and he wanted to downplay the primary. He knew the election was just beginning. "What is in order is more roast beef and more whiskey."

"Whatever, Dad," Danny chuckled, his arm around Jessie's shoulders. "We can make a toast if we want. Here's to a job well done!"

"Cheers!"

"Here! Here!"

They tapped each others glasses and drank.

Brady felt cautiously exuberant. "Thank you."

"Hey, are we missing something?" Gary Lake asked upon entering the kitchen. Pam Naughton trailed him, briefcase in hand.

"We forgot about you," Mark said as he twisted a cap off another beer.

"People always do," Pam said with a smile. "King County is done for the night."

"We were making a toast," said Danny.

"I don't want to be a party-pooper, but this is far from over. Don't be shocked if Newirth goes negative and nasty right away."

"See?" Brady looked around the room. "I told them not to toast me yet."

"Well, I guess it's okay. You did make it through the primary," Lake smiled. "Maybe you should say a few words."

"Speech! Speech!" Jessie exclaimed.

Brady made a face at Lake. "Thanks a lot Gary."

Sarah laughed. "Come on now." She took his glass and poured more Jack Daniels.

"I'm not about to give a speech. But, I think we all know why we're here." He accepted the drink from his wife and held it up. "I'd like to make a toast to Beth."

"To Beth," they said as a chorus. The room became quiet as all attention shifted to the deep-sleep breathing of Emily on the couch with Art the Bear.

Toby's nails clicked on the kitchen floor as he sniffed about for food.

"And no more food for the dog," Brady scolded. "I've been guilty of throwing him scraps, too, but, doesn't he look fat?"

"Hey, look," said Mark. He grabbed the remote and turned up the volume of the television, which had been muted. "McNamarra won the Republican primary."

"Not surprising. We'll be seeing tons of him in the next few weeks." Gary Lake grabbed his suit coat off a barstool. "I'm outta here."

Sarah moved next to Brady and rested her head on his shoulder. "Hi."

"Hi." He put his arm around her. It felt good.

Brady sensed Sarah's physical presence the rest of the evening. A nudge here, a touch there, as he tried and failed to awaken Mark as he slept upright on the sofa next to Emily.

"We need another blanket," Brady said softly.

Her hand was on his shoulder. "I'll get one," she said, walking a little unsteadily from the room.

Brady made another drink then began cleaning the kitchen, nibbling on crackers and cheese as he did so. "You really are a bum," he said to the dog. Toby sat a few feet away, watching and waiting for a crumb. Brady tossed a nugget of Swiss cheese.

"Who are you talking to?"

"The dog."

"Oh." Sarah gently lowered a patchwork quilt onto Mark and Emily then joined him in the kitchen. "Excuse me," she said from behind him as he rinsed dishes at the sink. Her hand momentarily landed on his lower back. He moved aside so she could pull the garbage can from under the sink.

"You brushed your teeth," Brady said to her image in the kitchen window.

"Yes. So?"

He dried his hands on a towel. "I'll get that," he said, taking the garbage bag from her. He went to empty it in the garage. When he returned, Sarah was sipping his drink.

"That's mine."

"I thought it was mine too. You know, since what's yours is mine, right? And vice versa, of course."

"Ha."

She pulled a cigarette from the flip-top box and placed it between her lips.

"Don't," he said.

"Don't what?"

"That." He moved towards her and plucked the cigarette from her mouth. "Don't smoke."

"I can do what I want," she answered and plucked another cigarette from the box.

"It's nasty."

"So?"

"It smells bad."

"So?"

"You just brushed your teeth."

"So?"

Brady moved close to her as she lifted the cigarette to her smiling lips.

"So, suppose somebody wanted to kiss you?"

"Somebody who?" She grinned. He backed her into the dishwasher, placing his hands on the counter on either side of her.

"You mean, some politician?"

He kissed her then on her toothpaste and whiskey mouth. She kissed him back.

"It's been a long time," he said.

Sarah's face grew serious. "I really am sorry."

Brady hugged her, kissed her neck and breathed in her perfume. "Shh."

As Sarah nuzzled his neck, Mark let out a sighing snore from the sofa. His chin had flopped down to his chest. Toby slept sprawled at his feet.

Sarah giggled. "His poor neck is going to hurt tomorrow." She moved away from Brady, picked up his drink and took a gulp. "Think they're okay on the couch?"

"The couch was fine for me," he said sarcastically.

"Ha. Ha."

His arms encircled her waist. "I've missed you."

Again, Mark coughed and snored.

"Okay, okay," Sarah whispered. "Let's go upstairs. You can stop missing me behind closed doors."

"How does it feel to be married to a politician?"

"You're not a politician yet."

"No. But I will be. I can feel it."

\* \* \* \*

THE NEWIRTH CAMPAIGN went negative. By Friday after Primary Tuesday mailboxes across the district were stuffed with hit pieces on John Brady.

Did Mr. or Mrs. Average Constituent want to elect a pawn of the timber industry?

Did Mr. or Mrs. Hard-working American want a part-time Senator? A man whose entire career had been with a billion-dollar business which also happened to have one of the largest lobbying groups in Olympia?

How could John Brady, a novice in the political arena, not be at the beck and call of Big Timber when he received a paycheck from them?

Brady and Sarah had received two pieces of mail each. Big, glossy 8x10 postcards. The first was a grim black and white grainy photograph of deforestation. Hill upon endless clear-cut hill. The mailing insinuated that Brady was the cause of the devastation. John Brady could not possibly be for the environment.

The second piece was another black and white photo with basically the same message. The picture was of a forest peppered with green dollar signs standing big as trees. In the midst of these money trees stood a chess board pawn: John Brady.

Brady felt angry and defiled. Neighbors and friends and co-workers would get these mailings, and knowing him, dismiss them. But the majority of the district; why not believe them? If it's in print it must be true.

* * * *

"I KNOW I'M naive, guys, but these are bad," Brady said holding up the mailings. "It's like slander, isn't it?"

"Libel, actually," Joe Booth answered. The State Senate Chief of Staff had called the strategy session. "And its part of the business. And it's why we're here. We have to hit back. And fast."

It was Saturday morning and the offices of the Senate Republican Campaign Committee were swarming with young, clean-cut staffers. Footsteps echoed in the narrow, marble-tiled hallways. Stark white paint against the dark mahogany wainscoting and doorways gave Brady the impression Harry Truman or another politico from that era should be walking the floors.

Gary Lake, dressed like Brady in khaki pants and blue oxford shirt, pulled papers from his briefcase. "Okay, I've been working on some mock-ups. Pam and I have some pretty good stuff."

"I'll be the judge of that," Booth said with a wink at Brady.

Pam Naughton placed her coffee cup on Booth's desk and gestured at Lake's papers. "Now, John, you're going to think these pieces are going overboard. Too much. But the thing is, we have to hit back hard. Okay? And we're not going to lie. This is all true stuff."

"I'm feeling queasy that I have to be warned," Brady said.

"Okay," Lake began, "the first piece will be: HAZEL NEWIRTH IS SOFT ON CRIME. She is for rehabilitation, not prison time for most offenses. She is for letting prisoners out early to free up jail space. That kind of bullshit." He showed the mock-up to Brady. "It ties directly to you and your history with Beth. Jeffries, Jr. getting out early, etc. We'll have a photo of a jail guard opening a cell and letting a prisoner out. That kind of thing."

"Good," said Booth with a nod of his head.

Pam watched Brady scrutinize the mock-up. "What do you think?"

"I don't like it, and my wife will hate it," Brady said as he handed the piece to Booth. "But it's the truth, and given what they have resorted to, I can live with it."

"Good. Actually, there are three negative pieces in addition to the five positive pieces designed to answer her attacks," Said Lake. "We're thinking, ten days out, the jail piece hits. One week out we do a tough compare-contrast piece, also on crime." Lake handed Brady another mock-up. "Then the weekend before the general the big one drops. She won't have time to respond."

The headline read: COMMUNITY ALERT! THESE DANGEROUS SEX OFFENDERS MAY BE IN YOUR NEIGHBORHOOD! It looked like an official document; something law enforcement might issue to warn people. The front of the oversize post card included mugshots of three seedy looking men. The text said that due to Hazel Newirth's votes in Olympia against mandatory life sentences for sex offenders, these criminals were running free in south King County.

"What the hell?" Brady was incredulous. "This is going to scare people to death!"

"Exactly," Booth said. "It will break through the noise at the end of the campaign, put her on the defensive, and keep the focus on our main issue."

John Brady shook his head. "That's just as sleazy as the stuff they did on me. Are those guys actually criminals who might be in our area?"

"No, listen," said Lake, "Those are stock photos, but she really did cast those votes, and you know she's soft on crime."

"But you are intentionally misleading and scaring people," said Brady. "I can't do this."

"You don't have to." Pam Naughton moved her chair close to Brady. "Your name will not even appear on the piece. Most of the mailings will state 'paid for by John Brady for Senate Campaign,' just like in the primary. The three negative pieces will have, 'paid for by the Washington State Senate Republicans,' our campaign committee."

"Deception," said Brady.

The phone on Booth's desk rang. "Joe Booth here."

Lake gestured towards the door. "Let's step into the hall."

They closed the door behind them. As they stood in the hall, Brady heard footsteps in the stairwell. "I'm really not comfortable with this."

Pam nodded her head. "We knew you wouldn't be. That's why it won't mention your name or the campaign."

"Bullshit! It will reflect on me, and you know it!"

"It's a common practice! Newirth has done it before," Lake responded. Both men were becoming agitated.

Pam nodded. "You won't have anything to do with it."

"Give me a few days to think about it."

"That's all you get. All three pieces need to be done and to the printer in about, oh , seventy-two hours," said Naughton.

"Two things to think about, John," Lake began, his voice rising. "First, everything in these pieces is true. Second, do you want to win or not? We have to stay on the attack and keep the focus on crime or you *will* lose. Period!"

Lake's attitude angered Brady and he began to respond when Pam cut him off.

"Come on, boys," Pam coaxed. "Let's get some caffeine and calm down."

* * * *

BRADY HEARD HER crying the moment he set foot in the preschool. Most of the children were busily at "work," each with his or her own activity. Spatial and motor skills. Eye-hand coordination. A number of children looked at Brady in wide-eyed wonderment.

He walked towards the office where a cluster of children bunched about the doorway.

"Who are you?" asked a little girl, her hair in braids. In her fingers she held an eye-dropper. She was transferring cobalt blue liquid from one glass beaker to another.

"I'm Emily's Grandpa."

"She threw up," said the girl.

"Oh dear, well, we'll take care of her."

"Okay."

The pre-schoolers moved aside for Brady. Emily lay upon a cot in the office, a large red bowl at her side. The room smelled of Lysol.

Wearing a red corduroy jumper, Miss Janice peered at a thermometer inches from her face. She saw Brady and jumped. "Oh, hi! Thank you for coming so quickly. We have a sick little girl here."

"How's she doing?"

"She has a fever of 101.5 and she's thrown up twice. Poor thing. This bug is going around."

He knelt beside Emily. "Hey there, how's my girl?"

Emily sniffed back a sob. "I threw up," she said through tears. "I wanna go home."

Brady felt her forehead with the palm of his hand; hot and damp. "Okay, honey." He remembered that his own kids would get scared when sick. They wanted the familiar.

Suddenly one of the boys in the doorway came over to the cot. He wore blue jeans with a stretch elastic waistband. "You okay?" he asked Emily. She shook her head and grabbed Brady's hand.

"Okay, Em," Brady began gently, "I'm going to pick you up and get you to the car."

"I threw up cause I was sick seven days ago," the boy informed Brady.

"It's yucky being sick, isn't it?" Brady asked.

Miss Janice put her hand on the boy's shoulder. "Come now, Brendan, let's get back to work. Emily's Grandfather wants to take her home now. She'll be better soon."

The preschooler hugged his teacher's legs. "I met Emily's Daddy before. I don't have a Daddy. I have a Mommy, though."

"Well, that's good." Brady smiled.

"Bye Emily!" Brendan shouted.

Brady's granddaughter was limp as he carried her through the school. The clammy skin of her face was wedged in the crook of his neck and strands of wet hair stuck to his cheek. Her breath came in quick little gasps that smelled rancid and vomit tinged.

"Excuse me, kids," Brady remarked on his way to the door.

"Bye Emily."

"I hope you don't throw up anymore."

"She's sick, stupid."

Miss Janice held the door open. "Thank you, Mr. Brady. We hope all is well soon."

"Oh, it will be, thanks," Brady heard himself say as he tried to refrain from sucking in vomit fumes.

*It'll all be fine.* The phrase, like a cheerful children's song ran amok in his head as Emily threw up in the back seat. He listened to the refuse of his granddaughter's stomach splash into the bowl Miss Janice had graciously given him. The stench from the back seat was immediate and overwhelming. He lowered his window and gulped in fresh air.

"Good girl, sweetie. I'm sorry you're sick. We'll be home in a minute" *It'll all be fine. It'll all be fine...* "Art the Bear and your buddy Toby are waiting for you."

Emily emitted a small gasping moan. "I want Mommy."

How to respond to that? "I know, honey. I know." *...I want Mommy too, Goddamit. What do I do with a sick kid? I forget this stuff. I don't want this stuff. She needs her Mother..*

"Hold on. Two more minutes."

"Kay," she answered with a voice that broke his heart.

*Goddamit. Goddamit. Okay. This is it. I'll do it. I'll okay those sleazy mail pieces. Newirth's going down. I've come this far. I've got to win for Beth and this little girl, and if this is what it takes, so be it.*

"Okay, Emily, we're home."

As he pulled into the driveway he heard Emily's stomach lurch as she readied to vomit again.

\* \* \* \*

THE NEGATIVE MAILINGS on both sides during the last two weeks of the campaign caused an uproar. Letters to the editor screamed heartfelt and heated words from voters attacking Brady and Newirth, but people seemed more angry at Brady. How could he turn the campaign into a typical mud bath and try and frighten people? People had thought he was different. How could he resort to politics as usual? One letter, penned by a working mother, a Boeing engineer began, "Oh, what a tangled web we weave when first we practice to deceive…"

Was he deceiving voters? Were the mailings untruthful? No; he could and did justify the pieces with the fact that Newirth had voted just as the mailings claimed. Crime was a legitimate political issue. Her beliefs were not in sync with the district. But did that really matter?

Brady decided that what did matter was getting past the final, ugly stage of the campaign. It could not be taken back or erased. It was out there. He thought of a judge during a trial telling members of the jury to disregard a comment, yet it was that comment that inevitably stood out. At that moment he knew his mailings were sitting on thousands of kitchen tables and counters, waiting for conscientious voters' perusal this weekend before the general election.

*Oh God how I hate hypocrisy.*

That morning Brady had heard sound bites on the radio of Newirth lashing out at his attempt to scare voters. He was ashamed of himself.

He tried not to focus on his shame as he taped his hands; layer upon layer of the thick white material over and around his knuckles and thumbs creating a forceful tightness when he made a fist.

After pushing his hands in the comically large boxing gloves, he approached the bag swinging. A direct hit to the rectangle of faded newsprint duct taped to the bag was a direct hit to the profile of William Jeffries Jr. Brady had kept the photograph and the accompanying article from the arraignment in his wallet until that afternoon. He had accidentally pulled it from amongst his credit cards while paying for gas. An urge had come over him to destroy the greasy, pony-tailed image.

Having been folded and unfolded countless times, the paper had the consistency of tissue, ripping and shredding with each hit. The power emanating from Brady's fists felt both inhuman and cathartic, purging his soul of pent up anguish. He knew the entire campaign had been an effort to release these emotions; feelings so powerful they would consume if not purged.

Hit. Jab. Punch.

The chain holding the bag rattled as scraps of newspaper fell to the garage floor.

Right. Right.

Left.

Right.

An oblong strip of paper sank into a small puddle of oil which had dripped from Sarah's car.

Left.

Left.

Muscles throbbed. Adrenaline rushed. If only he had a picture of Roger to tape to the bag. That too would be cathartic. That too would feel good.

Punch. Right-left.

Or plaster the bag with Hazel Newirth's mailings. No.

Right. Right.

He wouldn't be able to hit a woman. He wouldn't even hit a picture of a woman. Sweat down his temples and the small of his back. The force in his fists came from some unknown place deep within, yet he felt outside himself. A bystander watching.

*I let the damn staff gloss it over. I knew it was wrong and I let them talk me into it. Oh God. God, I'm sorry I let this happen. I mean, I want to win, I think. If you want me to win, of course. Just help me make the right choices. Help me stay on the path.*

Punch. Jab.

Left. Right.

Shreds of silver tape dangled from the bag. He continued pummeling the white letters on the red leather: EVERLAST...ETERNAL. LASTING. IMMORTAL. UNDYING. DEATHLESS. Synonyms flashed like neon signs on the screen of his brain.

Suddenly there came an image, a profile of Beth. Peaceful and luminous and beautiful. It was so realistic it made him gasp. He ceased the barrage of punches and stood frozen next to the swaying bag.

"You okay?"

He blinked away the vision. Sarah stood in the doorway, arms akimbo, surveying him.

"What?" he asked. He grabbed the bag, holding it as if hugging an opponent. Music from the local TV newscast wafted out to him, as did the scent of sautéed onions.

"Her fever's broke," Sarah said with relief.

"Oh. Thank God." He realized he was breathing very hard. Sweat was dripping off him, and he thought how awful it would be to have a heart attack.

She looked at him quizzically. "You sure you're okay?"

"I'm fine."

"She says she's hungry. That's always a good sign."

"Good."

"Dinner's about ready."

"Okay."

"Pork tenderloin. Red beans and rice."

"Great. Be right in."

The door closed and all he heard was his own breathing and the creaking chain. He sat on a step-stool, removed the cumbersome gloves, and began unwrapping the tape. White sticky residue lined his hands. Then, as he picked at the glue with his fingernails, the furnace began grumbling and clicking to life. He watched the blood-orange flame of the pilot light dance ethereally behind the small circular window.

Brady felt as if he were in a trance as he stared at the pilot light, then shifted his attention back to the letters on the punching bag. A shiver coursed through him.

ETERNAL FLAME. ETERNAL PEACE. ETERNAL LIFE. EVERLAST. EVERLASTING LIFE.

\* \* \* \*

IT WAS 6:00 P.M. on election day and Brady had been standing on the triangular asphalt island at the apex of the busiest intersection in the district, waving his yard sign for two hours when he noticed the pink and purple pacifier next to the curb. Binky. The term came back to him. When Beth and Danny were young he had always carried spares in his pockets. He remembered the helpless, sweaty, mortified feeling of being binky-less while in line at the grocery store or while in stop and go traffic. Nothing soothed intense emotional outbursts like a piece of rubber to suck.

He walked to the curb and picked up the plastic device; familiar yet strange. The rubber tipped ball of the sucking end had marked etchings; small scars from a teething mouth. He envisioned a single mother pushing her baby in a stroller. Waiting for the walk/don't walk sign to change and not realizing her youngster had tossed the peacekeeping binky away. Brady put the pacifier in his jacket pocket with his cell phone and his bottle of Tums.

Beth had not believed in pacifiers. She thought they stunted emotional development.

Suddenly his cell phone rang and it was Gary Lake sounding small and far away. Brady had to cover his ear to drown out the traffic noise. "I can't hear you," he said.

"It's great news!" Lake shouted. "Can you hear me Senator Brady?!"

"What? What's going on?"

"It's a goddamned Republican landslide! That's what's going on! Polls are closed back east and Democrats have already conceded the White House, which means the trend is moving west. You understand? Democrats here will figure, why bother? They'll go home after work instead of going to the polls."

Brady stood on the triangular island letting the information sink in. A car horn honked and made him jump.

"You there? John?"

"Yes, I'm here."

"Buddy, your race would've been too close to call, but this will gain us a few percentage points across the board. You're going to be a Senator!"

"But the polls are open for two more hours." The don't walk sign flashed beside him.

"Exit polls are confirming a huge Republican turnout. You gotta believe me. Pam and I should be to your house by the time King County posts the first numbers. Okay? John?"

"Okay."

"And John? Go home. Have a drink and relax."

* * * *

BY ELEVEN THAT evening Brady, Mark, and Danny had each polished off a bottle of champagne.

Danny, filled with political questions, turned to Gary Lake. "You know, it really doesn't seem fair. It seems somehow unconstitutional. Why are news organizations allowed to announce winners of national offices before polls are closed here?"

Lake nodded. "I agree. I think it's wrong too. Just so happens THIS time it worked in our favor."

Danny laughed. "And now I have to call Dad 'Senator.'"

"How about 'Your Honor,'" Brady quipped. "Or how about 'The Honorable.'"

"My ass," Sarah giggled as she sat down next to her husband.

"What about your ass?" asked Brady. "It's fine just the way it is."

"Okay, you guys are gross," Danny said. "And Dad, you're blushing."

Jessie entered the room carrying two cups of coffee. "Who's gross?" she asked, handing the cups to Brady and Sarah.

"My mom and dad," Danny answered.

Jessie sat down beside Danny, "Why are they gross?"

Pam Naughton laughed. "Come on, Gary, let's go see if the last numbers are up."

"You don't think it will change much, right?" Brady asked as he gingerly sipped coffee in avoidance of another scorched tongue.

"Relax. Over 90% of the precincts have reported. We've already won. Trust me." He punched numbers on his cell phone as he followed Pam out of the room.

Brady turned to Sarah. "I won't believe it 'till its over."

"The Honorable is very stubborn," said Sarah.

Danny plucked a wisp of hair off Jessie's cheek and tucked it behind her ear. "What were you and Mark talking about in the kitchen?" He looked at Mark reclining on the floor beside the couch where Emily slept. Mark seemed deep in thought as he stared at the ceiling. "It seemed serious."

"Beth," Mark said. "We were talking about Beth and what she would think of all this."

All the conversation in the room ceased instantaneously, and they focused on the noises around them. The local newscast coverage of election returns. Emily's sleep-induced loud breathing. Toby's nails clicking on the wood floor of the hallway as he pondered a spot by the front door and plopped down.

"God bless Beth," Sarah said quietly. "My Elizabeth," she added, then drank her own private toast with a sip of coffee.

Mark lifted himself onto one elbow. "She would think this is awesome. I know she would."

Danny laughed. "She'd never believe dad's a Senator."

Simultaneously, phones rang in the kitchen and the upstairs office. Brady stood. "It's me they want."

"Oh, the Honorable," Sarah mocked.

"Yeah, yeah."

When he answered the phone, the older woman's voice on the other end caused Brady to pause. The hair on the nape of his neck prickled.

"John Brady, please."

"Speaking."

"Mr. Brady, Hazel Newirth here."

"Oh. Hello." *Oh my God. How must she feel? Why did I agree to those negative slams?* He had a vision of Newirth: large, old, and chagrined. In his vision she wore her gray raincoat, enhancing her similarity to an elephant.

"Mr. Brady, I just wanted to extend my congratulations."

"Oh. Well, thank you." There was an apology wavering on the tip of his tongue. "Republicans were lucky tonight. I just got lucky."

"Yes, I would agree."

"Yes."

"Well, good luck to you."

"Senator Newirth?"

"Yes?"

"I just have to say I'm sorry. I'm really sorry about the last mailings."

There was a pause at the end of the line. "Mr. Brady. One must have a thick skin to survive in this game. Even at this level. You're going to need to learn that."

It was two in the morning when Brady walked Gary Lake and Pam Naughton to the door.

"You're Joe Booth's hero, John," said Lake. "Republicans have the majority in the both houses; 25-24 in the Senate. Unbelievable. And we have a new Republican Governor. I need sleep. I think I'm dreaming."

Awkwardly, Brady reached out to shake Lake's hand. "You guys know I wouldn't have won without you." Then he gave Pam a quick hug.

"The new golden boy," Pam giggled on her way out the door.

Everyone was asleep when he returned to the living room. Brady looked from one face to the next. Danny and Jessie were cuddled on the loveseat. Sarah, curled up under a blanket on the over-stuffed chair, mumbled something in her sleep. Mark slept soundly on the floor by the couch on which Emily lay still, holding Art the Bear.

Without waking anyone or turning off lights, John Brady crawled onto the couch, snuggling in behind Emily, the movement causing her to roll onto her back. Art the Bear fell to the floor.

Staring at her profile as she smacked her lips, swallowed, then continued sleeping, he was again overcome with the aura, the essence of beauty and angelic innocence.

His eyes watered as he looked at her face. A small pinched pain at the base of his throat made him swallow back tears. Just by looking at her, he knew that God had a reason for everything. Every detail of his life, of his family's life, had been planned. And he knew that he was on the right path. He felt it. He looked at Sarah and Danny. Then he focused on Emily again, mere inches away. And he felt happy.

# PART III

## RESOLUTION

*Doubtless a great anguish may do the work of years, and we may come out from that baptism of fire with a soul full of new awe and new pity.*

George Eliot

SENATOR-ELECT JOHN BRADY sipped frothy Budweiser from a plastic cup and remembered the afternoon when he, then a thirteen year old boy, had shot a robin dead with his BB gun. He'd checked on the decomposing carcass in the tall grass for several days until finally, one day, it was gone. The teenage Brady had walked under a black cloud for days, morose, pondering death. That small death had shaped his life-long view of guns. As an adult, he believed in the $2^{nd}$ Amendment, the right to bear arms. But he did not have to like guns. He did not have to own a gun.

Brady guessed that a good number of the people mingling about him at the Bullseye Ranch were gun-owners. The manicured grounds about the house and stables were teeming with casually-dressed Republican Senators, their staffs, and family members.

The Bullseye Ranch in rural Pierce County was owned by the state's premiere firearms lobbyist, Quentin Lamont. A bear of a man who resembled Grizzly Adams, Lamont was missing two fingers from his left hand, one from his right, and his upper right incisor.

The barbeque was an annual event and Brady had heard stories of Lamont and his hospitality.

In the shade, things sparkled with frost, and breath emanated from warm bodies like smoke. Not even a week into the new year, wreaths and mistletoe still adorned the barn and stables. He felt strange, shivering in the cold of a January morning, drinking cold beer before lunch.

The Senate Republicans had held their re-organization meeting just before Christmas, where Brady had the opportunity to meet most of the members. Still, he was grateful for the name tags they were made to wear. Brady, felt, however, that everyone knew him. He didn't need a name tag. He was the new one. The rookie. The freshman.

Many guests lingered by the pastures a few hundred yards behind Lamont's house where two firing ranges had been set up. One range showcased handguns; the other rifles. Lines of people waited at each as a uniformed guard, Brady imagined some sort of gun expert, strode down the line, explaining safety do's and don'ts.

"This is awesome, Dad!" Danny exclaimed. "Loud, though."

"I know." Brady drank his beer and shivered. "Your mother would hate this. Absolutely hate it."

Danny nodded. "Well, don't tell her, but I'm going to try the pistol. Not the rifle. The pistol."

"Okay," said Brady, although he wished his son was still young enough that he could tell him no. "Look, okay, this is the one I was telling you about." With a nod of his head, Brady gestured towards a woman peeling off her coat at the front of the line. She wore a shoulder holster and her own gun. "Senator Paula Moore. Ultra religious conservative. From Kelso or Vancouver or somewhere in the southern part of the state."

Moore pulled her gun from its holster and showed it to the guard in charge of the hand gun range. Then she slammed in a clip with authority.

As Brady and Danny watched, a cloud of cigar smoke overcame them. "They don't say a whole lotta Moore for nothing!" exclaimed Senator Jonah Johnson removing his cigar in order to laugh. He wore a tweed coat with leather elbow patches and grey snakeskin boots. "I'll tell you who wears the pants in that family," he whispered knowingly.

Brady was impressed at the ease of Jonah Johnson's mannerisms. He seemed down to earth and honest. He was the only fellow Senator he had taken a liking to thus far. Johnson grew apples in eastern Washington the majority of the year, and Brady found that admirable, never having known a farmer.

"How are you doing Jonah?" Brady offered his hand. "This is my son Danny."

"Nice to meet you." Danny put out his hand.

Johnson's grip was vice-like and he chewed his cigar as he spoke. "How do you do, son? As you can see, your Daddy, here, has become part of a very interesting group of people."

"I agree," Danny nodded.

"I feel like I'm in a fishbowl. Members and lobbyists all staring," said Brady.

"You're the new kid. New blood. We all went through it," Johnson remarked. "Where do you stand on guns?"

"Haven't fired a gun in over thirty years," Brady answered.

Danny shifted his weight to his other foot. "I went hunting with a friend once. But I've never shot anything."

They all watched as Paula Moore fired round after round, consistently hitting the middle target mounted on a bale of hay seventy-five yards out. There were two other targets at fifty and one hundred yards.

"Well, she does know what she's doing," Johnson said squishing the cigar between his lips.

Moore stood with her feet shoulders width apart as she emptied her clip then stood smugly as a range attendant presented her with the paper target riddled with holes like a piece of Swiss cheese. She chuckled with a group of onlookers while holstering her gun.

"Modesty," snickered Johnson.

"I'm going to try it," Danny said. "Don't tell mom."

"Good boy," said Johnson.

"Hey, give me the beer." Brady reached for the cup in his son's hands. "Great. Drinking and guns."

Brady and the Senator watched Danny receive instructions from a man wearing camouflage pants and a bright orange jacket.

"Senator Brady!" Quentin Lamont wore a sweatshirt exclaiming: GUNS DON'T KILL. PEOPLE DO. "And Jonah. I hope you boys are enjoying yourselves."

"Quentin!" Johnson barked. "Great turnout! As usual."

"It's the weather. Cold. Crisp. Just beautiful!"

Wearing goggles and large headphones over his ears, Danny began firing shot after shot into the target seventy-five yards out.

Johnson grinned, the two-inch long wet and expired cigar in his teeth. "Senator Brady's son there is quite the marksman!"

Lamont took in the scene as if surveying the making of a fine wine.

Danny's clip was empty and Brady was stunned. "God knows where he learned to do that."

Lamont laughed. "Some people just have natural talent, like Jonah, here. A hunter. And a good shot." The gap in his teeth showed when he laughed. "Okay, Senator Brady, what's your take on guns?"

"Everybody's curious, aren't they?" said Brady.

There was a twinkle in Lamont's eye. Save for the missing incisor Brady thought his host would make a great Santa Claus.

"I think there should be some gun control," Brady said.

Lamont nodded. "Like?"

Though Lamont was genial and friendly Brady felt patronized. "I'm not sure. Take gun shows, like at the fairgrounds each summer. Anybody can walk into one of those and walk out with an assault rifle. That's not right. Joe Citizen does not need an assault rifle."

"Most people who buy at gun shows are licensed firearm dealers and NRA members. They've already passed background checks. They're on file," Lamont's demeanor was calm and condescending, as if he had put Brady in check in chess match.

Danny returned and took his cup of beer from Brady.

"Where on earth did you learn to shoot like that?" Brady asked his son.

Danny laughed and shrugged his shoulders. "I don't know."

"You're a natural," Lamont remarked. Then he laughed. "Now your father, on the other hand, I need to work on him." Then Quentin Lamont slapped Brady on the back. "Ha! Just kidding. Now let's eat, boys!"

Brady felt like punching him, but he just smiled.


"One would think it would be a cinch to make legal fireworks legal."

"One would think," Brady agreed.

"Every session. Same thing. For several years we've tried to pass a statewide law making fireworks legal everywhere. A blanket law. Just the "safe and sane" products. We're talking sparklers and "whistling Petes." Not skyrockets and sticks of dynamite. Not the stuff sold on the reservations."

Bill Freeman was the lobbyist for Independence Day, a Washington State fireworks group. As he talked he ate potato salad, and a small chunk dropped onto his lapel next to an American flag pin. "Damn it," he said wiping the spill.

"I've never understood the current laws." Brady agreed. "Families can have 4$^{th}$ of July barbeques and have neighborhood fireworks display in one city, while in the next city over fireworks are illegal"

"There is no logic," said Freeman.

Suddenly Senator Paula Moore was standing with them, holding a heaping plate of food. She bit into a cheeseburger and listened.

"Paula, how are you?" Freeman asked as he wiped his mustache with a napkin.

"Hey, Bill, you working on our newest member?" She took a mammoth bite of her burger.

"You betcha."

"You're quite the shot, Senator," Brady said.

Moore scooped baked beans into her mouth. "Well, I shoot every day, so I better be a good shot. I didn't see you shoot."

"No, I'm not a gun man," Brady laughed. He could see her holster and gun inside her coat. And he knew she knew he could see it. The realization of how un-attracted he was to her made him laugh. She was a woman who relished her manliness.

Moore wiped her mouth and turned to Bill Freeman. "So, what are your chances this session, Bill?"

"God knows. Fifty-fifty. That's why we need this new senator here." He tapped Brady's shoulder.

"I imagine Senator Brady has his own agenda," Moore remarked.

"Doesn't everyone?" asked Brady.

Jonah Johnson laughed and coughed as he lifted a cellophane-wrapped cigar from the inside pocket of his tweed coat. "Of course. Everybody wants to do something. Everybody has an agenda." He unwrapped the cigar with too-long fingernails. After biting off the cigar tip he spat then sucked the stogie as he lit it. Puffer-fish kisses.

"Well, there won't be any extra money this session," Moore said matter-of-factly as she tossed garbage into a can. "McNamarra's got to have his tax cut."

"Yes," Brady agreed, "but he also agreed with me on the jail problem. He ran on that issue because of my daughter's case."

"He also ran on tax cuts," Jonah laughed. "He told the voters want they wanted to hear."

\* \* \* \*

TOBY CIRCLED THE cage perched upon the coffee table. The agitated dog's tail wagged precariously close to a Waterford crystal vase.

Within the steel cage, a scared black bear hamster was burrowed in a trench of pine bedding, only its snout protruding. Its whiskers twitched as it sensed the large mammal's moves.

In his mind, Brady pictured the scene from JAWS when Hooper is inside a huge underwater shark cage. The mammoth great white appears out of the blackness, dwarfing the cage and the man inside.

What must the little black hamster, yet unnamed, think of the large-toothed, dog-monster with the hot breath? Toby circled and circled the cage; sniff-blows dredging up wood chip litter.

He marveled that Sarah had agreed with Mark's insistence of Emily's need for another pet; a rodent in particular. She'd had to remind him that Beth and Danny had cared for a hamster when they were children. Each generation must have its own opportunities. Responsibilities. A chance, as Emily had now, to squeal with delight as her hamster rolled about the room in a fluorescent plastic ball, or ran on its squeaky wheel all night long.

After shooing Toby across the room and forcing him to lay on the rug, Brady opened the cage. Then, as if his was the hand of God reaching into the cage of Life, he plucked up the hamster and gently stroked it with his fingertips until it ceased trembling.

\* \* \* \*

WAS IT THE ethereal lighting of the stormy afternoon sky casting a dreamlike essence to his office walls? Brady gazed out his window at the expanse of evergreens moving in the wind. Tiny pellets of rain tapped on the glass pane. Nostalgia was a funny thing. Though he would still be employed by Northwest Timber after the legislative session, it felt to him that ties had been severed. He was moving on. He felt his life had become a journey; a quest.

Sitting at his desk, he surveyed his office as he would a sepia photograph. Awards of merit. Framed professional and personal pictures. Business-related trophies and trinkets. The clock on his wall, a cross-sectioned portion of tree trunk. His bookcases housed volumes of Northwest Timber history. Rules and regulations, employee payrolls, insurance carriers; medical and dental. Steel-toed boots and hard hats to be worn when visiting mills and harvest sites.

A knock at the door jolted him out of his reverie.

"Whoa! Didn't mean to scare you, John!" Jimmy Young, the company's lobbyist was standing in the doorway.

Brady laughed, rising from his chair. "Hey Jimmy, come in. As you can see, I was in another world."

Young leaned against the doorjamb, hands in pockets. "You excited for the swearing-in?"

To Brady, Jimmy Young had heretofore been an obscure employee. They had exchanged pleasantries for years, yet never talked shop.

"Kind of surreal, isn't it?" Brady asked. "I'm trying to tie up loose ends here. It's a little overwhelming."

Young casually jingled keys in his pocket. "It must be. But top brass here is fine with everything. There shouldn't be any conflicts of interest. Everybody here supports you."

"No bribing to keep my job?" Brady laughed.

"Nah. You're too smart for that. We need you here too."

"People think I have an agenda. Working here and being on the Natural Resources Committee."

"That's to be expected," Young said as he shifted his weight. "People need to bitch about something."

"True."

Young looked at his watch. "I've got to run. I have an appointment, but I'd like to get together for drinks in Olympia next week. See you later, Senator."

Within seconds, another knock. Brady looked up, expecting to see the lobbyist again.

"Hey, John," his boss greeted from the doorway. "Can I come in for a minute?"

Brady felt the goosebumps on his arms. "Sure," he answered. "Have a seat."

"Thanks," Roger said meekly.

Brady had not let their paths cross since he'd learned of the tryst. So it was the first opportunity to scrutinize his boss, his friend, as the man that had tried to take his wife. Feeding on her vulnerability; a vulture.

As he watched Roger take a seat, he wondered, not for the first time, what Sarah had seen in him, this pathetic, thin, impeccably dressed man. A man Brady had always thought somewhat feminine. A man with perfectly manicured hands. A man he could not imagine chopping wood. Or hunting. Or wearing a flannel shirt. Or fucking his wife.

Yet, Brady had been afraid to face Roger. Even though his insides burned with a violent, infectious feeling that flared and festered each time he thought of the man. Wasn't he supposed to be macho? Defend his manhood by beating him up? It was a question of male virility; chivalry. His wife was part of his home and castle.

Roger cleared his throat. "I haven't congratulated you."

Brady had the feeling that Roger was referring to more than his Senatorial win. He knew at that moment what he'd suspected all along: he would not lash out at Roger. He would turn the other cheek. The man in front of him was a defeated, guilt-ridden, unhappy shell of a man. Roger had gambled on Sarah and lost. Could he blame another man for loving his wife?

"Thanks, Roger. And don't worry. I'll be on top of things here. I've delegated what I needed to and, of course, I'll still be available."

"I'm not worried," said Roger.

An awkward silence ensued and became uncomfortably weighty when Brady's phone rang. "John Brady," he spoke eagerly. "Yes. Yes. Oh, hello."

Roger rose from his chair and moved to the window, gazing at the evergreens beyond the parking lot.

"Okay, is she really upset? Yes, okay." Brady glanced at the timber chunk of clock on the wall. "Her father's still in school, so, okay, I'll be there in about twenty minutes. Okay? Thanks." He hung up the phone. "The thrills of being a grandfather."

Roger turned from the window. "Something wrong?"

All he wanted was for Roger to leave. He didn't want his apology. *What in God's name do I say if he says 'I'm sorry John.' 'Oh, it's okay? Don't worry about it?' Go to confession, man. I'm no priest. I have no authority to absolve. Two centuries ago I'd have challenged you to a duel...but you've lost. I've won. Go away.*

"Oh, that was Emily's preschool. Seems there was a little incident and I need to go pick her up."

"She okay?"

"She's fine. A little boy managed to get his toy truck tangled in her hair. They can't get it out and they don't want to be the ones to cut it out." Brady sighed and almost laughed at the picture of Emily's predicament in his mind. "Children."

"I'll let you go," Roger said. "But, oh, one more thing: How's Jimmy Young treating you? I saw him leaving your office."

"He's a nice guy. Funny how I'd seen him for years and never really spoke to him.

Roger nodded. "It's funny how things work out." He shoved his manicured hands into his pockets. "Well, good luck. You know, on the bill about Beth and everything."

"Thank you."

"John, I hope we can be okay. You know?"

John Brady pitied the man cowering in front of him. Though he admired his boss for attempting an apology – and he knew in time he would forgive Roger – he couldn't give him the satisfaction of a handshake. Or a smile.

"I know, Roger. I hope we can, too."

\* \* \* \*

MISS JANICE WORE a necklace of chunky white and black numerals. It reminded Brady of photographs of African villages in National Geographic. Bone necklaces.

"I'm so sorry about this, Mr. Brady. We could not just cut her hair. You know the wheels on those little matchbox or Tonka trucks? The friction? You pull them back and they go forward? Anyways, one of the little boys was playing with Emily and somehow he managed to get his toy all tangled up in her hair."

Brady imagined the boy rubbing the toy through Emily's hair in a show of victory. Pre-schooler male testosterone.

With red-Ked-tennis-shoed feet, Miss Janice led Brady into her office. At a small desk beside a big desk, Emily sat coloring, a huge tangled mass of truck in her hair.

"Oh my, looks like we have a little problem here!" exclaimed the stylist with bright orange hair. She approached Emily and held out her hand. "What happened?"

Emily sniffed, tugging at the tangled nest of hair at the nape of her neck behind her right ear. "Joshua chased me and then he got it stuck."

"Well, come over here. I've got a big-girl chair for you. It's really cool." The stylist pumped the lever at the base of the chair with her foot then pushed a booster seat onto it. "I bet Joshua felt bad."

Emily climbed into the chair and put her hands in her lap. Staring at her reflection, she turned to the left, then to the right, making the wad of hair swing to and fro like a huge dreadlock. The stylist draped a cape about Emily's shoulders.

"I don't want to look like a boy," stated Emily.

"You won't. I have a daughter with short hair. She has a really cool haircut. I cut her hair. She's in preschool."

"What's her name?"

"Rachel."

"I'm in preschool, too."

"Thought so. My name is Sheryl. What's yours?"

"Emily," she stated confidently.

Sheryl carefully appraised the complicated muddle of hair and truck, then began pulling up twists of Emily's hair, securing them with plastic clips.

"You look beautiful. You look like a flapper," said Sheryl.

"I'm not a flapper!"

Sheryl laughed and dropped her comb, whereupon she reached for a new and sterile one out of a glass container of blue liquid. "Do you know what a flapper is?" she asked as she took final tiny snips with quick flicks of the scissors.

"I don't want to be one," Emily stated defiantly.

Sheryl surveyed her work. Emily's bangs and back of her hair had been cut short, leaving the sides tapered to chin-level. The cut accentuated her cherubic face and ornament-like eyes.

"A flapper was an independent woman in the 20's. That was a long time ago. Not that you'd understand. But their hair was new and stylish. It was cool. You look cool."

Emily studied herself in the mirror. "Do you like it Grampa?" she yelled across the room.

Brady crossed the room and stood by her chair. "I love it!" he exclaimed truthfully.

"Do I look stupid? Do I look like a boy?" she asked breathless.

"No," Brady chuckled. "You could never look stupid, or like a boy."

Emily smiled. "Joshua's stupid, cause I got this!" she exclaimed triumphantly holding the small plastic truck with wisps of hair twisted in the axels.

Later that evening, Brady spied his granddaughter after her bath, standing naked and pot-bellied before the bathroom mirror. She tucked her dripping wet, newly-cropped hair behind her ears then plucked some dangly earrings out of Sarah's jewelry box. Holding them to her ears, she admired her profile, left and right. She smiled at her reflection. "Hello," she said seductively. "My name is Emily."

\* \* \* \*

IT WAS NOT a magnificent specimen like Charlotte of the Web, in fact the opposite was true. It was unremarkable and small and approximately the size of his fingertip. Brady wondered what it subsisted on.

For nearly two weeks he'd woke to the hypnotic rhythm of Sarah's breathing and studied the minute maneuvers of the spider on the ceiling above their bed. His wife would have shrieked knowing it hovered as they slept. And yet, he did not tell her of it. It was his secret. If he spoke of it, the spider would disappear.

Brady's initial reaction was to kill the spider. But without someone pleading for him to extinguish it, he'd hesitated. Thought twice about it. He remembered the cup of tea he'd recently made. After the tea had steeped he pulled out the tea bag and noticed writing on the paper tag: IF YOU CANNOT SEE GOD IN ALL, YOU CANNOT SEE GOD AT ALL.

He had consumed the same tea for years and had never noticed the small quotes on each bag.

His mind kept returning to the small nuggets of wisdom. THERE ARE PEOPLE WHO HANDLE SITUATIONS AND THERE ARE PEOPLE WHO ARE HANDLED BY SITUATIONS. Philosophy to ponder while sipping tea.

Subsequently, Brady applied the words from the tea bag to the spider. When he saw it in the morning it actually made him smile. He felt a connection to the spider as he had with the ladybugs in the bathroom months earlier.

Then the inevitable happened. He awoke to the sound of the toilet flushing. The bathroom door opened and Sarah stuck her head out. "Honey, you awake? There's a spider in here. Could you come kill it?"

Brady scanned the ceiling. The walls. Nothing. *Can I come kill it? Why should I kill it? She's asked me for years and I've obeyed. Programmed to smash them. Smear their guts on the walls with a tissue. Stomp them with a slippered foot. Automatic. No questions asked.*

"Where is it?" he asked pulling on his sweatpants.

Sarah was applying toothpaste to her toothbrush. "There," she pointed.

It was the spider from the bedroom ceiling. His spider on the tile wall of the shower. He pulled a tissue from the box and gently brushed the spider onto it. Confused, it crawled about nervously then froze.

"What are you doing?" Sarah asked awkwardly, her mouth full of toothpaste.

"I'm putting it outside. Setting it free."

Sarah spat into the sink. "Why?"

"I don't know." He moved past her, gingerly transporting the spider on the tissue. "Why not?"

\* \* \* \*

A PULSE IN his brain, behind his eyelids. Pure, taught chords pulling at the fibers of his muscles and joints. A live thing that made his eyes water. An unknowledgeable novice of music, he found the genius of Bach or Mozart or Beethoven miraculous; humbling. What a gift, what inspiration. A summons to immortality.

His heart quickened with the repeating waves of notes and he wondered what God must be like to have allowed such creation. Benevolent. *I pray my Beth is with you. With such Grace she is okay.*

Brady opened his eyes as the piece ended. He pushed stop on the remote and sat up. He knew of a quote from Bach: "The objective of music shouldn't be more than the glory of God and the awakening of the soul."

He would be sworn-in to the State Senate in less than six hours. He picked up the black leather-covered Bible on the coffee table. *I will swear to you, God, on this, your word, that I will do my best.*

Pushing a button on the remote, he began the same piece again. Listening carefully, Brady honestly felt a genuine link to God; the sonata an umbilical chord of life. And when the music ended he whispered, "Amen."

\* \* \* \*

BEING A FRESHMAN senator, John Brady's desk was in the back row of the chamber. He sat quietly, hands resting on his family's Bible, taking slow, deep breaths to help calm his nerves.

From the rostrum at the front of the magnificent room, the Lieutenant Governor called out the name of the senator-elect from the 31st district. Brady watched the novice Democrat make her way down the center aisle.

Up above, on each side of the chamber, were the galleries in which church-like wooden benches were packed with guests and family members. As each name was announced, the spectators erupted in applause and whistles. Cameras flashed.

Although he knew that all the members of his family, each dressed as if for Easter, occupied half of a bench, Brady refrained from looking up. He did not want his emotions to rule. Instead, he focused on the historical factoids he had learned about the Senate chamber. In years gone by, when smoking was permitted in the chamber, the galleries were frequented by politicians and their various tobacco habits. Stinking masses of smoke hovered like rain clouds below the ceiling.

Another name was called to more applause. Thirty-seventh district Republican.

He looked at his hands on his Bible on his desk; one of the original mahogany desks from when the capitol was finished in the 1920s. Adorning the front of each desk was a cast-iron grille, behind which a kerosene heater had warmed the politicians before the modern HVAC system had been installed.

A tug from the past, a pull from the present. Brady eyed the luscious carpet awash in deep grays and pinks and greens. Rhododendron blossoms, the state flower. The rich colors of the carpet were offset by the highly-polished black marble walls, which, upon inspection were full of delicate rivulets of pink and white.

His gaze went back to the Bible. *Thy will be done.* Snippets of the Lord's Prayer had played in his mind all morning. *As we forgive those who trespass against us.* He lifted his sweaty hands off the black leather cover and watched damp handprints slowly disappear. HOLY BIBLE in gold embossed letters. *Our Father, whom art in heaven, hallowed be thy name…* It played in his mind like a ticker tape. A mantra.

Then, unable to stop himself, he looked up at the gallery and found his family. Sarah, Danny, Jessie, Mark and Emily were seated in the second row. Sarah and Danny waved.

Emily sat on Mark's lap loosening and tightening the knot of his tie.

*…Thy will be done. On earth as it is in heaven…as we forgive those who trespass against us…* Brady blinked and tried to focus on the oath of office being administered at the front of the chamber, but snippets of the prayer were unremitting. *…As we forgive those…as we forgive…* He felt his hands sweating on the Bible. His skin tingled as he sensed sounds and hushed voices. Physical energy and emotion. The symphony of individual and minute sounds created an electric hum. And he heard everything. Anything. Omnipotent. The honk of an older gentleman blowing his nose. A cranky child in the gallery to his left. Someone's leather shoe creaking with each step. Papers shuffling. He could have heard a pin drop. Felt a breath…*Jeffries trespassed against me. He's in Walla Walla maximum security prison for life. I think I do forgive him. Isn't that what you want, God? As we forgive those…and deliver us from evil, and thy will be done…*

Suddenly, Bach's piece he'd listened to the night before washed into his thoughts. A reprieve. An accompaniment to his prayers. The pure notes of the violin played deep inside him. His heart strings. He was conscious of a calmness descending on his body and mind and he felt unabashedly at peace. With himself. With his place in the world. His understanding was unrestricted.

*I forgive him. I don't hate him anymore. Let go. Let go of the hatred. It only rots the soul. The soul of the one who hates me… I forgive him. I forgive Sarah for being with Roger…yet, the other thing…more importantly, I think, …is it okay to say that I forgive You? Because You know that I hated You for letting it all happen. I really did. Can You forgive me? Absolution. Clemency. Forgive me for being blind to all that I still have…so, with all that I am, I accept Your will…*

Brady peered at his family in the gallery. They were clapping. Danny gave him a "thumbs-up" sign. The soundtrack of Bach ceased. Everyone on the Senate floor was turned towards him, clapping and cheering as the Lieutenant Governor called for Senator-elect John Brady to come forward.

Eyes burning, Brady blinked several times, determined he would not cry. Justice Nathan Abrams of the Washington State Supreme Court held Brady's Bible and asked the Senator-elect to rest his left hand on the tome and raise his right hand.

Brady wished for a drink of water. He thought of his family watching and of Emily's Gumby figurine in his pocket. He wondered why justices and judges and priests, for that matter, wore robes; to look like a scribe or a Pharisee, or perhaps, Jesus? *Thy will be done.* He wondered if Beth could see him.

"Sir, repeat after me," Abrams began, "I, John Brady, do solemnly swear that I will support and uphold the Constitution and laws of the United States,"

Brady spoke as commanded, though with no idea if he was speaking correctly.

"…the Constitution and laws of the State of Washington,"

Was he correct in thinking that one side of Abrams mustache was longer than the other?

"…and will, to the best of my ability, faithfully perform the duties of the office of State Senator,"

*…Please, God, I think you brought me here for a reason. Help me do the right thing…*

"So help me God," Justice Abrams ended.

"So help me God," Brady said firmly.

*…Thy will be done.*

\* \* \* \*

BRADY HAD CHOSEN Douglass fir seedling kits from Northwest Timber. The ceremonial practice was a Senate tradition: before a freshman's first speech on the Senate floor, it was customary to present his or her colleagues with a small gift. A trinket representative of themselves or their district. A senator from eastern Washington had dispensed small bags of apples from an orchard in his district. Another member from LaConner, just north of Seattle, had presented quaint boxes of tulip bulbs.

The seedling kits were lightweight containers the color of mud and the consistency of an egg carton. Each held a packet of seeds and instructions for growing and transplanting one's own tree. The biodegradable container, itself, the planter. Once the seeds were planted, the kit was to be kept indoors until seedlings sprouted. Then the entire contraption was transplanted outside. Part of Northwest Timbers re-forestation program, the kits were successful marketing and educational tools for schools and civic groups.

"Nervous?" Karen Callahan asked as she grabbed a few kits from the box. Brady's legislative assistant, Karen had been a Republican Senate staffer for fifteen years and knew everything there was to know about the legislature. Brady had been told repeatedly that it was a lucky thing her former boss had lost re-election.

"Can't wait until it's over," he answered as he adjusted clutter on Senator Paula Moore's desk to make room for a seedling kit.

"Don't touch her stuff or she'll shoot you," Karen grinned. "No, really, she'll have a hissy fit."

He thought of Moore at the shooting range and how she stood with her holstered gun. "Hey she likes me. She co-sponsored my bill."

"Of course she backs your bill. Doesn't mean she likes you," she said seriously as she looked about the chamber. "Think that's it. Any more kits?"

"There's a few extra."

"I'll keep them at my desk for constituents." She picked up the box. "Hey, good luck."

"Thanks, Karen."

As he watched her cross the chamber floor, he felt a profound sense of gratitude for the career staffer. He guessed she was in her late forties, yet her steel-gray hair belied the fact.

While she was moving between empty desks, a young female page, a bespectacled and pimpled teenager flagged Karen down. Though unmarried with no children, Karen was a mother figure to many in the Senate Office Building, and presently, she seemed thrilled to be of help to the teenager.

Karen Callahan was comfortable in her surroundings. She was part of them. She excelled at her job, and knew the workings of the legislature inside and out. She was content with her healthy salary and state benefits. She was a Senate lifer.

Brady stood at his desk arranging several note cards. Key words and phrases. He only needed to see the word and by rote, the sentence came. Having spoken on the bill so many times, the language on SB 3271 came easily. He had memorized every inch of Beth's Bill like he had his multiplication tables in school. He knew it by heart. Like a tape recorder: press a button, a trigger word, and the rehearsed lines flowed.

"Good morning, Senator."

Brady looked up to see a page passing by. The boy's white dress shirt was too big around the collar, his tie askew. Light glinted off his braces when he smiled.

"Good morning," Brady nodded, still not used to the deference and respect.

The chamber was coming to life. Senators, holding steaming cups of coffee, took their seats. Voices echoed in the hallway beyond the chamber door. In the air was the dank scent of damp raincoats and umbrellas.

"This bill, put forth by our new colleague Senator Brady, is just another waste of taxpayer dollars. We're all sorry for his loss, but it doesn't mean we must throw more money at jails. We don't need more jails. What we do need is to improve our schools. Pay our teachers more. Create a better education system so troubled kids who end up being criminals don't fall through the cracks..."

Brady listened as a junior Democrat from Seattle belittled Beth's Bill and marveled at the philosophical differences between Democrats and Republicans. Embarrassment at his past naiveté was total. In hindsight, he realized how passive and juvenile his political beliefs had been. Sure, he lived by family-instilled morals and values, but when it came to the big picture, he'd been like Switzerland. Neutral. Non-commital. Now he saw the immaturity in such a stance.

*...Have a backbone and stand up for a belief, for God's sake...a conviction is a good thing to possess...*

Most of his life had not been lived under extremes. No black or white system of thought. No Democrat or Republican agendas. No conservative or liberal ideas. He'd always gotten by just fine in shades of gray.

And now? His bill was strongly supported by Republicans. By prosecutors. By the counties.

Therefore, the bill was vehemently opposed by most Democrats and liberal social service groups. They could not vote for more jails. They did not believe in them. People needed to be reformed, not locked up. They wanted more money for education and rehabilitation programs.

Brady knew he was not a true-believing Republican on all issues, yet he truly didn't understand how a person could believe violent criminals could be reformed.

*…If only Jeffries would have gone to a school where the teachers made a little bit more money. What a Goddamned joke.*

He read a note card on his desk: Not enough money in their budget to operate a new jail. It sits empty, while other facilities are overcrowded.

*…then let the criminals out that have just about served their time…those least likely to re-offend; like Jeffries…*

At present, Senator Jonah Johnson had the floor, espousing Beth's Bill as an undeniably important piece of legislation. In his distinctive elbow-patched tweed coat, the boisterous senator bellowed, "If you do the crime, well then ladies and gentlemen, you do the time!"

Next, the chairman of the Senate Judiciary Committee, Senator Bill Foster said a few words praising Brady and the work he had put into the bill.

Another note card: Divert 1/10th of 1% of the sales tax away from the state and back to the counties to operate jails. The state would retain 99.9% of the sales tax currently have…

Brady stood, ready to be recognized. Senator Foster moved for SB3271 to be adopted then took his seat.

*…counties operate their own jails…not state run. Most counties just can't afford more capacity, they need help…*

As Brady unclipped the microphone from its holder, the Lieutenant Governor banged his gavel. "We recognize our colleague from Kent, Senator John Brady."

Brady told the Senate Chamber the story of Beth and how his bill was born. His speech was passionate and poignant and when he concluded there was jubilation and applause by Republicans. Several senators gave Brady high-fives or a slap on the back.

After the vote, he was giddy as he dialed his cell phone outside the chamber.

"You see me on cable?" His voice echoed in the cavernous hallway.

"You did great!" Sarah exclaimed. "Was it party-line?"

He had to cover his other ear to drown out footsteps on the marble stairs. "Not quite. We got two D's. 27-22. I can't believe it! I think this is really going to happen!"

"It's happening right now."

A tap on his shoulder. "Senator Brady?"

He turned to face a local TV reporter, plastic credentials dangling from his neck. Beside him a cameraman was adjusting his equipment. A bright light clicked on.

"Senator, what do you think the chances are of Beth's Bill sailing through the House, too?"

"Gotta go, Sarah." Brady slapped his phone shut and quickly searched his memory for an appropriately rehearsed sound bite.

\* \* \* \*

THE TRAY OF assorted doughnuts and muffins remained untouched at the center of the ornate conference table. A scattering of Senate and House Republican leaders and staff ringed the table, drinking coffee and talking on cell phones.

Governor McNamarra entered the conference room laughing with his chief of staff, Tad Brighton. "Sorry people," he addressed the room. "I know we were supposed to meet in the mansion, but they're in the process of terminating the bat problem."

"Lovely," Joe Booth commented. "The perks of the office."

"The wife does not find the flying rodents humorous," McNamarra quipped.

"I guess your predecessor was incompetent when it came to cleaning house," smirked Senate Republican Leader Alex Daniels. "But, then, he was a Democrat."

"And because of that, we've had nothing but tax increases year after year. This administration is going to change that. This session. Okay, people, where are we?" McNamarra took his seat at the head of the table and poured a cup of coffee from a carafe. "I think Tad, here, is ready with some numbers for us."

Brighton flicked on an overhead projector at the front of the room. A chart of a projected budget appeared on a screen suspended from the ceiling. In pin-striped pants and white shirtsleeves, he pointed to a column of numbers. "Okay, you each have this same graph in front of you. Now, our estimates show we need roughly another hundred million to pay for our promised tax cuts."

Joe Booth clicked the tip of his pen up and down. Up and down. "Great. A hundred million. What the hell do we cut?"

"Don't tell me," sighed Alex Daniels. "Let me guess. Right there on the screen. Senate Bill 3271. Beth's Bill. Or should I say, John Brady's bill?" The Senator sat back in his chair, visibly deflated. "No way."

"Now, Senator—" McNamarra began.

"Governor, sir, with all due respect, I can't do it. I can't kill that bill."

"And," Joe Booth added, "it sailed through the Senate and it's already in the House."

"Where it's expected to pass," Daniels said. "Governor, you yourself ran on that bill."

"Dammit! Don't you think I know that?" McNamarra loosened his tie as if he needed air. "How about King's gravel bill?"

"Negative," Speaker of the House Richard Lenhart interjected. "We promised it to him last session and besides, it doesn't save us nearly enough money."

Daniels drained the remainder of his Diet Coke and slammed the empty can on the wood table. "All I know is I promised to deliver that bill. If I kill it, it'll split my caucus."

"Suggestions?" the Governor queried the room.

Lenhart cleared his throat. "Brady's bill is the only significant new spending we factored into our original budget numbers, and it gets us the money we need. It's the obvious answer. We can kill it in the House; that'll take some of the heat off you, Alex. Stall it in Judiciary, then kill it in Rules. Jenkins is the chair. She'll do it if I ask her."

"You mean if there's something in it for her."

"Naturally."

Alex Daniels snapped shut his briefcase and stood to leave. "And what's in it for Senator Brady?"

"Alex, you and I both know what happens with the base if we don't pass this tax cut," said McNamarra. "Who would you rather piss off, one Freshman Senator or one million conservative voters? You know we have to do this."

The Speaker of the House grabbed Daniel's arm as he walked past. "There's always next session, Senator. Brady's only a Freshman."

Daniel's leaned from the waist and whispered into Lenhart's ear, "Screw you."

\* \* \* \*

VINYL, IRON-ON BADGES.  Shiny black paw prints traversing orange t-shirts.  Each print signifying an achievement: a good deed done, a personal goal reached, a craft or project completed.  The pattern of prints on each of the first grade boys, or Tiger Cubs, shirt bore testimony to the artistry and creativity of their parental unit.

In the future, as the boys grew in size and responsibility, and if they yearned to become Boy Scouts, they would acquire real badges like those sewn above the breast pockets of their leaders.  Cub Masters.

Tom and Gwen White wore the khaki military shirts of the Boy Scouts of America along with blue jeans and tennis shoes.  The husband and wife team had baseball caps like their charges; orange and white with the head of a tiger resembling Tony the Tiger on the Frosted Flakes cereal box. "One size fits all," the hats fit snugly on the adults, but were out of proportion on the small boys whose faces were obscured and whose heads looked too large.

The Whites were parents of two of the Tiger Cubs in the rotunda of the State Capitol.  Identical twins.  Tow-heads. The only difference between the two was that one wore glasses.  The twin with the glasses enjoyed the sound his echoed whoops made off the vaulted marble ceiling.  In fact, most of the boys were incredulous as to how their voices and whistles and claps bounced off the columns and statues and cathedral ceilings.  Bats in a cave.

John Brady laughed and nodded at the senior citizen security guard strolling by.  "First grade Tiger Cubs," he informed the guard.

"I can see that, Senator.  Rowdy bunch today?"

"Big field trip.  Okay boys, gather 'round."  At their feet, inlaid in marble, was a bronze seal of the State of Washington.  "What do you think of this?" Brady asked pointing at the floor.

"Cool.  That's George Washington."

"I know that, dummy."

"Hey boys, listen up," Den mother Gwen said, then raised her hand, index and middle finger in the air.

"Shh!" several boys whispered raising their hands to make the same sign. "Shh."

Tom White was bespectacled like one of his boys. Knowing he was a Boeing engineer, Brady could picture the man wearing science lab goggles while working with bubbling test tubes. Microscopes and Petrie dishes. "Thank you for meeting with us, Senator Brady," he said.

"The boys are so excited!" Gwen White exclaimed, as she pulled a disposable camera from her pocket.

"I can see that," said Brady. "This is a fun part of my job. And you know what, boys? My son, who is in college now, was a Boy Scout when he was little."

"Really?" asked a boy with a large freckle formation on his nose. "How old are you?"

"Old enough," laughed Brady. "But there were no Tiger Cubs then. He started as a Cub Scout. So, what do you gentlemen think about your State Capitol?"

Echoed whoops and cheers undulated within the Rotunda. A skin-and-bones boy wearing elastic-waisted Wrangler jeans put his hand up in the air.

"Yes sir," said Brady.

"Do you know the President?"

The adults smiled and the Tiger Cubs looked curiously hopeful.

"No," Brady answered. "But I do know the Governor."

"Cool!" barked one of the boys.

"What's all this racket, Senator Brady?" Senate photographer Stan Smith approached the group with a mockingly stern expression on his face. He rifled through the pockets of his olive green vest for film, his ominous camera with its impressive zoom lens dangling from his neck.

Brady had imagined the photographer at home on the savannahs of Africa, although he thought the state legislature could be comparable to life in the wild. Or a zoo.

"You men ready to have your official picture taken?"

"Sure!"

"Boys, this is Mr. Stan Smith. He's our official photographer here in the Senate," said Brady. "Say hi to Mr. Smith."

"Hi, Mr. Smith!"

A small hand waved in the air.

"The young man has a question," said Brady.

"Do all the Senators sleep here?"

"That's a very good question," Brady answered as he jingled change in his pocket. He felt Emily's Gumby figurine. "Many senators and house members live far away, on the other side of the mountains in eastern Washington. Now, during session – which is right now – many of them rent apartments here, in Olympia. Some have houses. They certainly cannot drive to and from work every day. Now myself, I live at home in my district. Only a few miles from where you kids go to school. I have an hour commute each way."

A boy with a large watch on a small wrist, picked his nose as he asked, "Are you rich?"

"No, I'm not rich."

Stan Smith snapped candid shots with a flash.

The same boy wiped his hands on his pants as he inquired, "Do you know the Pope?"

"No," Brady answered. "Do you?"

He loved the honest simplicity of their questions. To them, he was a big shot, someone who mingled with the rich and famous. Most people had no idea what being an elected official entailed. He himself had not known. Intricate schedules of small things. Hours and hours of committee meetings. Phone calls. Breakfasts with district leaders. Lunches with lobbyists. The problems and grievances of constituents. Anything from wrongful insurance claims to building permits to child custody fights. Then there were never-ending piles of letters requiring his signature. Busy work.

Yet, amidst the mundane, there was no way the Tiger Cubs, or any of the score of schoolchildren he'd met in the Rotunda, could know the feeling, the sensation inside his bones when he was called "Senator." When he received mail or packages at home addressed to "The Honorable John Brady." The feeling he had when there was roll call on a bill and he had to vote "yay" or "nay" on the rhododendron patterned carpet of the Senate floor. He would have been embarrassed to voice it out loud, but the thing he felt was patriotism. A loyalty. A responsibility to his district and state and country. Allegiance to the will and spirit of his daughter and family. Proud.

"Boys, did you know that Senator Brady has a very important bill that may become a law?" Tom White asked his troop. He nodded to Brady and whispered, "I've done my homework."

"I see that," Brady said. "Right now, though, my bill is stalled in the House."

"What is the law that you're trying to make?" asked the twin with the glasses."

"It's basically a law to keep really bad guys in jail."

"That sounds like a good law," the twin answered.

"I thought so too," Brady agreed.

"Why would they want to let bad guys out anyways?" chimed the nose picker.

"Very good question. I'd like to know the answer to that one," said Brady. "Okay, I think it's time for my friend Stan, here, to take a picture."

The photographer clicked his flash a few times to get the boys attention.

"Hey, where's Tony?" someone said.

"Tony!"

"There he is!" The boys laughed and pointed.

Gwen White's surprise turned to horror as she saw the truant Cub perched atop a large bronze bust of George Washington, tennis-shoed feet dangling just under the first President's nose.

John Brady marveled at the boy's stealth and agility as Tom White strode quickly across the marble floor of the Rotunda.

"Oh man!" someone whispered.

"That's awesome! How'd he do that?"

"Tony's dead."

Brady stifled a laugh as he thought of visions from his own childhood. Third or fourth grade. *Oh my God, that was about forty years ago. Forty years. It seems like yesterday.*

Though he had lived in Maryland at the time, his class had taken a half-hour bus ride to the Washington National Zoo in D.C. Just thinking about it conjured up the sound, the smell of the school bus. Claustrophobic and hot with used-up air to breathe. Every other window open just an inch, the remaining windows locked shut. Teachers and parent chaperones, fingers to lips; "SHH. INSIDE VOICES."

He remembered the two kids, boys, who never obeyed. Trouble makers. Bullies. Class clowns of the type who would surely have prescriptions for Ritalin now.

*Dean and Sean. One put in the back of the bus, one in the front. There were two incidents, but which kid did which? One taunted the orangutans until one hawked and spit right through the bars of the cage and onto the boy's shirt front. The other kid tossed a bag of orange circus peanuts into the polar bear cage exhibit. The bear ate the entire bag, including the plastic wrap. We all got in trouble and the boys cried and the teachers were mortified.*

Brady watched the boy named Tony climb down from George Washington's head and onto the shoulders of his den leader.

"Is Tony in trouble?" a Cub asked Brady who hid a smile.

"You boys know we must respect public property."

"Like my brother got punished for taking my skateboard without my permission and losing it."

"Exactly," Brady agreed, making the boy's cheeks glow with pride.

It was then Brady's aide Karen arrived with souvenirs for the troop: miniature Washington State flags. She passed them out to the troop just as Tom White returned with renegade Tony. The chagrined boy, his pride crushed, wiped his eyes as his mates waved their small green flags.

*I still have the souvenir from the D.C. zoo. A peacock feather. In that box of odds and ends in the hall closet. Blue, green, almost a phosphorescent sheen. The man at the souvenir shop had said the feather was good luck. A circle pattern on the top of the feather looked like and eye. Like the eye of God. Like the arts and crafts popsicle stick and yarn ornaments we made in school. I haven't though of that forever. I kept it in the cups of pens and pencils on my desk in my room and used to touch for good luck, like before going to bed. I did the same with the crucifix on my wall, and with a rabbit's foot key chain. Now with Emily's Gumby. Do we ever finish growing up?*

"Okay, boys, picture time!" Stan Smith yelled then clicked the flash of his camera several times, calling the boys to attention by blinding them.

\* \* \* \*

TURDS, THE SIZE of rice grains, adhered to the interior surface of the exercise ball. A few bits of excrement, older and therefore harder, pinged about the plastic sphere and the black bear hamster like corn kernels in an air popper.

Emily had placed Hamlet inside the ball in the late afternoon. Being nocturnal, the hamster rolled himself unnoticed behind the living room couch and went to sleep until the house was dark and quiet.

It awoke in the desolate downstairs, aware that it was not confined to its pine-litter filled cage with the squeaky wheel. Hungry and restless, it pushed its tiny feet against the plastic concave surface, moving the ball and his refuse forward.

With a whir of air through slotted holes in the ball, the animal maneuvered into the hallway; a thoroughfare of hardwood into the kitchen and den. Bobbing and spinning and turds pinging. Then still, quiet. A life form instinctively gaining its bearings.

Across the night-light illumined room, by the sliding-glass door, Toby was sprawled, fidgeting in slumber. The dog had become more of an awkward, big-boned teenager than a puppy.

The hamster, protected by a safety wall of plastic, rolled toward the familiar scent and banged into the dog's snout. Toby jumped to his feet and sneezed. Then, tail wagging, he breathed in the small animal's smell and licked the ball. It spiraled backwards across the floor and under the kitchen table. Hamlet sat quiet and unmoving, save for the twitching of whiskers.

Small excitement over, Toby yawned and stretched and lumbered to the sofa. He eased himself onto a corner cushion, curled up and closed his eyes, comfortable with his place in the animal hierarchy.

On the other hand, the hamster's place in that hierarchy was more of a limited existence. Lower on the totem pole of life, his realm was ground level.

So, as the bigger mammal drifted in and out of sleep, it opened its eyes every so often to check on the nocturnal member of the household as it repelled off a chair, a tennis shoe, a pile of Barbie accessories. Excrement pellets fell about the carpet.

John Brady pulled the car into the garage, the car's grille inches from the punching bag. Without cutting the lights, he stepped from the car and went to the bag. With a nudge of his fingertips, it swung forward then returned, banging into him. Soft jab. Soft jab. Without gloves, the leather hurt his skin. Burned. Impact jarring the bones in his hands; a good hurt. *Damn them! Fucking liars. All of them!* Hard jab. Dust motes in the headlights. *Fuck them.* Too hard. His wrist jammed on contact and there was an audible snap. Wincing in pain, Brady cradled his hand against his chest then kicked the bag for good measure.

2:12 AM by the clock on the microwave. The bulb from inside the refrigerator spread an eerie cone of light across the kitchen. He snapped open a can of beer and downed half. *Damn them all. Walking clichés... back-stabbing, putrid politicians ... I am totally screwed.*

As Brady transferred the sandwich makings from the refrigerator to the table, the dim light glinted off the hamster's exercise ball on the far side of the den. The ball was moving towards him. Then Toby, smelling food, stretched and climbed down from the couch.

The kitchen became shadows when he closed the refrigerator door. He flicked on the light above the stove before he slumped onto a chair, banging his hand as he did so and yelping in pain. Toby sniffed at Brady's clothes, curious from the scents of the day's travels. Sitting on his haunches, the dog stared at the food on the table. Toby would wait patiently, sometimes to the point of humor, for a mere crumb to fall.

Ham and cheese and mustard and mayo. Brady assembled a sloppy sandwich and absent-mindedly tossed the dog a piece of American cheese. Eating the sandwich in angry bites, he thought over the last several hours. *Sneaky sons of bitches...stringing me along. And they already knew...they knew the bill was dead.*

A thud against his foot. Hamlet in the ball next to his chair. Toby extended his neck and sniffed the rodent.

"Somebody forgot to put you away, ay, Hamlet?"

He ripped a sliver of ham from his sandwich and dropped it on the floor at Toby's paws. The dog looked at the meat inches from his snout. Then, satisfied the morsel was his to have, he hobble-crawled to it and ate it. He licked his lips.

"Fat dog," Brady muttered. He picked up the plastic ball, unscrewing the circular opening. "Carnivores everywhere. Okay. Atta boy," he cooed then gingerly lifted the squishy animal from its prison. The creature sat motionless in his palm, nose and whiskers twitching. Brady offered it a shard of meat, whereupon it lifted itself on his hind legs, praying-mantis-like, grabbed the ham with both front paws and began nibbling voraciously.

As he watched the hamster in his hand he said, "You know, freshman Senators and hamsters are a lot alike." The Hamster continued chewing the ham. "Fuck you," Brady said sharply, and the hamster jumped. "Not you."

Having consumed the ham shaving, Hamlet sniffed about the hand which held him. The hamster didn't weigh much, in fact it seemed almost weightless. It's feet were tiny and pale pink and cold and each toe had a tiny claw. Nocturnal feet which reminded Brady of vampires.

He, John Brady, was a pawn of the Senate Republicans and the Governor. He'd done their bidding. He'd promised to vote with leadership on the budget. On everything.

"Fuck them twice," Brady whispered. "Okay. Back to your cage."

Quietly, he ascended the stairs, hamster still in his palm. He turned on the bathroom light so he could see in the bedroom where Emily and Mark slept. The air in the room was stale and close with night-breathing.

Returned to familiar surroundings, Hamlet sucked on the straw of his water bottle contentedly. A line of bubbles rose in the bottle. Finished, the hamster scurried into a corner of the cage and burrowed under the pine bedding.

Brady crossed to the window and carefully slid it open a few extra inches to allow in some fresh air. Then he stood and looked at the sleeping forms of Mark and Emily. An overwhelming sense of love and responsibility came over him and he thought he might cry. He wondered when they would find a place of their own. He hoped it wouldn't be soon. It was okay with him if they just stayed. Just stayed put.

Before turning off the bathroom light, he poked his head in the master bedroom and took in the sleeping form of his wife, noticing the curve of her hip underneath the blanket. Tip-toeing to the bed, he contemplated her for a moment. He gently stroked her hair laying on the pillow. Confirmation that she was real.

Brady went back downstairs and turned on the water at the kitchen sink and felt it with his fingers. Tepid. Warm. Hot. He pumped the liquid soap into his palm; antibacterial.

He envisioned Lady Macbeth washing away her deeds. A need for purity. Lather, clean smelling, on his hands and between his fingers and on his wedding ring. Working the soap into his pores. Gently around his sore wrist and a few inches up his forearm. He thought of surgeons preparing to operate as he washed rodent germs and the garbage of the day down the drain.

Brady dried his hands then went into the darkened living room. He took off his shoes and stretched out on the couch. Seconds later, Toby came into the room and lay on the floor beside him. As he tried to calm his brain, he noticed the working tick of several clocks about the downstairs, something he never noticed during the day.

The events of the evening played over and over in his mind. Senate Majority Leader Alex Daniels had summoned him. Just off the Senate floor, the Majority Leader's office was large and ornate. A different ballgame, another league than that of a freshman senator.

Reminding Brady of a movie set, Daniel's office was equipped with a sidebar. Ice bucket and glasses and a large assortment of liquor bottles. He accepted a scotch-rocks, taking a large swallow as if it were a shield. Battle armor. They sat in matching leather chairs.

"John, thanks for meeting with me," Daniels said.

"Of course."

"I'm not going to screw around with you. I've got bad news about your bill."

Brady felt blood pulsing in his neck. He wanted to loosen his tie and unbutton his shirt at the collar. Sip of scotch. "How could that be? I thought leadership wanted it."

Daniels concentrated on his right leg crossed over his left. The tassel on his shoe. The glass of scotch dangled from his hand draped over the arm of the chair. From the light of the table lamp, Brady could see the amber liquid separate from the melting ice. Oil and water.

"What's going on?" Brady asked. "I was told – have been told – it was a sure thing."

"I know. But, leadership, as you know, has been negotiating the budget with the Governor. And the House. We can't fund it the way it is. We've tried everything. God, John, it's the first time in twenty-five years that the R's have been in complete control. There's no choice. We have to deliver on McNamarra's proposed tax cuts and we need another 100 million for that and a balanced budget." Daniels took a lengthy pull from his drink as if punctuating his speech.

"McNamarra campaigned on Beth's Bill."

The Majority Leader nodded his head. "I know. I know. And he's not the only one. But there's only a few days left in the session, the House Rules Committee killed it today."

"You mean McNamarra forced them to kill it."

"John, I fought for you. I did. But the Speaker's being a hard-ass and won't budge. We tried to trim the tax cut."

Somewhere in the room a clock ticked. Ice melted, clinking in the cocktail glasses.

Daniels leaned forward, cradling his drink in both hands. "I know you're disappointed. I am too. But listen, you're only a freshman. You can try again next year."

Brady shook his head. "Unbelievable," he said, perplexed. "Why this bill? It's a good bill. With a budget of over twenty billion, this bill goes down. It goes down when there are dozens and dozens of garbage, total shit bills that pass. Total bullshit bills. They become LAW."

Daniels said nothing as he watched Brady stand and begin to pace on the ornate carpet.

Brady lifted his glass towards the Majority Leader as if to make a toast. "There are a few bills in particular that I like. How about the nearly $500,000 to fund an ombudsman to settle disputes at mobile home parks. Important. Or the $300,000 to market wine-or this one kills me: the Agricultural Fair Study. Let's study the economic contributions of county fairs. That one's only about $75,000 of the budget. Now that's a deal. Much more important than putting bad guys away and making sure the criminal justice system works."

"John, listen to me. Next session, believe me, you'll have a better chance," Daniels said. "Some of the bills you just mentioned have gone down in previous sessions. Some of those senators are due."

"Oh, okay, so it's just shut-up and wait your turn. The content of a bill doesn't matter. What's right or wrong doesn't matter. Don't patronize me," Brady fumed. "I just need to do my time first, right? Pretty ironic, considering my bill."

Daniels rose and went to his desk. He set down his glass and began shuffling papers. "We're having a press conference tomorrow afternoon to announce the final budget."

Brady downed his drink. "Hooray," he said. "That bill is the only reason I'm here." He turned and left the room.


The morning newspaper thwacked against the front door waking John Brady and his dog. Toby growled and stared at the door as if something else could be expected.

After a few seconds, having oriented himself, Brady said, "Shh, don't wake the house." He stood and stretched and thought how sleep never felt as refreshing on the couch. His wrist throbbed and he looked at it momentarily, then remembered the punching bag. "Just brilliant," he muttered.

He opened the front door. It was getting light outside. The air was clear and cool and it had rained in the night so that everything was wet, and the newspaper was sheathed in an orange plastic bag.

Brady saw the bird droppings on the aggregate when he bent down for the paper. Looking up to the ledge on the pillar of the porch, he saw there was a new nest. What looked like a female sparrow eyed him, unafraid. Opposite her on the ledge of another pillar sat a bird which was presumably the father.

Wondering if sparrows mated for life, he realized that he was glad that the birds had chosen his porch. He felt protective of the small bit of nature. Responsible. An obligation to the tenants of his domain, be it animal or human.

Somewhere in the neighborhood a dog barked and on the threshold of the doorway behind him, Toby growled. The dog wagged his tail and sauntered towards Brady and nuzzled against his leg.

King of his realm, on his front porch as the world came to life, the dog actively sniffed the morning air. His ears twitched at the cacophony of bird calls from the depths of a giant cedar a few houses away. Suddenly, the bird in the nest above fluttered her wings. Toby looked up and growled.

"Hush, fat dog. They have a right to be here. Just like you." Brady scratched behind the dog's ear.

Across the street the porch light went out and his aged neighbor-Marine stepped outside the door in his bathrobe. In his hand was his American flag on its pole.

Toby growled.

Carefully, reverently, Ernest unfurled the Stars and Stripes and pushed the pole into the bracket on his house. The old man watched the flag for a time then pulled a handkerchief from his pocket and blew his nose. Then he surveyed his front yard. His street. His neighbors' houses. He noticed Brady and waved.

Toby barked.

Brady waved. "Good morning," he called, his voice loud upon the quiet morning air.

"Yes it is," Ernest nodded, then he turned and opened his door. "Have a nice day, John," he called, then disappeared inside his house.

"You too sir," Brady whispered as he watched the flag move in the breeze. He sat on his stoop causing the birds above to make adjustments and Toby, at eye level, to lick his face.

*Moral conscience. Choices.* He thought about Ernest. Eighty-five years old. He put up his flag every morning and took it down every night because he knew it was a good thing. The need. The want. It was his personal duty. And whether it was for himself or his country or God, it was his decisive action. His conviction.

Brady thought of all the decisions, the choices he had made over the past year. So many he'd had to wrestle with and had to listen to his inner voice to overcome. And for the most part, hadn't he made the right choices? He knew that all of his decisions had to do with Beth, and that if things had been different, his marriage, his career, never would have changed.

But things were what they were. Things happened for a reason. He and Sarah were doing better. Becoming a Senator was a good thing. A chance for real improvement. Real change. And Beth's Bill was so close to becoming law. So close.

He realized how far he had come on his journey, his quest on Beth's behalf. But he knew, if he was to live right with her memory, with his own conscience, with God-he could not quit. Not ever. God wanted something from him.

When the front door opened Toby got to his feet, tail wagging.

"There you are," Sarah said from the doorway.

"Here I am."

"Coffee?"

"Oh my God, yes. Thank you." Shooing Toby aside, he reached for the mug and made room for her next to him.

Sarah sat down and her thigh, under a thin veil of nightgown, pressed against his. When he turned towards his wife, with her tousled-morning hair and sleepy face, he knew his quest was not over.

\* \* \* \*

JOHN BRADY WAS sure the knowledgeable woman at the pet store had claimed the life span of a black bear hamster, any hamster for that matter, was two to three years. He was so certain that the statement played over and over in his mind as he hurried after his hysterical granddaughter.

"Hamlet! Hamlet! Grampa!" Emily sobbed, snot dribbling from her nostrils into her mouth. "Something's wrong with Hamlet!"

The cage was on the bottom bunk. Within its pine-bedding interior, the hamster was sprawled half-in, half-out of the food bowl. Black-bead eyes open and void. The creature's breathing was laborious, his mouth opening wide, allowing in big gulps of air. Brady thought of taking deep breaths as a doctor held a stethoscope, cold and metallic, on his bare back.

"Oh Em," he whispered, knowing that a death was imminent.

Emily looked at his face and surmised the outcome. "No! No! No Hamlet!" She grabbed Art the Bear off her pillow and hugged it to her chest. She wiped her face on the bear's head.

Kneeling by the bed, Brady opened the hinged door on top of the cage. Upon contact with the hamster, his fingers recoiled. It was cool. Almost cold, the body was already semi-rigid. He could see the tiny fang-like teeth.

Emily was kneeling next to him, sniffing globs of snot back into her nose. "Don't die. Don't die."

Brady curled his fingers around the hamster and lifted it out of the cage. "Oh, poor guy."

"No!" shouted Emily.

"Shh. Shh. Sweetheart." He held the hamster out to her. "Here, honey, he's sick. Just hold him and tell him it's okay. Tell him you love him."

Summoning all the bravery she could muster, she wiped her face on Art and dropped him to the floor. Then, hands cupped, she reached for Hamlet.

"There, there. Good girl," whispered Brady.

The hamster was prostrate in her hands. Emily's bottom lip quivered as she watched Hamlet's mouth open and close. The fur around its eyes was wet and Brady wondered if hamsters cried. Did the animal understand what was happening?

"Oh Hamlet, please…you're such a good boy…don't go away," Emily slobbered and coughed. She transferred the dying animal into the palm of one hand so she could stroke it with the other.

"Just tell him you love him."

"I love you buddy. Tell him you love him, too."

"I love you, too, Hamlet." Brady swallowed hard in an effort to hold back tears. *My God, leave it to me to pick a faulty hamster. Diseased. No death warranty.* "It's okay, Em, he knows you're here."

As she pleaded with the hamster to live and as Brady knelt beside her, helpless, Hamlet's mouth opened and did not close.

Brady waited, horrified, for Emily to realize the situation. He wondered how God could let this happen. Did Emily really need another lesson about death? He wanted to scream obscenities at God.

When the lid was raised on the jewelry box, a miniature ballerina twirled on a pedestal to Tchaikovsky's Swan Lake.

"See?" Sarah asked as she showed Emily a small metal key. "We can lock the box and you can keep this key forever."

Emily reached for the jewelry box and placed it on her lap. She opened the box and closed the box. Opened and closed. Twirling ballerina-Tchaikovsky-silence. Twirling ballerina-Tchaikovsky-silence.

"But what about the ballerina? She'll be in the way," Emily stated.

Nodding her head in anticipation of the question, Sarah said, "It can come off." She showed her granddaughter how the figurine could be pulled off her post.

Emily smiled. "We can put her in the box and she can keep Hamlet company."

"That's right. She can keep him company," Sarah agreed. "Hamlet would like that."

Mark entered the room. "Hey, Em, how's this?" In his hand was a cross, a grave marker. Popsicle sticks and rubber bands. On the crossbeam "HAMLET" was printed in black letters.

Emily surveyed her father's handiwork. "It's good, Daddy." She placed it on the bed. "Look. This is what we're going to put Hamlet in." Picking up the ballerina figurine, she added, "he'll have a friend with him until he sees Mommy."

Mark stepped on the shovel, pushing it through layers of bark and soil. He made a small pile of loose dirt and pebbles near a small rhododendron in the front garden bed. A larger rock rolled off the pile, falling back into the beckoning hole.

Emily held the jewelry box-casket. The lid was open and they could see the dead hamster, frozen, paws reaching. Tucked inside with the deceased was the ballerina and a few of the little girl's personal tokens. A cats-eye marble. A wind-up toy from a McDonald's happy meal. A piece of bubble gum.

They stood in a semi-circle around Mark as he dug the hole. Rain started to fall. It sprinkled the contents of the jewelry box. It started a pattern on Mark's back. An ink-blot test on a cotton t-shirt. The rain fell into the freshly dug orifice.

"Good?" Mark asked considering the depth of the hole.

Brady remembered making holes for tulip bulbs with the metal bulb-digger. Mark's hole was much bigger. "Good," Brady answered.

Mark carried the shovel back to the garage and returned with a golf umbrella. He held the cover over them as they said goodbye to the hamster.

Sarah handed Emily a white linen napkin. "I thought he might like a blanket."

"Oh, that's good," Emily nodded tucking the cloth about the rodent and ballerina and personal baubles as if tucking in a bed. Then she closed the lid and Sarah helped her lock it.

Emily knelt upon the damp earth and solemnly inserted the jewelry box into the grave. She scooped small handfuls of dirt and delicately sprinkled it on the lid, the sound not unlike the raindrops hitting the umbrella.

Mark handed Brady the umbrella than knelt beside his daughter. Together, they pulled the earth and pebbles back into the void. They patted and smoothed the mound.

Poking the popsicle stick cross into the dirt at the head of the grave, Mark said, "There. That's nice."

"Do you think God will let him come back if he wants to?" asked Emily.

"He'll be in heaven with God and his mommy and daddy and all his hamster friends," said Mark.

"That's right," Brady agreed.

Brady remained at the garden grave as the others went inside. He liked the sound of the rain and he wanted to think.

At what point would there be only skeletal remains? Could a body stay warm after the soul has departed? If yes, for how long? He thought of the time that had passed since Beth died. Time in general. Life; a limited time. Minutes and hours and months. Of choices. Of being chosen.

He put down the umbrella and lifted his face to the sky. He watched the raindrop bombardment. Felt them spatter his face, the reflection of which he scrutinized lately. Wrinkles and creases and seams. Endless and breeding. Multiplying. He envisioned rain running like rivulets across his time-chiseled epidermis. How much time before his skin, as the peel of aged, ripened fruit, cultivated age spots like bruises? A rotting corpse.

He closed his eyes and listened. Rain in trees and bushes. Individual leaves touched. Water trickling down the metal rain spouts. Tires on wet pavement and suddenly a horn blast burst his meditative state. Opening his eyes he witnessed neighbors with their children waving as they drove by. Brady returned the wave enthusiastically, like a child caught in the act of something embarrassing. He watched the car turn at the corner then regarded the fresh grave with the cross.

He felt youthful and ignorant and buoyant at the same time. Then, laughing out loud, he held his face up to the baptismal rain. Opening his mouth to the rain, he tried to imagine how a kid would feel. Swallowing intermittent drops made him feel revitalized. A solution flashed in his brain. An answer. A band aid. He was going to buy Emily a new hamster. And one more thing: he wasn't going to give up his fight.

* * * *

SEVERAL DAYS LATER the Republican budget, having sailed through the House, was on the Senate floor. John Brady sat at his desk in his best navy wool suit busy with paperwork; an effort to stop members and staff from offering condolences on his bill's failure.

He picked up his phone and punched the numbers to his office. "Okay, tell me again. What's going to happen?" He spoke quietly and felt as if he were doing something illegal.

Karen Callahan, too, whispered, as if she would be heard on the chamber floor. "They're about to vote?"

"Yes."

"Okay. It's the budget. It'll be totally party-line, so the Floor Leader will change her vote so the bill can be reconsidered."

"What happens to me?"

"Don't worry. It buys us time."

Members took their seats, speaking quietly amongst themselves or on their phones. The Secretary of the Senate began the roll call on the final passage of the budget.

"Anderson?" the Secretary called over the chamber sound system.

"Aye," replied the junior senator from Chelan.

"Bentley?"

The freshman Democrat from Bremerton sat directly in front of Brady.

"No."

"Brady?"

*What am I willing to do?*

"No," Brady stated firmly.

In the split-second of silence that followed there seemed to be a rush of air, then an audible, all-encompassing gasp. Every head turned towards Brady with expressions of shock.

Then, as the Secretary tried to resume the roll call, life on the floor turned to chaos. Republican leaders rushed towards Majority Leader Daniels desk as several Democrats laughed out loud.

"Oh my God, what the hell is he doing?" Senator Paula Moore yelled.

"Cramer?" the Secretary called.

"No."

"Dougherty?"

"Aye."

The Majority Leader hurried to Brady's desk. "What are you doing, John?" Daniels whispered as he leaned over Brady.

*What am I willing to do...h*e did not look up from his paperwork. *What am I willing to do...Please, God, let this be the right thing.*

"Foster?"

"Aye."

The Majority Leader stood ram-rod straight and signaled to the Floor Leader, Senator Genie Frye. She, in turn, whispered to the other members of leadership huddling about her. The Secretary continued to read the roll call.

Daniels leaned in again. "What do you want? What can we give you?" When Brady ignored him, the Majority

Leader hissed, "Jesus Christ!" then stormed across the chamber among snickering Democrats.

Within minutes the vote was over. All Democrats voted no. All Republicans voted yes. Except Brady. The final tally was 24-25. The bill had failed.

The Floor Leader jumped up. "Mr. President!"

"Senator Frye?" the Lieutenant Governor asked from the rostrum.

"Mr. President, Frye changes from "Aye" to "No.""

Brady sat in wonder at the scene erupting about him. He could feel the contemptuous glances of several fellow Republicans. They had been packed and ready to go home to their districts seeing as the budget was the final vote of the session.

*I guess this is what I was willing to do...meant to do. Look what I've caused.*

The Lieutenant Governor was conferring with the Secretary of the Senate. Returning to the microphone, he said, "Senator Frye votes "No." Are there any other senators that wish to change their vote? No? If not, the Secretary will announce the vote."

"Mr. President, there are 23 "Yeas" and 26 "Nays.""

The Lieutenant Governor cleared his throat. "Having failed to receive a majority vote, Engrossed Substitute House Bill 1125 is declared lost."

Once more, Floor Leader Frye jumped up. "Mr. President!" she yelled.

"Senator Frye."

"Mr. President," Frye began forcefully, "having cast my vote on the prevailing side, I give notice of my intent to reconsider the vote by which House Bill 1125 failed to pass."

The chamber had become relatively quiet. All eyes were on Senator Frye, standing solidly, microphone in hand, awaiting the Lieutenant Governor's response.

Brady watched in total confusion, amazed at the seemingly routine mechanizations of the legislative process. Partisan process.

All the while, he felt the stares, the looks of disdain boring into him.

*They hate me. They thought the budget would pass. Session done. They're outa here. But no. And what did they think? I'm a wimp? A loser whose not going to fight? Be strong, damnit. God bless Beth. Can she see me now?*

"Engrossed Substitute House Bill 1125," the Lieutenant Governor stated, "will remain on the Senate's Third Reading Calendar, pending reconsideration."

This time, it was the Republican Caucus Chairman, who happened to be Senator Jonah Johnson, that stood up. "Mr. President, there will be a Republican Caucus immediately."

All was commotion on the floor.

"Quiet, please!" the Lieutenant Governor bellowed. "The Senate will stand in recess for the purpose of caucus meetings."

And as the President of the Senate banged his gavel, John Brady felt the heat of humiliation amidst the curses and laughter of his comrades.

The Majority Leader leaned against the wall near the caucus room as Brady approached.

"John, can I talk to you for a minute before we go in?"

Brady shrugged his shoulders and put his hands in his pockets, trying to appear at ease. A few senators, talking amongst themselves, brushed past them.

"Asshole," one of them hissed.

"Nice," Brady nodded. He felt the Gumby figurine in his pocket.

"They're pissed," said Daniels.

"So am I," said Brady. "I was voting my conscience. Is that against the law?"

"No. You just never told us. We're supposed to be a team. We assumed you were with us."

"And I assumed you were behind my bill."

Daniels sighed. "Okay, John, is this about your daughter? Because there's no fucking way you're getting that bill. It's too damn much money! And I tried, by the way. I did. I tried to change McNamarra's mind."

"I was strung along like a puppy."

"Is this about you? Let's think here. What can we give you to change your mind? How about a bill out of Natural Resources? For Timber? Help your company with tax credits. Something."

Brady was incredulous and he wondered if it showed on his face. Wasn't this the sort of thing people went to jail for? Wasn't this corrupt? Graft? Weren't minimum security prisons full of people who succumbed to such deals?

"Or what about a committee chairmanship?" the Majority Leader continued. "Does your wife like to travel? There's a new committee on trade we're creating. Lots of overseas trips."

He pictured clips on the evening news. Politicians. Lobbyists. CEO's of huge corporations wearing suits and handcuffs. Making plea agreements to serve shorter terms in prisons that were more like day care centers. Day camp where they could read and exercise and weave baskets. Learn culinary arts or study law. Or get off with a slap on the wrist, pay a fee or wear a home-monitor bracelet for a few months.

"Don't," Brady said holding up his hand.

"What?"

"You know what I want," said Brady.

"It's not going to happen," Daniels shook his head. "We can get you a better office-with a view? Or how about a better parking spot? Or both?"

"You're kidding me, right?"

There was much commotion from inside the caucus room.

"I think they await me in the lion's den," Brady snickered and started into the room.

Inside the large ornate room was a gargantuan oak table with twenty-five upholstered chairs that reminded him of something from Sir Arthur legends.

Many chairs were taken by exhausted senators; deflated and angry. Others, including Senator Paula Moore, empty shoulder holster over her blouse, stood shouting derogatory remarks. "Who the hell do you think you are?" she called to Brady as he entered the room.

Brady knew that firearms were illegal on the Capitol campus, so he wondered why Moore wore the holster anyway. Some sort of statement, he imagined.

"Bastard!" somebody yelled.

Caucus Chairman Jonah Johnson sat at the head of the table. He banged his gavel three times.

"Senators! I will have order in this room!" he boomed authoritatively.

Somewhat grudgingly, the members quieted down. Senator Moore shook her head as she found a seat.

He felt like a defendant as he sat down....*they'll find me guilty and Paula Moore will pull her gun from under her skirt and shoot me.*

Jonah Johnson had removed his tweed jacket. A few cigars and a ball-point pen were visible in his shirt pocket.

"Okay, folks," he began as he rolled up his sleeves. "We have a problem here."

"Cause of Mr. Shithead over there."

"Okay, now John, would you like to tell us what just happened out there?" Johnson asked in an even-tempered tone.

Senator Moore banged the table with her fist. "What happened is he made us look like fools! The majority party can't even pass their own budget!"

Senator Johnson banged his gavel. "Paula, I'd like to hear from Senator Brady, please."

Moore slumped into her chair.

The stares from around the table felt like needle pricks on his skin. *This is what I am willing to do.* He stood and placed his hands on the table in front of him for support as he looked about the table, meeting the gaze of each member.

"Folks," he began. "As you know, I am a novice here. And I know I just broke a cardinal rule-"

"Damn right! Why the hell didn't you tell us you were gonna vote no?" asked the senator from eastern Washington, the one who had distributed apples at the start of session.

"Okay. I'm not your typical politician. I didn't come here for a career change. I don't know that much about budgets and taxes. I came here as a father. You know my story. I don't want your pity. I just want a little justice. I came here to pass "Beth's Bill-"

"And we got you elected," Majority Leader Daniels chimed in.

"You did not get me elected!" Brady yelled. "The PEOPLE voted for me! They connected with me, my plight, and sorry to say, they AGREE with me! Something needs to be done for the victims, for innocent, everyday people. We've been here for four months and I've been a team player all along. What did I get for it? I got screwed."

"Fuck you!"

"What makes you so holier than thou?"

Jonah Johnson slapped the gavel down. "That's enough!"

"Yes, it certainly is," Brady agreed evenly then turned and left the room.


Outside his office window, he watched the lights come on across the Capitol campus illuminating raindrops racing down the pane of glass.

Karen Callahan entered the office and deposited a cardboard box of files on his desk. "You've got messages from THE TIMES, THE DAILY NEWS and Eric Glass. Oh, and your wife. Glass wants you for his show tomorrow."

"What the hell should I do?" Brady asked.

"We've got to brainstorm. They have to give you something."

"Like what? Their committee chairmanships? A new office? Tax breaks for Northwest Timber-hey, that would be great. They'd probably raise my salary. Or give me a bonus." He pushed back in his chair and put his feet on his desk. "God, I'm tired-I don't know. You see, I didn't come here for that stuff. I don't care about it. And I don't want it. I just wanted to do something good. Something for Beth. For victims like her, you know?"

"I know," Karen answered. "Listen, I've been talking to Booth and the Governor's staff. The budget is absolutely closed."

"Meaning?"

"It's closed. Done. They can't re-open the budget discussion in order to figure out how to pay for your bill or it all falls apart. Plus, it's a dangerous precedent. They give you that bill as a freshman, then what about Senator so and so's bill. And so on and so forth. We need to come up with something else you want. It's not a lost cause."

"What's not a lost cause?" Pam Naughton interrupted as she stormed into the office, her hair wet from the rain.

Brady knew that Pam was twenty years or so Karen's junior and because they shared the same no-frills, no-nonsense, no-makeup ways, they could have been mother and daughter.

"The session. I'm trying to tell the Senator that he has leverage."

"She's right, you do have leverage; for now," said Naughton. "I've been sent here to deliver a message.

Leadership wants to work with you, but you can't get Beth's Bill and the clock is ticking. There are Democrats who are willing to be the 25th vote on the budget in exchange for their favorite little piece of pork, and they are willing to deal for a whole lot less than the $100 million you want for your bill. No one wants to go that route, but everyone wants to pass the budget and go home." Naughton paused dramatically, then added, "You have until 3:00 p.m. tomorrow to tell Daniels what you want. So, what's it going to be?"

Brady breathed a heavy sigh. "That's the big question," he said.


Hours later, through a fog of fatigue and frustration, it came to him. He had been pouring over drafts of dead bills when something caused him to really look at the file in his hand: DEPARTMENT OF HEALTH AND HUMAN SERVICES: ABANDONED NEWBORNS.

"Oh my God."

"What is it?" Karen asked as she set down her cup of rancid institution coffee.

"I know what I want to do." He felt his pulse quicken. "Remember the baby in the dumpster story? McDonald's several months ago?"

Pam looked at Karen then back at Brady. "Yeah."

"The girl lived a few streets away from our house. I'm not sure what happened to her, but I know the baby lived. Thank God. This is what I want to do. Something so this sort of thing doesn't have to happen. My daughter would like that." *Is this what God wanted all along?*


It was four o'clock in the morning. He was reading the computer monitor in front of Karen when Pam Naughton rushed in.

"This is fantastic! Okay, there are several other states that have laws making it legal for parents of unwanted newborns to drop them off at designated safe places without fear of prosecution. Hospitals. Shelters. So forth. In fact, there was an obscure "Safe Baby Bill" introduced by the D's two years ago. It died in committee."

"We can re-work it. Introduce it to Daniels tomorrow. He'll be thrilled," Karen said.

Brady fought the urge to jump up and down in glee. "So, why would they give this to me? How much would it cost?"

"That's the beauty of it," Pam smiled. "It won't cost the state a thing. Adoption agencies, social services and Child Protective Services all want to do this. All we will be doing is giving them permission by making it legal!"

* * * *

*She muffled his whimpers, his gasps, his noise with her long woolen scarf speckled like a berber carpet. In soiled and bloodied clothes, the young girl held the newborn boy to her chest and cried.*

*Having severed the umbilical cord with a nail file from her purse, a puddle of red-jelly afterbirth pooled at the base of the toilet. Light-headed and nauseous, she felt herself bleed, and prayed for it to cease.*

*The door to the restroom banged open, letting in a blast of restaurant noise and the smell of French fry grease. A burst of water then a woman's voice. "How in the world did your hands get so dirty?" And, "You were going to eat with these?"*

*"I don't know," answered a small and meek voice.*

*The girl hummed to the tinny music seeping from a circular speaker in the ceiling so that the baby would not be heard.*

*"Germs, honey, germs."*

*She could see the child's tennis shoes under the stall door. As the small feet crossed the floor, red lights twinkled in the soles of the shoes. As the electric dryer whirred noisily, the newborn fidgeted against her and she covered his face with the scarf.*

*"Come on, Daddy's waiting," the woman said. Then the feet were gone and the door slammed and the dryer shut off. Quiet, save for the music from above and squeaks from the lifer in her arms.*

*Cold. Trembling. Exhausted. She went over the plan in her head and wrapped the scarf about the baby tighter. She did not look at its face. Her cell phone rang.*

*"I'll be right there," she whispered.*

*Perched on a lamppost in the McDonalds parking lot, the mottled gray and white seagull took notice of the small wriggling bundle which had been tossed into the open dumpster. It made noise. Taking off from the post as if from a diving board, the bird sailed slowly across the littered asphalt, landing on the dumpsters metal edge. The bird cocked its head to and fro, in the cold drizzle, curious. As it watched, the gull nabbed a wilted French fry from the debris and swallowed it whole.*

*Gasping and choking beneath the woolen scarf, the baby cried in small bursts. Small, angry eruptions.*

*As darkness descended, the lamps in the parking lot buzzed on. Two more seagulls joined the first on the dumpster. One of the gulls hopped onto a trash bag near the live bundle. Business picked up in the drive thru.*

*A mini van pulled into the lot and parked near the dumpster. A mother in tennis shoes, jeans and a hooded rain coat emerged, slinging an oversized purse over her shoulder. She slid open the side door of the van. Two teenage girls in cheer uniforms and pony-tails giggled as they emptied from the vehicle. Next, two smaller children, a boy and a girl, bickered as they got out.*

*"If you two can't get along, we'll go home to eat!" the mother scolded.*

*"But it's her fault!"*

*"I didn't do anything!"*

*The mother grabbed the boy by the arm. "Enough!"*

*Embarrassed by the familial outburst, the teenagers started for the door of the restaurant. "We'll get a table, Mom."*

*The woman closed the van door and had just told her son to zip his coat when she heard something. A sound she would recognize even in her sleep. The sound jerked her attention away from her offspring.*

*There were no other children in the parking lot, yet the sound was that of a baby. Close-by. Then she heard the gulls. It had always seemed strange to her to see or hear gulls anyplace other than the ocean. Out of place. Several of the birds were in and about the dumpster.*

*"Hold hands," she ordered as they crossed to the restaurant. Then something, a force, made her look at the seagulls hopping suspiciously about the garbage. As she sensed an eeriness envelope the situation, the sound came again. She felt dread when she realized the sound came from the dumpster. Within the dumpster. HOLY GOD. HOLY GOD. HOLY GOD.*

*"Holy God!" she yelled. Her hands began to sweat. She stopped the children and looked into their faces.*

*"What's wrong, Mommy?"*

*"Mommy's not sure." Again, a baby's cry from the direction of the dumpster. "Go inside. Tell your sister to call the police. Do you understand?"*

*The woman's daughter, her youngest, began to cry. "Mommy!"*

*A baby. The caw of a gull. Another bird landed on the heap of trash.*

*"Go!" the woman yelled, more at the scavenger birds than at her children as they ran to the door of the restaurant.*

*It was with dread that she ran to the dumpster, yelling at the birds as she began to climb the ladder. Two of the seagulls lifted off noisily and flew to the roof of the McDonalds. A third joined them. Spectators now.*

*From the top of the ladder, she looked into the garbage. A stench of dirty metal and grease filled her nostrils, making her hold her breath. Her eyes darted across soiled napkins and cups and half-eaten cheeseburgers. Spoiled lettuce and onions. Throughout the garbage was the wet sparkle of liquid. Ketchup? She thought of blood, yet in the early evening light, she saw no color. Directly in front of her a fourth seagull stood, frozen as a sculpture, atop a pile of pickles.*

*A slight movement. A warbled gurgle. There was a dark shape near the gull's talons. Out of place; a blanket. No, a scarf. It moved again. The seagull looked at the bundle then at the woman, who had the feeling the bird might attack her if she tried anything.*

*Then there came a quiet and small whimper, and sure now, the woman was up and over the side of the dumpster with an agility born of adrenaline. The solo seagull fluttered above and about the scene in an agitated air dance.*

*Knee-deep in the wet refuse, she made her way, sluggishly, wading, her lower extremities like dead weight in water. In the filtered light of the lamppost, again she saw movement. Another burst of sound. A cry of hunger.*

*The curious seagull landed again on the rim of the dumpster and cocked its head, watching.*

*As the woman reached for the bundle, her fingers felt electric.*

*"Hey lady! What's going on?" A man's voice. Hurried footsteps in the parking lot. Sirens in the distance.*

*"The police. The police," she said. IT WILL BE OKAY. IT WILL BE OKAY. She felt a blanket of calm come over her as her fingertips touched wool. HOLY GOD.*

*"What's in there, lady?"*

*"Mommy! Mommy!" her two small children screamed. Then her teenaged daughter yelled, "Mom? What's going on?"*

*As she tried to gain her balance, her foot slipped on a large ketchup can. Steady. Carefully, she turned the bundle over, slowly unwrapping the scarf. The baby's face was pinched as it grimaced in the cool evening air. The shock of black hair, sticky with afterbirth, had flecks of lettuce and onion throughout. Rosebud lips searched for splayed fingers of its tiny hand. OH WHAT A BEAUTIFUL, BEAUTIFUL BABY. OH MY GOD, THANKYOU. IT'S OKAY. IT'S OKAY. IT'S A BEAUTIFUL BABY.*

*"Mom!"*

*"It's a baby! And it's alive!" She half-yelled, not wanting to scare the newborn. With a gentleness that felt holy, spiritual, she lifted the baby and cradled it close to her chest. She thought of Jesus in a manger. A baby in the garbage.*

*"Mommy! Mommy! Can I see? Can I see?"*

*Babe in arms, she waded carefully to the edge of the dumpster. "Sweetheart, look, it's a beautiful baby."*

*"Who put the baby in the garbage, Mommy?"*

*Police cars converged in the parking lot. The static of radios.*

*Suddenly, there was another movement across the refuse. The seagull on the edge of the dumpster, which had been eyeing the bundle in her arms, turned its head at the same time as the woman. The rodent, fat and hairy, dove under the garbage, its long, skinny tail disappearing seconds later.*

*A policeman stood at the top of the ladder. "Okay, ma'am, right over here. Paramedics are here."*

*She tried to push the vision of the rat from her mind.
"Oh, good. Thank God."*

*"Mommy?" her son asked again, "Who put the baby in
the garbage?"*

*Seagulls. Rats. An unwanted pregnancy. Against all
odds, the baby had lived. The woman realized that she was
crying as she handed the baby to the officer. Climbing out
of the dumpster she was hit by a wave of dizziness. I came
to McDonalds to buy cheeseburgers, but God had other
plans.*

*Her children surrounded her when she hit the pavement.
Her cheerleader daughter and her friend hugged her. "Oh
my God, Mom, who would do this?"*

*"I don't know, honey. God knows." God knows.*

Brady awoke in a sweat, his face sticking to the papers
on his desk. As he lifted his throbbing head, he found his
neck was stiff.

Stretching, he looked out the window. Night was over
and the rain had ceased. The wet parking lot glistened in
the morning sun. Cars scurried about, like insects, every
which way, weaving into assigned places. A new day.

He looked at the draft for his new bill. He thought of his
own children's births. Severed umbilical cords tied off with
plastic clamps; small clips like alligator-jawed barrettes to
stop the flow of blood and amniotic fluid. The stuff of life.
The clamps held on to the shriveled and black length of
tissue, resembling the stem of a rotten banana, until it fell
off.

He again remembered the automobile accident Danny
had been in when he was eighteen. His son had been
speeding when he crashed and totaled Brady's car. At the
scene, standing beside the twisted and smoking scrapheap of
metal, Danny repeated the words, "I'm sorry, Dad. I ruined
your car. I'm sorry, Dad. I ruined your car."

How could his son realize the gut-wrenching panic at the phone call from the police? That all he cared about was his son, in one piece, standing before him. Arms and legs and fingers and toes intact. He had scanned Danny's body as he had when his son was newly born. A father's joy that his child was fine.

Alive. A life. He found it hard to fathom the helplessness of a parent willing to toss the miracle of possibility away . Tossing a baby into the garbage. There needed to be hope. Hope versus evil. Hope amidst the refuse and scavengers of society.

He picked up the phone and dialed home. Sarah was quiet after he told her of the new bill in full detail.

"What would she think?" he asked.

"Beth?"

"Yes."

"She would be proud."

"It's not as big, not as important as "Beth's Bill.""

"It's huge."

"What about you? Are you proud of me?"

"Do you want me to be?"

"Yes."

"Well, I am," she said.

"Thanks."

"So, the "Safe Baby Bill," huh?"

"Leadership thinks I'm nuts. "Beth's Bill" would've cost millions. This one is like a freebie."

"You'll vote for their budget?"

"Yes. They thanked me for being a cooperative team player."

"What a team," she said with sarcasm.

"What a game," he said.

\* \* \* \*

JOHN BRADY'S FIRST session ended the following day. In a flurry of quick votes in the House and Senate,

Senate Bill 3279, the "Safe Baby Bill" and the state's two-year operating budget both passed. The budget was party-line. Brady's new bill passed 31-18 in the Senate, and 65-33 in the House as hard core conservative Republicans voted no, ironically calling Brady soft on crime.

That afternoon, the weather, typical of the Pacific Northwest, could not decide what to do. Subsequently, clouds deposited rain as the sun shined.

Standing under cover on the steps of the Capitol, Brady could see a rainbow covering part of Olympia while members of news crews held umbrellas over cameras and reporters exposed to the rain.

Governor McNamarra laughed at a question dealing with disturbances within the Republican ranks. "What we really experienced was honest political debate. And that's a good thing."

The reporter re-phrased his question. "Sir, what about Senator Brady's first vote on the budget? Didn't the whole problem stem from Republicans killing "Beth's Bill? And Governor, didn't you say you would help pass that bill if you were elected?"

Brady stood behind the Governor, among several Republican senators and leadership. He could sense the media honing in on him.

"I did," McNamarra said, "but to be honest, cutting taxes became my priority. I will urge Senator Brady to offer "Beth's Bill" next year. If our long-term revenue forecasts are accurate we should be able to fund it in a supplemental budget."

"Senator Brady, what do you think about all this?" The lights and microphones were in his face.

"I think I will pass "Beth's Bill" next session. It's not going away because it is a good issue. And in a smaller victory, the "Safe Baby Bill" will allow justice for the smallest and most innocent of victims."

The Majority Leader stepped next to Brady and the microphones. "Believe me, Senator Brady is no longer a political novice."

The group of Republicans laughed.

Brady laughed, too. "I think what Senator Daniels means is that I did everything I could to get something good done."…*What I was willing to do…I came here to punish criminals and I end up passing a bill to spread compassion…Thy will be done.*

\* \* \* \*

*RELAX. RELAX AND regulate.* He willed his breathing. *Breathe in. Breathe out. Regulate.* In boxer shorts and T-shirt, Brady lay upon the bed. The room was stuffy and hot, and the shades were drawn to within inches of the sill, an invitation to any breeze.

His heart beat irregularly against his rib cage. At least he pictured it doing so to the metallic whir of the ancient oscillating fan on the dresser. Hot air seemed less oppressive when pushed about. Keep it moving.

Eyes closed, he lay very still, urging his mind to empty of thoughts. Visions of capillaries and veins, blue and red, like the wires in back of his stereo components. Red and white blood cells. Nerve endings tingled in his fingers and toes. Were they really there at the end of his limbs? If he focused intently, nothing was there. No hands. No feet. No being. Only a numbness.

He couldn't sleep. Looking at the digital clock, he thought, *okay, next time I look if it's still 1:33 something is going to happen…*

He lay very still and thought that he didn't feel fifty years old. Half of one-hundred. A few days prior, he had become half a century old. The statistic scared him as did the maddening party favors. Black balloons and crepe paper. Black cups and napkins and ghoulish frosting that made everyone's teeth look rotten. Over the hill and down towards the finish line.

He looked at the clock. 1:34. *Thank God.*

For his birthday, Sarah had reserved the small banquet room of his favorite Italian restaurant. The whole evening he had felt a morbid sense of irony. His newfound fascination, or preoccupation with death and religion was amplified that evening as they commemorated his life amid the restaurant's collection of Catholic memorabilia. Photographs of Popes, past and present. Cathedrals. Saints. Movie stars playing saints. Paintings of Jesus and Mary. Dashboard ornaments and refrigerator magnets. A hologram of Pope John Paul II where one step to the right raised the Pontiff's hands and a step to the left lowered them.

Brady had taken it in stride. He'd smiled, bit his lip and thanked everybody for their consideration. His favorite present had been from Emily: a water-snow globe with a miniature Pope John Paul in his Pope-mobile entrapped within.

"Oh my!" Brady exclaimed as he admired the bauble.

"You like it, Grampa?" Emily asked, dunking a breadstick into a bowl of butter.

Sarah laughed. "She saw it in the gift shop up front and had to have it for you."

Brady shook the globe and the Pope and the Pope-mobile were encased in a snowstorm. "It's magnificent. I love it!" He smiled at his granddaughter and she basked in his attention.

Their waitress appeared carrying a candelabra like Liberace's. The flames bent and smoked as she walked. The party erupted in a chorus of "Happy Birthday" and ended in clapping and whistling.

Pasta, Chianti and family made Brady feel nostalgic. Warm and fuzzy. "Do I have to blow these out yet?" he asked. "It adds quite the ambiance."

"Okay. I guess that's fine," the waitress laughed. "I mean, until we need it for another birthday party."

"He's just sentimental," Danny teased.

Brady poured Chianti. "No, I just need to get my wish right before I blow them out, or it won't come true." He took a sip of the dry red wine. "Everybody knows that."


The whir of the fan. Time had passed. Moments of memories. He realized he had done it. He had regulated his breathing. Calm. Regulation. Rules. Rules of being. Rules of Life. And if you play by the rules, what then? Beth had always followed the rules. *You never know. You can't afford to procrastinate. Danny's doing the right thing. He knows Jessie's the real deal. Why wait? Thank you, God, for today. It's a happy day. Thank you for Danny and Jessie. Thank you for Mark and Emily. And Sarah. Especially Sarah. And for letting us get through everything. And about Beth. I know her soul is with you…If you could let her know that we are happy today and we feel her with us today. Thank you for that. Amen.*

Brady let his thoughts go and fell asleep, only to be awaken moments later by voices, laughter in the backyard. Then there was hammering and chunks of music. Clapping. Toby's bark.

Brady smiled then, knowing his quiet time was over. Stretching, he got up and went to shower and shave and don the rented black tuxedo hanging from a hook on the bathroom door.


Emily held the bubble wand too close to her lips and tasted soap. She spat onto the grass, an action which belied the fact she wore a fancy taffeta dress, and dunked the wand into the small plastic bottle.

Tail wagging, Toby barked agitatedly, waiting to catch and destroy the floating effervescent spheres of soap. Bubble ropes floated to the dog and he ate them. They popped on his head. They burst on his snout causing him to bite and sneeze.

Jubilantly, Emily obeyed her pet's unspoken order to produce more bubbles. She blew them down at the grass. She blew them up into the sky. Above the rows of empty chairs. Under the big white tent.

She became ecstatic with her expertise. Subsequently, each bubble became a serious invention. Lips pursed in an O, back bent and neck craned, she blew breath slowly, oh so slowly through the plastic circle. It was then that a bubble of particular merit was born. Gelatinous and wobbly, it was the size of a not-too-full balloon.

It was as if the floating globule were an animate, thinking organism, purposefully rising just out of the canine's reach. Excited and crazy, Toby followed the bubble across the yard, through the bed of rhododendrons and azaleas, and back into the grass.

The bubble landed, then, gently, intact, atop the cut blades of grass. It perched, balanced, as if on a golf tee. Witnessing this, Toby slowed, shrunk to the ground and crept forward. Slow. A predator on target; prey in sight.

Just then, a touch of wind, a mere breath of air lifted the bubble as if by divine, deliberate plan, sending it zigging and zagging through the uniform rows of white folding chairs.

The dog yelped and continued the chase until the bubble sailed towards the perimeter of the yard and rose up and over the fence. Flabbergasted, Toby stood beside the fence looking skyward. He yelped then looked at the wood planks as if he could see through them. Suddenly, a large bee, enticed by the perfumed flowers of a nearby rhododendron caught Toby's attention and he bounded towards it.

John Brady stood on the small aggregate patio by the back door and watched the bubble escape the yard of it's conception, rising into the sky so brilliant blue it hurt his eyes. The bubble sparkled in the sun several yards away then disappeared.

He remembered his last dental visit and how he had seen bubbles outside the window, rising, ten floors above the streets of Seattle. At any point in time, how many bubbles floated above the Earth? How high could they float before bursting out of existence? And could the souls in Heaven see them? He liked to think so.

"It's like a fairy tale. Absolutely perfect," Sarah remarked stepping outside. "How is the groom's father holding up?"

Brady turned and gasped at the sight of her. "Oh my God, you look beautiful," he blurted.

The dress she wore was of shimmering silver silk, strapless and fell just above her ankles. Her hair was swept up off her face and neck, accentuating the dangling diamond earrings. She laughed and blushed and the earrings twinkled in the sun. "You flatter me. You look quite dapper yourself. Where's the rest of your get-up?"

"Get it Toby! Get the bubble!" Emily yelled. She was seated on one of the folding chairs, the taffeta dress puffed-up about her.

"God knows why, but the photographer was taking pictures of my jacket and tie and stuff on the stairs." Brady had stood back in the hallway as the man used his light meter then, crouched and peered through his lens. He hadn't understood why his cuff-links, bowtie and tuxedo jacket thrown on the stairs should be subject to photographing and he did not ask. Click. Flash.

"He looks like quite the character," Sarah said quietly.

"Yes." The man had been recommended, though obviously Brady thought, not for his appearance. Short in stature, sixty-ish, his hair and beard unkempt and grey. His blue pit-stained oxford shirt was un-tucked and his loud tie came to a halt far above his belly. A little boy tie. Possibly a clip-on.

Sarah nudged him as the photographer came out the back door.

"Don't mind me," he said, equipment dangling by straps over his shoulder. "I'm taking shots before the ceremony." The man peered about the yard. "This is beautiful."

"Thank you," Brady said.

The man ambled up the few steps of the deck where five eight-foot tables stood. Four more tables were set on the grass. Adjusting the equipment hanging from his shoulder, he squatted and focused his camera on the accoutrements adorning each white-linened table. Bowls of nuts. Plates of mints. Small plastic bottles of bubbles, the kind Emily used. Small packets of bird seed tied with a ribbon. Flowers: white roses, baby's breath and carnations dyed purple in honor of Elizabeth. The last item on each table was a disposable camera, giving each guest an opportunity to make memories for the bride and groom.

"These are all gone," Emily stated as she placed the wand into the bubble bottle and screwed the cap shut. "Gramma! I love your dress! You look like a princess." Her small hand stroked the silver silk. "Can I go see Jessie?"

"Go ahead," Sarah laughed. "The girls are doing her makeup in the upstairs bathroom."

"Oh!" Bending, Emily placed the bubbles on the deck and ran for the door.

"Don't get in the way!"

"I won't!"

"Emily!" Brady called.

The taffeta dress swished back and forth like a bell as she halted. "What?"

Brady went to her and lowered his lips to her ear. "You, my dear, look like a princess, too."

She giggled and ran inside.

The photographer crossed over to the quarter of yard covered by a huge white canvas canopy strung with miniature white lights, under which a bearded man was laying down wires and hooking up stereo equipment. The two men shook hands. Toby dashed under the canopy, tail wagging, and sniffed at their feet.

Brady looked at his wife. "Everything looks perfect."

Sarah sighed. "Oh, I hope so. I keep thinking we've forgotten something."

"You know, at this point, it really doesn't matter. All we need is the bride and groom. And the priest, of course."

There was a pack of cigarettes and a lighter on the deck railing. With an anxious movement, Sarah reached for them. She had to finagle her finger about inside the pack in order to retrieve one. After lighting it she inhaled deeply, almost desperately. Her hand trembled slightly as she held the cigarette in her fingers.

Brady imagined her lungs turning ugly and black and stone-like within her chest, like the pictures he saw as a teenager in health class. He turned from her and witnessed Toby urinating on a bush. "We better put him in the garage soon."

"What time is it?"

"About that time. You know, you look like you should be in a Humphrey Bogart movie. The dress. The cigarette and all."

She narrowed her eyes at him. "Ha. Please don't reprimand me on smoking. Not now."

"Okay."

"Really. I'll quit soon."

"Okay."

"I need it now."

Brady whistled for the dog. "I'll put him in the garage."

"You think the candelabra, you know up at the altar, will be okay?" Sarah asked as she surveyed the yard. "You think they'll stay lit?"

He moved behind her and kneaded her bare shoulders with his fingers. Her neck looked delicately thin with her hair pulled up. "You worry too much. Everything's wonderful. Danny's in awe of what you've done."

"Can you believe our little boy is getting married?" She asked, voice quavering.

The taught, tight muscles near her collarbone seemed to relax under his touch. "It's a good thing. A very good thing. But no, I can't believe it."

"Hey guys, the caterers are here," Danny announced from the door. Wearing black tux and tails and freshly shaven, Danny's cheeks glowed like an excited adolescent.

"My God, you look like a grown man," Sarah said then laughed.

"Gee thanks, Mom," he answered. "I'll take that as a compliment."

Brady smelled his son's musky cologne. He smiled and felt happy for him.

"I think you're quite dashing," Sarah whispered in Danny's ear. Then she pecked him on the cheek. "I need to speak to the caterers." She dropped her cigarette onto the patio and squashed it under the sole of her sandal.

After his mother left, Danny tried to act relaxed by jamming his hands in his pockets.

"Nervous?" Brady asked.

"I guess. I don't know. It's more like I'm nervous because I'm supposed to be. That and everybody keeps asking me. You know, if I have cold feet."

"Don't worry. That's natural. I'm proud of you. So is your mother. Jessie's wonderful. You are making the right move."

Danny smiled and shrugged his shoulders as Toby barked at the photographer taking pictures of the make-shift altar.

"Okay, that's enough." Brady whistled and the dog came to him. Shooing the pooch into the house with his foot, he looked at his son. "It's exciting, isn't it?"

"What?"

"All this stuff." He gestured at the backyard. "Life."

"I guess so. I just hope I'm ready."


Tissues. A compact, travel-sized pack of tissues in his coat pocket. The sun beat down as he witnessed the ceremony from the front row of folding chairs, and Brady thanked God for tissues. He had not planned to cry. In fact, he'd promised himself to keep his emotions in check. Yet as he watched his baby boy-turned-man at the altar with Jessie, his eyes and nose leaked involuntarily. He felt dizzy and ethereal and humbled in the midst of family and friends.

Brady wiped his nose and watched Father Boyle in white and gold vestments open his Bible as he stood in front of Danny and Jessie.

*You do the best you can with what you're dealt. Bad health. Accidents. Marital problems. Deaths of loved ones. You do the best you can and go on with your life. There's always more. There's always something else to do; to look forward to. Then, when all is said and done God will judge you accordingly.*

He watched the profile of his tall and handsome son as he recited his vows to Jessie. On his left, he felt Sarah's presence. The scent of her perfume. Memories. Mark sat on his right, Emily on his lap. And he felt Beth. He felt as if he could lean forward and look past Mark and she would be seated beside him.

After the ceremony, it was impossible to keep Emily away from the bride. Her new aunt, Mrs. Jessica Brady.

"She's a fairy princess!" Emily exclaimed to her friend Abigail, whilst twirling around and around in her taffeta dress. "Like Princess Aurora!"

Abigail was upset that her dress would not swoosh the same as Emily's.

Jessie beamed in her strapless bridal gown, the bodice an intricate pattern of tiny pearls. "I'm your aunt now. And you're my niece."

"Oh," Emily answered with a tinge of mystery in her voice.

"I'm Aunt Jessie now. We're family."

"Okay!"

The photographer, shirt still un-tucked, snapped a frame of Jessie removing the veiled wreath from her coiffed hair and carefully placing atop Emily's head.

"Oh! Oh, Jessie!" she exclaimed. "Gramma! Gramma!"

Jessie noticed the look of both adoration and hurt on Abigail's face as she watched her friend receive such attention. Then Danny appeared and the problem was solved.

"Mademoiselle," he announced elegantly and bowed before Abigail.

She wrung her hands shyly as Danny produced from behind him a lavender carnation from one of the table bouquets. "For you," he said and she blushed as he tucked the stem behind her ear.

She giggled and smiled broadly. "Emily!" she cried and ran through a throng of people to find her friend.

"Why husband, aren't you the charmer?" Jessie remarked coyly. She adjusted his bow tie.

"God. I'm actually a husband. Your husband."

"My husband."

The photographer snapped a picture. "Sorry, guys. Good picture."

Sarah felt the lump in her throat when she recognized the song the DJ had started. Adrenaline and emotion and champagne amplified memories of her daughter, at the enchanted age of four or five-not too much older than Emily- dancing in her pajamas to the same music. The music she now felt in her bones.

She watched as Mark offered his hand to Emily for the dance. The little girl's face glowed with love for her father. "This is my song! This is my song, daddy!" she exclaimed as she adjusted Jessie's veil and crown of flowers on her head. I KNOW YOU, I WALKED WITH YOU ONCE UPON A DREAM...

From her seat at one of the beautifully decorated tables, Sarah watched couples dance under the canvas tent. Sipping champagne, she closed her eyes and let the tune from Disney's Sleeping Beauty wash over her. She heard animated laughter and conversation and the tinkle of glass and silver.

Suddenly she was dizzy, envisioning Beth's face on Princess Aurora and Mark's on Prince Phillipe. Three kindly fairy-godmothers fluttered about.

Sarah opened her eyes and watched Emily stand on Mark's feet as they turned in circles. She heard her granddaughter say, "Daddy, you smell good."

Closing her eyes to bring back the visions, she saw Princess Beth twirling slowly, slowly, alone in the clouds. She clasped inches of her gown so as not to trip. *I know you, I walked with you once upon a dream...will we live happily ever after? The ever after...heaven...is Beth's soul content...is she okay? It's okay to let go. It's okay to let go.*

She opened her eyes as the song ended and a contemporary dance song began. Pouring herself more champagne, she thought it would be nice if fairy godmothers were real.

"It's like we're starting over."

"More like a jump-start," Brady said.

"I'm so stupid."

He squeezed her hand. "We both were," he whispered as the photographer entered the living room.

"This the place?" he asked, snapping a new roll of film into his camera.

"This is it," Sarah replied. She adjusted Brady's bow tie. "This feels so strange," she whispered. "I feel old."

Looking at her hands, he touched the solitaire diamond of her wedding ring. "You're beautiful."

"You're prejudiced."

"You're still beautiful."

Wearing a short-sleeved, Roman-collared black shirt, Father Timothy Boyle entered the room and spied an end table to deposit his plate of half-eaten food. He popped a meatball into his mouth and wiped his chin with a napkin.

Sarah put her lips to Brady's ear. "Thank you."

"For what?"

"Taking me back."

"I never let you go."

"But you could have."

The priest clapped his hands. "Okay, you two, let's go!"

As the commotion of the reception swirled through the house about them, Junior, Emily's new hamster came bumping and rolling into the room inside its exercise ball. In hot pursuit came Emily, giggling and flushed, Jessie's veil flowing down her back. Abigail and Toby chased Emily. The photographer took photos of the bedlam.

"My word!" exclaimed the priest.

Brady laughed. "Who let the hamster out?" He looked at Father Boyle. "Please don't mind it. It's harmless."

"Except for the droppings," Sarah giggled.

"Except for the droppings."

Emily returned, having ceased her pursuit of the rolling rodent. Approaching the priest, she tugged at his pant leg, panting and out of breath.

He squatted down to her level. "Yes, dear?"

Emily whispered the loud, audible whisper of a small child. Cupping her hand to the holy man's ear, she said, "Our Father who art in Heaven." Then she nodded as if she understood an important secret.

"That's wonderful Emily," Father Boyle smiled.

"I learned it in church-school." Emily stated. "Mommy's in Heaven too."

"Yes, she is."

"With God."

Father Boyle touched her cheek. "Yes, your mommy is with God. She is in good hands. You are such a smart little girl."

Emily smiled then ran from the room to find Abigail and the animals.

John Brady wiped his eyes and swallowed hard. "Today is just full of emotions."

Sarah squeezed his hand. "I've felt that way all week."

"I've felt Beth," Brady said to the priest. "That she's witnessing all this. I mean, this morning, we visited her grave. I know she's watching."

Boyle nodded. "I believe you. I believe, most definitely, that Elizabeth is here with your family. Today, tomorrow. Always."

"I do too," Sarah replied quietly.

In the backyard, a song ended to applause and shouts. Another song began. The caterers clanged pans and dishes in the kitchen. In the corner of the dining room, the photographer quietly looked at his camera.

"It seems like she's been gone a long time," said Brady.

Father Boyle looked out the window at the ongoing reception. "You two have gone through so much this past, what? Year? Year and a half? She is with you. And

Elizabeth would be so proud of you. Both of you. Getting through this. Being strong. Her death caused many other trials for you. But, your family, your beliefs, your marriage, why, they seem stronger than ever." He gestured towards the festivities. "Look at all you have here," he stated with a piercing stare. "Things happen for a reason. There is a divine plan."

The photographer snapped a picture of a piece of the divine plan. A true moment.

Brady took a deep breath. "Okay. Let's move on. To the plan at hand." He moved a step closer to Sarah and squeezed her hand.

"John and Sarah," Father Boyle began, and as his words flowed over them, Brady found himself focused on the dusting of dandruff on the priest's shoulders. His mind was dizzy and his thoughts were dreamlike. Could Beth see them right now? Was she a ghost, a spirit, in the house? Several times during the day, he had turned, thinking a presence was near him. Each time it had been nothing. Empty space.

He blinked his consciousness back to the present and said "I do" when asked if he wished to renew his marriage vow to Sarah. "In a heartbeat," he confirmed.

"A wonderful thing," the priest affirmed. "Kiss the bride and go celebrate. You have quite the party in your backyard."

"Quite the party," Brady repeated to Sarah. When his lips touched hers there was a jolt of nostalgia. Religious bliss. Perhaps it was a feeling of blessedness in Father Boyle's presence. An aura. And through that aura, God. Brady felt God and smiled at the legitimately holy feeling. Then he smiled at Sarah. She returned the smile.

John Brady hugged Father Boyle then shook his hand, passing him a few extra bills for service above and beyond his duty. "Thank you, Father."

"Blessing two marriages in one day? It's my privilege. Like I said, life goes on. There is always a cause to celebrate." And with his nugget of wisdom hanging in the air, he retrieved his plate of half-eaten food and turned to Sarah. "And where, my dear, could an old priest get a nice glass of wine?"